STREET SOLDIER

ANDY McNAB

STREET SOLDIER

DOUBLEDAY

DOUBLEDAY

UK | USA | Canada | Ireland | Australia
India | New Zealand | South Africa

Doubleday is part of the Penguin Random House group of companies
whose addresses can be found at global.penguinrandomhouse.com.

www.penguin.co.uk
www.puffin.co.uk
www.ladybird.co.uk

First published 2016

001

Text copyright © Andy McNab, 2016
Front cover artwork and design copyright © Stephen Mulcahey, 2016
Cover photography copyright © Jonathan Ring, 2016

With thanks to Ben Jeapes and David Gatward

The moral right of the author has been asserted

Typeset in 13/17.5 pt Adobe Garamond Pro by Jouve (UK), Milton Keynes
Printed in Great Britain by Clays Ltd, St Ives plc

A CIP catalogue record for this book is available from the British Library

Hardback ISBN: 978–0–857–53469–9
Trade paperback ISBN: 978–0–857–53470–5

All correspondence to:
Doubleday
Penguin Random House Children's
80 Strand, London WC2R 0RL

GLOSSARY

ACOG – Advanced Combat Optical Gunsight
providing up to 6x fixed power magnification,
illuminated at night by an internal phosphor

Anti-tank rockets – man-portable rockets designed
to be able to defeat armoured vehicles. Usually
they are less capable than anti-tank guns and
missiles, but are useful against various targets
including buildings and fortifications

Army Reserve – formerly the Territorial Army or
TA, this provides trained soldiers who work on a
part-time basis to support the regular army

CQR – Close Quarter Recce

Flash-bang (stun grenade) – a non-lethal explosive
device used to temporarily disorientate an enemy's
senses

Foxhound – Patrol vehicle specifically designed and
built to protect against the threats faced by
troops in Afghanistan

GLOSSARY

Fusiliers – an infantry regiment of the British Army, part of the Queen's Division

Glock 17 Gen 4 – lightweight and accurate pistol with a magazine capacity of 17 9mm rounds

GPMG – General-Purpose Machine Gun, nicknamed the 'Gimpy'; belt-driven

IED – an Improvised Explosive Device, which can be placed on the ground or used by suicide bombers; sometimes activated by remote control

Infantry – the British infantry is based on the tried and tested regimental system which has proved successful on operations over the years; it consists of a number of regular battalions. The British infantry has a strong tradition of courage in battle

Insurgent – a person who fights against an established government or authority

Intel (INT) – army term for intelligence: information collected on, for example, enemy movements

Intelligence Corps – one of the corps of the British Army. It is responsible for gathering, analysing and disseminating military intelligence, and also for counter-intelligence and security

LASM – Light Anti-Structures Missile; a rocket launcher designed to be discarded after launch

MI5 – a British intelligence agency working to protect the UK's national security against threats such as terrorism and espionage

GLOSSARY

MoD – Ministry of Defence. Their aim is to protect the security, independence and interests of our country at home and abroad. They ensure that the armed forces have the training, equipment and support necessary for their work

MP5 – 9mm submachine gun built by Heckler & Koch

NATO – North Atlantic Treaty Organization: an organization whose essential purpose is to safeguard the freedom and security of its members through political and military means

NCO – Non-Commissioned Officer, like a corporal or sergeant

No. 8 Temperate Combat Dress – this replaced the No 5 and 9 Dress, in what is known known as the Personal Clothing System. It is based around a Multi-Terrain Pattern (MTP) windproof smock, a lightweight jacket and trousers with a range of ancillaries such as thermals and waterproofs

PE – Plastic Explosive

PRR – Personal Role Radio: small transmitter-receiver radio that enables soldiers to communicate over short distances, and through buildings and walls

Royal Logistics Corps (RLC) – provides support (e.g. vehicle parts, tools, ammunition and rations) to the Army, both in peacetime and on operations

RPG – Rocket-Propelled Grenade

GLOSSARY

SA80 – semi-automatic rifle made by Heckler &
Koch, the standard British Army rifle

SAS – Special Air Service, tasked to operate in difficult
and often changing circumstances, sometimes in
absence of guidance and within situations that have
significant operational and strategic importance

Screws – a prison nickname for a warder

Special Branch – units responsible for matters of
national security in British and Commonwealth
police forces. Acquire and develop intelligence,
usually of a political nature, and conducts
investigations to protect the State from perceived
threats of subversion

'Taking Point' – Assume the first and most exposed
position in a combat military formation

UGL – Under-slung Grenade Launcher, fitted to SA80

Warrior – a series of British armoured vehicles, origin-
ally developed to replace the older FV430 series of
armoured vehicles. A highly successful armoured
fighting vehicle, the Warrior can be fitted with
enhanced armour and is continuously being updated

YOI – Young Offender Institution, a type of British
prison intended for offenders aged between 18
and 20, although some prisons cater for younger
offenders from ages 15 to 17, who are classed as
juvenile offenders

Chapter 1

A helicopter roared in enemy airspace. Its searchlight speared out of the warm night and swept over the rooftop. Sean Harker swore and ducked into the shadow of an air vent.

He pressed himself against the rough, damp brick. He had dressed for the darkness, as per orders. Black jeans, black top, black hood pulled over his blond hair. If the light caught him, nothing would stand out more in its merciless glare than someone who was obviously trying not to be seen.

But it was just a routine patrol, not looking for anyone in particular. The light moved on and the helicopter didn't react to him. It disappeared into the darkness.

Sean stayed where he was until he saw Matt emerge from the shadow of another vent. Then he stepped out, just as Curly crept from behind the small generator shed. Sean had spent half the night crouching down, and his thighs cramped. He flexed his arms and back and gazed out across the graffiti'd maze of rooftops and alleys. Then he and Curly looked to Matt for orders. Matt jerked his head, and the three of them silently gathered together by the skylight.

One of its panels was cranked open, and fumes of oil and petrol and ganja rose up from the workshop into the summer night. Sean took a deep breath through his nose. They were the smells of his childhood.

The vehicle workshop was all lit up and the security shutters were down. Men in grimy overalls lounged in an office behind a glass partition, catching a last smoke and a drink before heading off. Even if they had looked up, they wouldn't have seen the three lurkers. They would be looking out of a brightly lit space into the night.

Finally it looked like they were leaving. One of them stood by the keypad to the security alarm, ready to tap in the code. Matt gave Sean the nod and Sean delved into his pocket for his phone. He had already loaded up the recording app. Slowly, so that no one down there would spot a sudden movement out of the corner of their eye, he stretched his hand through the open panel, holding the phone out to catch the sounds below.

Bleep, bleep, bleep. The electronic tones echoed around the workshop – they had the recording. They could play it back at their leisure to work out the code. Then they could let themselves in, switch off the alarm, and they'd have all the time in the world to get what they had come for.

Sean grinned at the others and began to withdraw the phone. Matt gave an approving thumbs up. A grinning Curly went further and gave him a nudge.

Sean's hand bumped against the frame of the skylight and the phone was knocked out of his fingers. He made a futile grab at thin air at the same time as he heard it hit the concrete floor.

Perhaps even that wouldn't have been so bad if he hadn't instinctively hissed, '*Shit!*'

A cry came from below. Curly and Matt flung themselves flat, away from the skylight. Sean was frozen for only a second longer, but it was long enough to be caught by the searching torchlight. More shouting below – not in English, but he got the gist of it. *There's someone on the roof!*

Running footsteps echoed. Without a word the three pelted towards the top of the fire escape, a vertical iron ladder with safety hoops around it . . .

And skidded to a halt. The workshop's back door was right by the bottom of the ladder and it was just opening. They wouldn't get down before the work crew emerged.

Sean ran over to the far side of the building. There was no escape here – it was a sheer drop into the forecourt.

The only other way was the narrow alley at the back of the shop. It couldn't be more than three metres wide.

'Oh shit oh shit oh shit . . .' Curly was muttering.

Matt cuffed him on the head. 'OK.' He backed away from the edge. 'They're gonna come up one by one. We're just going to have to pick them off one at a time—'

'No. No need,' Sean said. They stared at him. 'They only saw me. They don't know anyone else is here.'

'So what?' Matt demanded. 'We just let them take you? Fuck that!'

'No.' Sean shook his head emphatically, and pointed at the vents where they had hidden. 'Get back there.' He felt the excitement rise within him. A tense, nervous thrill, like his lungs and his stomach and his balls were all cramping into a tight knot. It was scary and weird and *good*. 'Go on!'

He grinned and ran back to the top of the fire escape. The first of the work crew had his foot on the bottom rung.

'Wankers!' Sean shouted, and ducked out of sight. He turned quickly to face the others. 'Guys. I can do this. Hide over there.' He jerked his thumb at the air vents. Matt took a breath, about to argue. Sean looked him in the eye. 'Please?'

Curly turned to Matt for orders. Matt just stared at Sean like he was mad, but he could see it was their only option. Slowly, not taking his eyes off Sean, he backed into the shadows, with Curly at his side.

Sean bounced on his toes, and felt his heart thud inside him. And as he heard footsteps on the iron rungs, he began to run back across the roof towards the alley.

His long legs ate up the distance in a few paces. He drew a deep breath into his lungs, leaped onto the low wall with a single bound, and flung his lean, six-foot frame into the darkness. Air soared around him . . .

. . . Except that he wasn't going to make it. He was dropping faster than the far wall was approaching. It was only three metres away, but he had picked a really bad time to learn that three metres was further than it looked.

His arms began to windmill, striving for that little extra momentum.

'*Shi-i-i-t . . .*'

His torso thumped into the wall with an impact that knocked the breath from his body. He flung his arms forward to get a hold. Pain flared in his armpits as his weight ground them into the sharp edge of the roof.

But he wasn't falling any more. With an effort, he hooked his elbows over the top of the wall, dug his toes into the cracks and levered himself up until he could fall forward onto the flat roof on the other side.

He rolled onto his back, stared up at the night sky,

and laughed. Pain stabbed through every bruised rib and he didn't care. '*Ha!*'

Angry, baffled yells behind him made him grin. The work crew lined the edge of their roof. They were three metres away and might as well have been on the other side of the city.

'You little shit!' one of them shouted. Another seemed like he might seriously try and jump over, but then he looked down and thought better of it. If Sean could barely do it with a run-up, no way was it possible from a standing start. None of the men had noticed the other two figures, still in the shadows on the other side of the roof.

But now one of them was fumbling inside his coat for . . .

Shit! Sean pushed himself to his feet and was running for cover even before he was upright. If the guy was armed, he wasn't going to hang around.

He ducked down behind the coaming of an aircon unit, breathing heavily. He hadn't thought much beyond this point, and had no idea if you could get down from this place. If there were skylights, then he would break in, risk the alarms, and smash his way out of a window downstairs before reinforcements arrived.

But he had to be quick. He only had a couple of minutes before they sent people down to ground level, and then back up inside the building.

He needn't have worried. His eyes lit on the railings at the top of a fire escape – a proper one: a metal staircase winding its way down into the next alley. He charged towards it, hearing the angry shout from across the way.

Sean threw himself down the metal stairs and kept his grip on the iron railing long enough to fling himself in the direction of the main road. The pain in his ribs he told to piss off, and for the time being it obeyed. The alley was an obstacle course of overturned bins and sagging boxes, all vomiting their contents across his path. Sean half ran, half hurdled, his whole life shrunk down to one aim: get to the main road; get out of here.

He burst out into the road like a cannon ball. The pavement was lined with the turning-out crowd – people heading home from a late screening or a restaurant. The air was rich with the sweet aroma of fast food. Faces loomed in front of him and then whipped away, just as shouts rose up behind him. *Shit.* They were still on his tail. At least they probably wouldn't start shooting in front of all these witnesses.

Sean put his head down and urged himself on.

He had to get away from this area. And there, up ahead, was his way out. A guy in black leathers and helmet, sitting at the lights astride a Kawasaki Ninja. They had just turned red. The stream of traffic was slowing down and Sean was running faster than the cars, so he took a left and dodged through a gap in the oncoming traffic. An angry horn blared as a car jammed on its brakes. It shuddered as the car behind kept going and ploughed into it with a metal crunch.

Sean summoned all his strength for a final dash between the streams of traffic before the lights could change again. The biker looked in his wing mirror and saw him. The helmet swung round to stare.

Sean didn't stop. He barged into the man with his shoulder, hard enough to knock him off the saddle. The guy bounced on one foot, arms waving for balance, and then sprawled in the road as Sean grabbed the handlebars and swung his leg over. And then the biker was back, wading in with hammering fists before Sean could get his hand on the throttle. He ducked under the first swinging punch, and the guy grabbed him with both hands, one on each shoulder. Sean saw what was coming and thrust his arms up in front of his face, just before the guy nutted him with his helmet. Sean's arms took the blow.

Whatever – no time to argue. Sean brought his arms down hard, knocking the hands aside, and in the same movement brought his knee up into the guy's balls. The biker bent double and staggered away, his yell muffled by the helmet.

It was the chance Sean needed to gun the throttle,

and the bike surged away. '*Yeah!*' He pumped the air with a triumphant fist.

He kept the gear low and the throttle at max, forcing power into the wheels while the engine howled. Adrenaline pumped through his veins like petrol through the engine. The white lines on the road blurred beneath him, and gritty, petrol-laden fumes washed into his eyes. He took a right, and pointed the front wheel towards friendly territory.

Five more minutes and he sensed that he was properly out of danger. Untrained eyes would have said it was just another shopping district, units lining the road on either side, some shuttered for the night, some still lit up for the late-night population. But Sean was finely tuned to the invisible barriers that carved up the city – different races, different religions, who was a friend, who wasn't. The style and language of the graffiti had changed. There were different tags on the walls. This was the no-man's-land between two sides. He wasn't home and dry yet, but there would be allies here. He could slow down, a little.

With the engine revving hard beneath him, Sean scanned the way ahead for landmarks. After a moment he knew where he was. The glowing neon sign of the fast-food joint where he'd had a quarter-pounder with fries last week. Curly had been trying to chat up the girl who took their order. She had replied with a remark about only serving burgers, not chipolatas. And she had held thumb and forefinger just far enough apart to make it clear what she was referring to.

Sean broke into a laugh at the memory. And then he was passing the restaurant and the memory came apart as he remembered what had happened next.

Two days later, the place had been blown up. One staff member and two customers killed, and a dozen others injured. The staff member had been Chipolata Girl.

The restaurant's plate-glass windows had been boarded up so he couldn't see into the blackened interior as he zipped past, but the devastation was clear. The brickwork was scorched where the flames had licked it. Weird that they had left the sign switched on.

In that brief moment Sean was too distracted to notice the car make its way out of a side street directly into his path.

He grabbed the Ninja's brake – too hard: the rear wheel skidded out left and Sean dropped onto the ground.

His body slammed into the tarmac and he pulled his arms in tight as he rolled. The road scraped his skin raw through his jeans. The bike continued on its way, slipping under the vehicle, with sparks flying and the creaking sound of metal on concrete echoing as it disappeared from view.

Running feet stopped in front of him. 'You OK?'

A tall black guy helped him stagger up onto legs that were bleeding and sore. Concern was stamped all over his face. Sean looked around desperately. The Ninja was a write-off and he wasn't going to get any more transport. His best chance was to spin a sob story and get out before the cops arrived. He drew in a breath to begin – and suddenly a police cruiser was there, screeching to a halt with flashing lights.

The driver had the window down. 'Hold him!'

The guy turned towards Sean and opened his mouth – but Sean was already running. Hands grabbed at him and he jabbed back, hard, with his elbows. He felt them grind into flesh and bone. The guy swore and the hands let go.

He ducked hard left into a shop. The door swung behind him into whoever was on his tail. More swearing.

Sean pushed on, between magazines and newspapers and canned food and bread. The only person in the shop was an old woman with a bucket and mop. She leaped out of his path and fell over backwards.

And there was the rear exit. Sean swerved towards it, but the floor was still wet. His foot slipped beneath him and he fell flat on his face.

He wasn't given a chance to recover. A body fell on top of him, then another. He howled his anger and tried to push himself up. A third body knocked him down again and drove the breath from his lungs.

Immediately his hands were pulled behind his back and pinned together. *Click, click.* Metal loops snapped into place around his wrists.

And, despite everything, he laughed.

It had finally happened. There was a first time for everyone, and this was his. Like getting laid – though doing that for the first time had been a lot more fun.

Breath, warm and heavy, fell across his right cheek. There was coffee on it, stale and sour.

'Share the joke, son?' the voice murmured.

'Yeah,' Sean gasped. 'My mum always told me a night out in Ilford would be shit.'

'She wasn't wrong.' Someone grabbed the back of his head and banged his face onto the wet tiles. The voice said the three words that Sean had always known he would hear one day.

'You're nicked, son.'

Chapter 2

Rain pattered against the small window above Sean's shoulder. The custody van had waited in the secluded yard outside the court with its doors open, so the air was damp with an October chill that soaked into his bones.

They had climbed in one by one, under the cold, watchful eyes of a couple of machine-gun-toting cops whose fingers danced on the trigger guards: they were clearly taking their jobs seriously.

The inside was like a normal minibus, except that it smelled of sweat and damp clothes, and each seat was enclosed by a small mesh cage. Sean had sat where he was told and the cage door had been locked behind him. After three schools and two foster families – he'd actually wanted to stay with the families, but they couldn't get rid of him fast enough – he had finally found somewhere determined to keep him when all he wanted to do was leg it.

A week earlier he had turned sixteen. He'd had better presents.

'What is this?' The angry, whining tones came from the guy seated behind Sean. 'No seat belt! We could get killed!'

Oh God. Sean closed his eyes. The prick had the kind of voice that was carefully tuned to pierce your eardrums. *Someone shut him up . . .*

His head was still throbbing from last night's farewell party. Matt had rounded up all the Littern Guyz – not just Curly, but Joe and Wayne and Spence and all of them – to mark Sean's last opportunity to get well and truly wasted for a good long time. They all knew, and appreciated, that Matt and Curly were free because Sean wasn't. But that was how it rolled. You took your hits.

It sucked that of the three people Sean loved most in the world – Matt and Gaz and Copper, his surrogate big brothers – Matt was the only one still at liberty to throw the party. But maybe it was also appropriate. Most of Sean's first life experiences – first drink, first smoke, first binger – had taken place in Matt's flat. A party for Sean's first custodial sentence kind of completed the deal.

He rested his head against the plastic around the window and tried to wish his headache away. His ears popped and another stab of pain entered his brain as the guard slammed the rear door closed.

The driver turned round and addressed his passengers. 'Hold on tight, ladies. Next stop, Burnleigh Palace!'

Sean rolled his eyes. He wished. Burnleigh Young Offender Institution might be an HM Prison, but it was hardly fit for royalty.

The van began to move, slowly trundling through the narrow tunnel, waiting while the metal gate rolled back to let it out into the world again. Then it was on the road and past the sculpted concrete blocks that acted as car bomb protection. It lurched as the driver shifted up, which simultaneously set off Sean's headache and his whiny neighbour again.

'Oi! You know we don't have any cushions?'

Sean closed his eyes. By the end of the journey, he suspected, turning round and planting his fist in McWhiny's face would feel like a really good idea. Apart from the mesh between them.

Peter, his caseworker, had explained it. No cushions because offenders ripped them off. No seat belts in case the prisoners hanged themselves. Sean had to grin at the image he had of a butcher's truck, corpses dangling from the ceiling when they opened the doors.

The cops had wanted him on remand. They didn't know about the attempted garage heist but they did have him for the bike. It was Taking Without Consent, not theft, because they couldn't prove he hadn't meant to return it. But they had fingerprints. They couldn't show that Sean had ever nicked a vehicle before, but they had him in several vehicles that had also been twocced.

But on the plus side, he had never been more than a few miles from Walthamstow in his life, and had no previous record for assault. His solicitor had successfully argued that he was not a flight risk, the public were in no peril from him, and the remand cells were already too full of far more dangerous cases. So, bail.

He had duly turned up for sentencing, hungover, in a borrowed jacket and tie, with a pair of armed cops lurking at the back of the stand. It must have taken all of thirty seconds. The judge had said he was taking Sean's guilty plea into consideration, and this was a first offence, but it had involved violence in that he had assaulted the Ninja's owner, and yadda yadda yadda . . .

Twelve months. Six in custody, six on parole in the community.

'A year!' his mum had sobbed. She and PJ, the latest boyfriend, had come to visit him in the holding cell with a change of clothes – his usual things, so that he didn't have to wear the borrowed clothes in jail. A bit switched-on for Mum, so probably PJ's idea. 'But it's OK, sweetheart, I'll come and see you whenever I can . . .'

Then she'd broken down in tears. Like she always did. Whatever life did to her, she cried. At least PJ seemed like someone Sean was prepared to leave her with, unsupervised. She had gone through a bad run of boyfriends who liked to hit her, which had finally ended when Sean grew big enough to start hitting them back. PJ seemed fond of her, and that was all he asked.

So Sean had given her a hug and a peck on the cheek, because she was a fat, soppy old cow – but hey, she was his mum. The chances of her getting round to visiting were, he knew, somewhere between zero and zilch.

Heavy drops were a metallic drumbeat on the roof as they rolled round the M25. The weather matched Sean's mood. He had been nicked during the summer. It was now an early evening in autumn. Summer had come and gone – and what a great one it had been: three months under curfew at home on the Littern Mills estate, with a tag on his ankle. At least it meant he had been elsewhere the night of the riots, and when the White Hart Lane bomb went off. That summer there had been a distinct sense of the world going to shit, even more than usual, and it hadn't all been because of his looming court date. With terrorist strikes getting closer to home, everyone wondering where the next one would fall, Sean was happy to be stuck on the estate.

Matt had joked that IS had a good sense of PR, so they wouldn't blow up Littern Mills in case anyone mistook it for doing the world a favour.

Eventually the van jarred to a halt; its way was blocked by more bomb barriers and a massive, solid gate set in a towering red-brick wall. The driver had a brief conversation with the guys outside. Then there was the sound of moving machinery and the gate slowly slid aside. The van edged forward into a tunnel, and the journey was over.

'Name?'

'Sean Harker.'

'S-E-A-N?'

Sean briefly considered responding with 'No, D-I-P-S-T-I-C-K.' But the glint in the eye of the large woman on the other side of the counter made him rethink. Her uniform blouse was stretched tight over the muscles beneath it.

'Uh-huh,' he said out loud.

'Date of birth . . . ?'

Reception into Burnleigh was about as welcoming as Sean had expected it to be. This was a prison and that meant punishment, not group hugs and a welcome party. The woman bashed at her keyboard like she was personally insulted that, of all the prisons in the world, Sean Harker had to turn up in hers.

The windowless reception room smelled of sweat and fish and chips. The intake from the van sat in a row of chairs down one wall. Half-arsed efforts had been made to decorate the place. There was a fish tank against the far wall, with grimy sides and three fish. A pot plant drooped sadly on a pathetic wire pedestal in one corner. The room's harsh strip lighting brought every badly painted corner, every bit of dirt, into sharp focus.

The piss-poor attempts at making them feel at home were given the deathblow by the poster on the wall which warned of the penalty for biting staff. It hadn't occurred to Sean that he would ever want to. Now he knew that if he did, he would get twenty-eight days added to his sentence. Presumably someone had needed telling.

A couple of uniformed guards – *screws*, Sean reminded himself, if he was going to fit in here – stood watch over them: white short-sleeved shirts with epaulettes, black clip-on ties. One of them had a brown and white dog – Sean was pretty sure it was a spaniel – which had made a fuss of them all as they entered, running around with its tail wagging, sniffing, letting them give it a pat. It had even butted its nose against Sean's leg as he waited in his chair, looking up at him with hopeful brown eyes. He had given its head a fondle because it seemed like the right thing to do.

One by one they had been called over to the counter, and now it was Sean's turn.

The woman gave the keyboard a final thump, and nodded abruptly to where one of the screws waited by a side door.

'Go through with Prison Officer King for the body search.'

Oh, shit. Everyone from the van, one by one, had been going through that door. Sean had seen each one of them hesitate, before a screw took them firmly by the arm and led them away. And now he knew why. If there was one joke at last night's party that Sean hadn't found funny, it was the one about the body search – lads miming snapping latex gloves onto probing hands.

Well, if he was going to tough it out for the next year, this was where he started. He nodded and let King guide him. The screw walked with all the grace and threat of an overweight Rottweiler. He had muscles, but he also had a belly straining against his shirt – not that Sean was considering having a go. What would be the point? Where would he go afterwards?

Through the door, a screw with a face like an angry rat waited in a small, bare room. His name tag read PRISON OFFICER CAGE. There was a table with a screen and some kind of kit on it, but Sean's gaze went straight to the thing next to it. It looked a bit like the electric chair used in all the movies.

'Remove everything except your underwear,' Cage

snapped. Sean realized he had just been standing and staring at the chair. 'Today, if you can.'

Sean stripped down to his boxers and passed the pile of clothes to Cage, then stood in the middle of the room for King to make a visual check that he had no contraband taped to his skin. Next the warder ran hard fingers through his hair, peered into his ears, and held his mouth open with a spatula. Finally he patted down Sean's thighs, arse and balls through the fabric of his shorts.

'Nothing of interest here,' he said with a huge smile. Sean guessed it was an old joke. 'And now we look where the sun don't shine.'

Sean swallowed, but he remembered how he had resolved to get through this. He hooked his thumbs into the elastic of his boxers and started to slide them down.

'Don't be soft!' Cage shot King a glare. 'Mr King likes to think he's a comedian.'

'Hey, it never gets old. The look on their faces!'

Sean felt his face flushing red and hid his confusion in as much anger as he dared show. 'So what do I do, then?'

'You keep yer knickers on and you sit down there.' King gave Sean a gentle push towards the chair.

'Just sit?'

'Just sit,' Cage confirmed.

'What does it do?' Sean asked. He carefully placed his arse on the hard plastic surface. It was even less comfortable than the seats in the van. At least those were roughly bum-shaped. This was just a hard, flat surface.

'Scans you. This is the Body Orifice Security Scanner – Boss for short. If the alarm goes off, we know you've got something inside you that you shouldn't have.'

'What, drugs?'

King shook his head. 'We've already checked that,' he said. 'You saw the dog, right?'

Sean remembered the dog. He'd thought it was just being friendly. So it was scoping him out for possession? Sneaky four-legged tosser.

'Nah, we're talking way more exciting than drugs,' said Cage. 'We've had weapons, mobile phones . . . one guy managed a grenade. Had to call in Bomb Disposal to give him an enema.'

'Mr Cage has been in this job long enough to remember when the only way to find out for sure was to have a good old root around ourselves,' said King. 'Progress is an amazing thing.'

'Christ, it made my fingers sore.' Cage pressed a number of buttons and looked at the screen. Sean heard a few whirs and buzzes, saw some flickering lights. 'Boss says you're clean.'

'That's it?' Sean had been through so much bullshit since getting nicked that he couldn't quite believe anything could only take a couple of seconds.

'Unless you'd like us to get the gloves and Vaseline out for old times' sake,' King said. 'This way. Bring your clothes.'

Next stop was a narrow room with another counter and a door at the far end. This counter had a grille from the top to the ceiling. They made Sean stand against a measuring stick stuck to the wall.

'Tall,' said the screw behind the counter. 'Shoe size?'

'Eleven.'

The counter screw pushed a pair of packages wrapped in cellophane through a square gap in the grille, followed by a plastic box.

'Your new outfit.' King pushed the packages at Sean. One was clothing; the other was a pair of scuzzy trainers. King pointed at the box. 'Everything else goes in there. Clothes, watch . . .' He tapped the ring in Sean's left ear. 'Jewellery, apart from approved religious items. If you're wearing it, take it off, and it'll be kept secure for you until your release.'

Sean stared at the box. On its side was a shiny new label showing his photograph and a number. His prison number. If any further confirmation was needed of where he was and what he was, that was it.

He pulled open the cellophane. There were even prison issue Y-fronts. How many other men's balls had been where his were going? He shuddered.

The rest of the clothing was basically a tracksuit, though the colour had faded from what must once have been a vivid lime green to something more like mould. The material was stretched and worn. He pulled it on silently, while the screw behind the grille catalogued his clothes. The new outfit was a size too large and it hung from his lanky frame like a baggy tent. Sean had to pull the drawstring as tight as it would go to stop the trousers falling down. He felt like a total prat and had no doubt that he looked like one too.

The box was taken back inside the grille – and with it went his last physical connection to his life outside the prison.

He signed a receipt for everything he had given up, and a last cellophane package was pushed through the grille.

King handed it over. 'Prison issue towel. Ready?'

Sean held the pack under his arm and nodded.

'This way.' The warder felt for the keyring chained to his belt and turned to the far door. It opened into a dark, wet night where rain hammered down on a covered walkway. 'Welcome to Paradise.'

Chapter 3

'*Fresh meat!*'

The cry went up as Sean stepped out of the rain into his new home. He blinked for a moment, eyes dazzled by the light. Then he felt King's hand on his shoulder, guiding him forward.

'*Fresh meat! Fresh meat!*'

It was a group of black lads gathered round a table. They could have been any group of teenagers hanging anywhere, except for the crap tracksuits and the absence of burgers or cans. Some sat; some stood, with a bad case of PBS – prison bitch syndrome, trousers hanging so far down their arses that if they wanted to take a piss, they would have had to pull them up to get everything aligned. They all thumped the table top in time with their chant.

The unit was built around a large triangular open space. Cells lined each of the three sides at ground level and on a higher level, and in between was the common area. All the cell doors were open. Sean didn't know what time they all got locked up, but he guessed that during the day they could move about. At least a little.

King just kept walking like the cheering lads weren't there. Sean glanced around, trying not to look worried. He couldn't see any other screws. There were prisoners watching TV, playing pool, just lounging on bean bags and jawing. One thing he noticed immediately: each race stuck together. Asians, whites, blacks, each clustered together. Just like the world he knew outside. And the whites were subdivided too. Body language and other subtle clues told him that the group of lads sitting at the table *there* were distinct from the group lounging *there*. The table lads, he was prepared to bet, were fellow East Londoners. The lounging ones had rangy bodies, lean faces, severe haircuts – he wouldn't have been surprised if they were East Europeans.

Everyone who was standing or walking had both hands shoved down the front of their tracksuit bottoms, apparently holding their bollocks. Maybe for protection, maybe for warmth, maybe to keep their PBS bottoms up . . .

For the first time in his life Sean realized that he had no idea. No idea at all.

Usually, you saw a gang of teenagers, and if you didn't know them, then you thought, *What the fuck are they doing here?* because they were strangers in your manor. So that kind of streamlined the process of deciding if they were going to be friends or enemies.

He had only a few seconds to size them up. He was taller than half of them. Also probably younger. OK.

He met the eye of the loudest, the largest, as he followed King. The other lad looked back and began to shout and thump even louder. A big cross dangled on a chain round his neck. Sean slowly raised his hand, middle finger extended, and turned it into a scratch behind his ear. Then he lowered the finger again, keeping it extended for as long as he could.

The other lad's eyes narrowed and he extended his own finger back.

That was the opening pleasantries dealt with.

Sean flashed his friendliest grin. 'No, but seriously, guys,' he said as he walked past. He turned to face them so that he was walking backwards. 'You're too kind, and I'd love to have you all queue up and suck my dick, but, you know . . .' He put all the fingertips of one hand to his mouth and gave them an elaborate, lingering kiss. He never took his eyes off the other lad. And as he turned, he tapped the fingers he had just kissed against his bum crack, and gave his hips an extra wiggle for good measure. The message was obvious.

Kiss my arse.

King glanced sideways at him but said nothing. Sean still had no idea if he had just made friends or enemies, but he had made his mark.

And then . . .

'*Seany!*'

Sean's head whipped round just in time to catch someone advancing on him like a runaway petrol tanker bearing down on a moped. He just had a chance to take in the shock of red hair and a pair of arms that could bend steel pipes, and then Copper had flung his arms around him in a bear hug and hoisted his feet off the ground, shaking him.

'Fuck me, it's Sean fucking Harker! So they sent you here, you poor dumb fuck?'

Copper was a lad with two very obvious defining features. The first was his short, but bright red, hair. And if anyone thought that taking the piss out of it was a good idea, then his other defining feature usually put them off: he was massive.

'Hi . . . Copper . . .' Sean gasped between shakes. And even though he was glad, all the usual Copper precautions were sliding into place. You put a smile on your face. You thought extra hard about everything you were about to say, because if he ever took offence, then there would be zero time to unsay it. With these defences in place, you could enjoy being around him.

Because, for all his faults, Copper was one of the three big brothers Sean had never had, along with Matt and Gaz. Copper had taught him to fight, and fight hard. And one or two other lessons, including 'Don't be like Copper'.

'Put him down and step away, Mulroy.' The warder's voice had suddenly taken on a harsher tone.

Copper slowly put him down and backed off. 'It's OK, Mr King. Sean and I go way back.' He ruffled Sean's hair. 'Right?'

Sean knocked his hand away, still with a grin. 'Right. Yeah, Matt said you'd be here.'

'Yeah? How's he doing, all on his ownsome?'

'Hey, Mulroy.' It was the big black lad calling, the one with the cross. 'Your friend has respect issues.'

'Ah, fuck off, Tag.' Copper didn't even look round, and Sean saw how Tag's eyes narrowed a little. OK. 'So, where you putting him, Mr King?'

The officer regarded Copper coldly, but there wasn't much point telling him to walk away. 'He's in twenty-two,' he said. 'This way, Harker.'

'Twenty-two, Sean,' Copper said with a wink. 'See you in thirty seconds.'

King led Sean up the steps to the next level, and stopped by a cell door. 'Your new home from home.'

Sean stepped in, trying to ignore the thick steel that he knew would close behind him soon enough.

The room was small and simple. It was lit by a strip light on the ceiling, and grey light seeping in from a barred window. A single bed stood against one wall. Another wall had a stainless steel toilet and a sink. There was a desk, where a brown envelope lay next to a box just about large enough for a pair of shoes, with a TV above it, bolted to the wall and spewing out the news. The rolling headlines mentioned a bomb alert on the Tube, a stabbing in Croydon, a strike by firemen and ambulance drivers until the police could offer them better protection on call-outs.

'I'll be back in half an hour for your first-night interview,' said King. 'Until then, just try and settle in as best you can.'

Then he was gone.

Sean chucked his towel on the bed, and tipped the contents of the envelope out on the desk. Two small bars of soap, a white plastic comb, two tubes of toothpaste and a pale blue toothbrush.

'Hey, Sean, look who's here!'

Copper filled the doorway behind him, but he pulled someone forward and sent him into the cell with a thrust of one powerful arm.

'Hey, Sean,' Gaz Dobson said quietly.

Big brother number three, and the one Sean was actually, properly, glad to see. He hadn't set eyes on Gaz since the raid that got him and his old man nicked for running one of the most profitable vehicle chop shops in London. Too much money had been passing through it for either of them to get probation. Losing both Dobsons in one go had hit the Guyz' income hard.

If Matt had taught Sean how not to get caught, it was Gaz who had taught him how to nick in the first place. Even when he was just a kid, Sean had known his way around a car engine, and how to break into one. It was the ultimate rush and the best way to pull girls.

'Yo! Gaz!' Sean strode forward with a grin on his face, hand held out to bump fists. Gaz had shrunk since they last saw each other. He seemed to stand a little wonky, even allowing for the stupid tracksuit. He took just a moment too long to return the fist bump.

'Good to see you, Sean.' He winced as Copper thumped him on the back.

'How cool is this? Three Guyz together – we are going to rule this place. Say, lucky you got nicked when you did. I'm out in January and Gaz is getting on. Few months later, you'd have missed us both.'

It took Sean a moment to work out what he meant. Gaz was pushing twenty-one, like Copper, while Sean had just turned sixteen. Another few months and Copper would be out and Gaz would be too old for a Young Offender Institution. Their paths wouldn't have crossed.

Gaz was more helpful. He nodded at the small pile of toiletries on the desk. 'You'll have to buy your own when they run out.' He had his arms wrapped around himself.

Sean nodded his thanks and turned to the box. Small boxes and sachets. Cereal, milk, tea, bread, jam.

'And that's your breakfast pack. Proper full English on Sundays, otherwise it's this stuff.'

'So, uh, Gaz . . .' Sean sat down on the bed, bounced experimentally. The springs creaked.

'No silent wanks in this place,' Copper said cheerfully, and laughed like a drain.

'How're you doing?' Sean finished his question.

Gaz looked at him like he had just said a very, very stupid thing. 'You mean, apart from being locked up? And the fact that there's a condition that I don't ever get to work with vehicles again?'

Sean gaped. 'Shit, no! But . . .'

There was no *but*. Cars were Gaz's life, end of.

Gaz just shrugged, and got another slap on the back from Copper.

'Ignore him. So, Sean, when we brung you up so well – how did you go and get caught?'

Sean pulled a face. He'd known this was coming. 'After you two got nicked . . .' he began. Copper encouraged him to keep going with a nod. 'Matt thought he'd give me and Curly a chance to step up . . .'

Copper's eyes had narrowed. *Oh, crap. When are you going to learn, Sean?*

'I mean, obviously, we'd never replace you,' he said quickly, 'but, you know, Matt needed the help . . .'

'That's how it goes,' Gaz said with a shrug, taking the sting out of it. 'And?'

'And he took us on a job. Patel's Quality Used Vehicles, off Ilford Hill.'

'Patel's, huh?' There was actually the ghost of a smile on Gaz's face. Patel's had been the chief rival to his old man's operation. 'Good choice.'

'Yeah,' Sean said heavily. 'You'd think.'

It should have been the perfect crime. Sean had been taught by the best in the business – Gaz's dad – that if you really want to make money, then you let the other guy do the work. You let someone else pimp a car up with all the flash gear, and then you take it all off again. Gaz's old man made more money selling off the bits – rims, stereos, body kits – than if he just sold the whole car. And Patel's parts would be untraceable. Half of them would be hooky too, with the old serial numbers filed off. They wouldn't have been going to the cops in a hurry.

Sean and the lads would have got into the shop, found the keys to all the cars, ripped off as many parts as they could, loaded them all up and driven them back to a secure lock-up at Littern Mills. Job done and Patel severely pissed off.

'Only it all went tits,' Sean added, carefully not mentioning who had been the one to drop the phone. Anyway, that twat Curly shouldn't have nudged him. He described the jump, and the motorbike, and what had happened next.

Copper howled with laughter. 'Oh, Harker, you stupid tosser. OK, well, it's done and here we are. You, me, Gaz – we're going to rule this joint. You'll see.'

Soon after that, King was back. He took Sean to the medical centre, where the doctor listened to his chest and back with a stethoscope, shone a light into his eyes and ears, and asked questions about his medical health. Then it was over to a small meeting room in the unit, where Prison Officer Jacqui Parker shuffled papers in a folder, gave him a patient, friendly smile that was just too switched on for his liking, and asked if he had ever thought of self-harm or suicide. She tried to convince him that if he behaved himself, he could get out of this place with a clean break from the past and never have to come back again.

After the interview, King took him for his first shower in captivity. Then he was able to grab some fish and chips – and finally it was back to his cell, his hair still damp. The sound of the door closing and locking behind him echoed around inside his skull long after he had gone to bed. At first he just lay there, staring at the ceiling. Next to the smoke detector there was a red arrow in a circle, with words in English and – he guessed – Arabic: *Qibla prayer direction*.

Then the lights went out automatically. After that he lay on his back in the dark and stared at the ceiling, where the detector and the arrow would be.

Ahead of him lay a week-long induction. Then the rest of his sentence. Beyond that, the rest of his life. But to progress to any of that, first he had to get to sleep. It had been a long day, the shittiest one of his life, but it was still way too early for bed, and his body was pumped full of adrenaline.

Burnleigh was too quiet. Sean missed the music and voices and road noise that you got on the estate. The silence was almost like a steady background roar, but it was enveloping. He could feel it surrounding him, and at last it brought sleep with it. His last thought was that, hey, it was shit but he had two friends here. Well, one friend and Copper. It might be all right . . .

An electronic scream blasted into his eardrums, and every muscle in his body spasmed. He sat up sharply and bellowed into the darkness. 'THE FUCK!?'

Alarms were blaring out in the corridor. *DRRR-DRRR-DRRR...*

He heard shouts, and booted feet running on lino. There was a crackle of static, and an amplified voice spoke.

'All inmates, stand by your beds and prepare for evacuation. All inmates, stand by your beds and prepare for evacuation...'

Evacuation? Sean threw his duvet back and clambered out. Something tickled his nose, and he paused and sniffed.

Smoke. Not tobacco smoke. *Smoke* smoke. The kind that smelled dirty and gritty and burned the inside of your nose. The kind where things were burning that weren't supposed to burn.

Fu-u-u-u-ck.

There had been a fire on the estate when he was little. A confused OAP with dementia, who didn't understand ovens, had been cooking his food on an open fire in the living room. It had got out of control. The block had been evacuated. Sean remembered the smoke creeping up the stairwells and through the vents. And he remembered weeping with fear and impatience as his stupid cow of a mum waddled her way down the stairs along with everyone else, not letting go of his hand and *not moving fast enough.*

To smell that strong, this fire had to be big, or close, or both.

Sean paced around the cell. The smoke smell was growing more intense. Outside, he could hear the sounds of keys in locks, and men shouting orders. *C'mon, c'mon, let me out of here . . .*

And then it was his turn. A screw pulled the door open. 'Assemble outside the front entrance—'

Sean didn't need to be told twice.

Out in the corridor, he understood why the smell of smoke had been so heavy. The air outside the cell next door was still hazy. From inside he could hear the bellowing gush of fire extinguishers. A dark-haired lad sat by the door, hugging his knees and laughing hysterically while two screws stood over him.

'You dumb prat, Omar!' shouted a familiar voice. Copper barged his way down the corridor, a scary sight in just his underwear. A screw tried to confront him and was bowled aside. Two more moved forward immediately, shoulder to shoulder to block his way.

'That'll do, Mulroy.'

'You could have killed us all!' Copper bellowed. Omar's laughing just grew even louder.

'Get a move on.' A screw gave Sean a shove towards the exit.

*

It was an hour before they were allowed back inside. The fire brigade had to check the building and confirm that all fires were out. Thirty minutes were spent shivering and trying to shelter from the rain under the plastic cover of the walkway, until the screws finally thought to bring blankets round.

Sean, Gaz and Copper huddled together in their own little group. Copper was large enough to act as a windbreak for the other two. He and Gaz filled Sean in on what was happening, though he had worked most of it out for himself.

Omar had set fire to his bedding and clothes. Those things were meant to be non-flammable, so he must have gone to a lot of trouble to get hold of something that would help them burn. And Omar had previous. This wasn't the first time.

'He's been in and out of the shrink's office more often than my dick's been in and out of your mum,' Copper explained. 'Fucking insane, that's what he is. Should be put away with the other fucktards.'

So fucking selfish, Sean thought as he pulled his blanket around his shoulders. There had to be ways of topping yourself that didn't involve killing everyone else.

Eventually they were allowed back into their cells. Five minutes later, the lights went out again.

Sean stared into the darkness.

He had known that this place would be different. He had known that he could take nothing from his old life for granted. This place would not be normal.

He hadn't realized just how far from normal it would be.

He had thought it might be all right. It wasn't.

He lay sleepless for the rest of the night, in a place where a lad just like him had been prepared to set fire to himself and everyone else rather than face another day.

Chapter 4

The wake-up call: a shrill, brain-shuddering metallic ring. One month in, Sean had learned the hard way to keep his eyes closed until the lights came on. Otherwise you were there in the dark with your eyes open when some screw threw the switch, and then, *Aargh!* Light speared into your eyes.

Light and sound combined were a pretty good way of wrecking the sleep of every inmate in the block. The screws' way of saying: *OK, you've had your beauty sleep, time to get on with the day.*

Sean grunted and forced his eyes open. Every morning he felt like it took a bit more energy. He couldn't remember the last time he had slept properly. His first night – well, thank fuck there had been no repeat of *that*. His second night, he had expected to be so tired he would just switch off.

No such luck. It wasn't that the bed was uncomfortable.

He had slept on worse – or sometimes just passed out, which was more or less the same thing.

It was just that he was in prison. End of.

But if he just lay there, he had the horrible feeling that he would be absorbed into the walls. He would become part of the place. An old lag.

Not going to happen.

He threw back the duvet and slunk over to the sink to wash his face in icy cold water. It was that, or wait five minutes for something lukewarm to trickle its way from the boilers to his cell and out through the hot tap. Sunken grey eyes stared at him from the stainless steel mirror screwed to the wall above the sink, beneath a fringe of blond bed-hair, all crushed on one side and matted to his forehead. It wouldn't get sorted out until it was his turn to have a shower. Face like uncooked pizza dough. Fucking hell, he looked ancient.

Sean stepped back and studied the A4 sheet of paper Blu-tacked to the wall next to the TV. He had listed the days of his sentence, 1 to 182, and put a smiley face at 23, 46, 69 . . . every 23 days, all the way to the end. Each one was roughly an eighth of the total. Days 46 and 138 – the quarter and three-quarter marks – had an extra smiley, and the halfway mark at day 92 had a big *PARTY-Y-Y!*

His mouth forced itself into a smile and he crossed

off day 33. Over one eighth of the way through, and in less than a fortnight he'd be at the first quarter.

'Yep,' he muttered. 'Sean's coming home.'

'Hey, Gaz! Heart-attack special!'

Sean put his tray down on the table and dropped into the chair across from his mate. Tables and chairs were all screwed to the floor, to deter anyone from thinking they'd be just the thing to use to cave in someone's head. The canteen air was rich with every smell the prison could throw at the inmates. Stale breath and sweat was mixed up with unwashed clothes, food, milk and coffee. Through this came the cold tang of air pushing in through open windows, bringing with it hints of the world beyond. Car fumes, damp earth. If the wind was blowing just right, Sean had sometimes caught wafts that reminded him of the baker's back on the Mills. Most days he'd have killed for a baked-bean-and-cheese slice, or just a decent mug of coffee.

But Sundays were a break from the breakfast pack that everyone ate in their cells. It was a decent fry-up in the canteen, even though it wasn't a real fry-up because nothing got fried. It was cooked in the oven – no one trusted inmates around hot oil. But at least it was a meal that filled you up. And it was a day off lessons. Weekdays, they were obligatory, starting at 8.30. The only good thing was you got 40p for every class attended to spend on chocolate or phone credits; Sean had never been one for school – as the three he had been to since age eleven could all confirm.

'Problem, bro?' Sean asked after a moment, when it became clear that Gaz was saying nothing.

The other lad looked up from his untouched tray and stared at Sean with dark, empty eyes. 'This place,' he said. 'It's doing my head in.'

'Uh, yeah?' Sean held his hands out as if presenting Gaz with the basic facts. 'It's supposed to. You just got to get through it. Don't let it get to you.'

Gaz shook his head. 'When you get out of here, Sean, what're you going to do? You're going to go back to the Guyz, right?'

'Hell, yeah!'

'Me, I'm only good at one thing, and that's what got me in here, and the court says I'll never be allowed to do it again. Any pig sees me working on a car that I don't own – I'm back here. Some little old lady breaks down and I help her change her fucking tyre – I'm back here. Except it won't be here, it'll be adult prison, which will make this place look like fucking paradise. So every day I spend here is just one less day of fucking boredom before I get out into a *world* of fucking boredom.'

'Proper Mr Sunshine, in't we?'

Sean said that because he wasn't sure what else to say. That first day they'd met, he'd thought Gaz was fine. Subdued, but fine. Everyone looked a bit down when they were standing next to Copper, drowned out by the big lad's optimism.

But even without Copper's presence to cloud the issue, Sean had started to notice the darkness there.

Back on the estate, Gaz had always been one of the quieter ones. He had let his expertise with cars do the talking. When he did speak up, he was always worth listening to – it was just that he didn't need to shout and act up and throw his weight around to get noticed.

But as the days and weeks had gone on, Sean started to realize that maybe Gaz wasn't cut out for this place at all.

He took a deep breath, knowing that the words forming on his tongue could be the end of a friendship. They were just not the kind of thing Guyz said to each other. But . . .

'Gaz . . . mate . . .' That used up the breath. He took another as Gaz looked at him quizzically. 'You know, you could talk to someone about it, right?'

The look Gaz gave him made him want to curl up and die, or cry, or both. And that was *so fucking unfair*! Sean wouldn't have said a word if he hadn't wanted to help. And yes, he knew he was sounding like the prison psychologist, and that meant he might as well just write TRAITOR in large letters on his forehead. But what else could he do?

'Talk,' Gaz said.

'Well – yeah. Talk.'

Gaz didn't blink. 'About what?'

'About . . . you know . . . Oh, forget it. Forget I spoke. Forget everything.' He attacked his breakfast angrily and a shadow reached over his tray. Sean took a tighter grip on his fork and raised it. 'I wouldn't,' he said, without even looking up.

'I wasn't doing nothin',' Copper said cheerfully. He sat down opposite Sean, next to Gaz, squeezing his bulk into the plastic seat. He reached again for Sean's fried bread.

Sean raised the fork again. 'I'll stab your bastard meat hooks if they get any closer to my tray, I promise.'

'Hey, Sean. Seany. Half that lot's wasted on a skinny shit like you. I need the fuel.'

'And I need you to keep off.'

Copper grinned. 'You know, you've changed.' He turned his attention to the pile of food on his own tray.

'*You* haven't,' Sean replied.

'Hey, once you achieve perfection, I say leave well alone, yeah?'

Sean smiled, couldn't help it, as Copper flexed a bicep

and kissed it. 'You really are fucked in the head – you know that, right?'

Sean talked to Copper like that because it was the only way to keep him normal. It was what he understood. And having a friend the size of Copper was no bad thing – it made other people steer clear. It worked on the street, it worked in here.

'Class A headfuck, me,' Copper agreed proudly. 'Right, Gazza?'

Gaz sighed, pushed his tray back, got up. 'Fuck off, Copper,' he murmured. He took the tray, still laden with food, over to the disposal slots.

Copper actually looked a little surprised, maybe even hurt. Then he shrugged and burped, long and loud. The stench of it rolled over Sean like a cloud of vom.

'God, you're hideous,' he said. Deep down, he meant it too. Was it worth pointing out that Gaz seemed unhappy? Would Copper even believe it? Probably not.

'You wait till this all comes out the other end.'

'I'll pass. Cheers.'

Copper pushed his own plate back and stood up. His tray looked like it had been licked clean. 'Laters, Seany.'

Sean nodded and watched Copper wander off, then turned back to finish his meal, though he knew he'd still be hungry even afterwards. He reached for his drink, just as someone barged into his back. Water spewed across his food.

Sean swivelled angrily in his seat and looked up into the face of the black guy he knew only as Tag. The big guy, the loudest of the *Fresh meat* crew, who had complained about his respect issues on his first day. A couple of other black guys hung in the background, like reserves. Tag was casually fingering the cross around his neck. Sean had found that, in here, a lot of lads discovered God in a big way, as a means of protection. They wore the big crosses for all to see. If Tag had found religion, it didn't seem to have made much impact on the rest of his life.

'Fuck you looking at?' Tag said.

'The twat who ruined my fucking breakfast,' Sean snapped back.

'Done you a favour then, haven't I?' Tag replied. 'Tastes like dog shit. You should be thanking me.'

Sean chucked his cutlery down on his tray. He had met plenty of lads like Tag. Lots of swagger, lots of over-the-top body movement to emphasize every word they said. It just made the lanky wannabe gangster seem even more of a dick.

A dick who wanted a fight. It wasn't coincidence that Tag had waited until Copper left. They both knew this couldn't end well, but Tag didn't care. He wanted to hurt

Sean – as a matter of principle and because it would earn him respect from his crew.

Respect was the only thing they both had. Sean and Tag were about equal when it came to education, cash, and prospects for success in the world outside. But Sean knew that he had the respect of the only people whose opinion mattered to him – Gaz and Copper and Matt, and all the Guyz – and he had earned it, so fuck what anyone else thought.

Tag had probably never earned a scrap of respect in his life, except through fear and being a tosser. He just claimed it, and picked fights as an easy way to get it from other losers like him.

'You're not even going to apologize, then?' Sean said, with not a lot of hope.

Tag sneered. 'You're having a laugh. I ain't apologizing to no one. You should be apologizing to me, man, for vexing me. And I don't like being vexed.'

Sean was tired. He was hungry. And he just wasn't in the mood for any of this. He rose to his feet, no threat, just calm and casual, but Tag bumped him back down into his seat.

'Reckon you should stay seated – know what I mean?'

Sean breathed deep and slow, taking air in through his nose, then exhaling through his mouth. He was reading Tag now, watching for any small signs of his next move. When it came, it wasn't much. A flex of the jaw, a tightening of a fist as an arm pulled back just a little.

Sean didn't wait. He ducked down and sprang away as Tag came in with his right hand white-knuckle tight. Only Sean wasn't there any more, and the movement sent him off balance. Now Sean was on his feet and Tag was stumbling forwards in front of him. Sean hammered down onto the back of Tag's neck with his right forearm.

This wasn't a street fight where you had time to go in for another attack. Here, you had to make whatever you were doing count, because the prison officers would be on you in seconds. No messing around. So all Sean's weight and strength went into that one forearm swipe. Tag didn't stand a chance: he crashed down onto the floor.

Tag's two reserves had already fled. Sean laughed and stood back. He knew what was coming next.

Before he'd even had time to put both hands above his head, three warders were on him, with two others closing in. He didn't fight back, didn't struggle. No point getting a broken arm on top of everything else.

Prison called it 'basic'. Sean called it 'solitary'. It lasted a week.

With all his privileges revoked, he was moved out of

his cell and placed in the solitary wing. A single cell, smaller, more basic than the usual, locked in for twenty-three hours a day. No exercise, no education. Just enough time to get showered, grab food, then back to the four walls.

Day one wasn't so bad. He managed a little exercise – star jumps, stomach crunches, press-ups. He read some of a book he'd been allowed to take with him. He had chosen it because he'd seen the film and it was pretty decent.

Day two came, and Sean started to notice something weird about his time. There seemed to be more of it. And no matter what he did with it, he couldn't get rid of it. Sleep didn't come easily. He was restless. Exercise seemed pointless. The book was dull.

Day three, he started to think about what lay outside the cell: the people, the noise, the endless space. A car might strike you down as you crossed the road. Some git a thousand miles away in some country you would never visit might decide it was your turn to die today, and a bomb would take your life without you ever knowing. Out there struck him as a dangerous place to be. Perhaps staying in the small cell made sense. Most of that day he spent perched on the bed hugging his knees.

Day four was the complete opposite. He paced about the little room, convinced it was getting smaller. Did the walls creep a little closer every time he took his eye off them?

He stood on the bed to peer out of the high, narrow window. Shit, there were trees out there. Trees! It was late autumn and the leafless branches made him think of bare bones clawing at the sky. Even so. He quite fancied climbing a tree. That would be fun. He couldn't remember the last time he'd done it, if he ever had. Funny, he thought, how here inside a prison he could see more trees every day than he'd ever seen in his whole life, and yet he still couldn't get to them.

Day five, he had a visitor, and his life changed for ever.

Chapter 5

'Uh – hi?'

Sean stopped just inside the door to his tiny cell. The screw who had escorted him from the showers gave him a shove in the back and closed the door, but didn't lock it.

A man stood in the middle of the floor with his arms behind his back, feet slightly apart, back straight, like he owned the place. Like he was the one receiving the visitor. Sean guessed he was in his late thirties. His face was worn and lined, his light brown hair cropped short. A furrowed brow sat above pale grey eyes that were frighteningly alert. He wore green slacks and a white T-shirt over a wiry, athletic frame. The shirt had some kind of crest on the left breast.

He smiled when he saw Sean, but . . . that smile. It wasn't a friendly, pleased-to-meetcha smile. It wasn't the sneer of a Tag or the mad grin of a Copper. It was . . . it was the way Sean might smile at a new Ferrari which he just knew he was going to wire later that night. Quiet, keeping it to himself, but supremely confident that he would get what he wanted.

'Sean Harker. Hi. Phil Adams.'

It was a London accent. Adams held his right hand out to shake and Sean clocked the tattoos straight away. The man saw where Sean was looking and held out the other hand. Both powerful forearms were heavily inked.

'Matching pair,' he said with another, friendlier smile.

Sean didn't return the smile. Adams lowered his hands.

'Mate,' Sean said. His voice sounded weird in his ears – the first words he had said out loud to another human for five days. 'If you get locked in with me for another twenty-three hours, then I'm keeping the bed.'

'They'll let me out. Do you want to sit down?'

Sean wasn't sure he did. They were about the same height, so he wasn't about to be intimidated, but it was clear from Adams's body language that neither was he. The man perched himself on the edge of Sean's table. Sean sat on the bed, a safe distance away, so that he could sit without craning his head upwards. Adams picked up a slim plastic folder from the desk but didn't open it.

'So. One month down, five to go, and you get yourself thrown in choky. Careless, any?'

Sean shrugged.

Adams opened the folder and made a show of browsing through it. 'Twelve months for taking without consent, and obviously not your first time, just the first one they got you for. Bit of a petrolhead, are we?'

Another shrug.

Adams went on. 'My sister's lad says petrol is a chemical for turning money into fun. Here . . . I've been dying to show this to someone who will appreciate it.'

He dug out his phone and flipped through screens until he had the picture he wanted, before holding it out to Sean. Sean waited – to show he was only doing this because he wanted to – then took it to see what the fuss was.

The screen showed a couple of smiling lads, maybe a bit older than him, apparently standing in a road while they gave a thumbs up to the camera.

He almost asked, 'Who're the losers?' but something about Adams's obvious pride said maybe he shouldn't. He read the status caption.

Hey, this is us on the Mulsanne Straight, hours before the 24-hour Le Mans cars were doing over 200mph down here!!

O . . . kay. He had to admit, that really was quite cool.

He handed the phone back.

'That's my nephew and a mate,' Adams said. 'They saved ages for that holiday.'

And suddenly it was clear. Sean grinned, without finding anything funny. Different way of doing things, same old bollocks. The prison was trying a new way of making him into a useful member of society.

'And . . . here it comes. The lesson.'

'And what lesson would that be?'

'You know, the lesson. *You don't need to steal stuff, Sean. All you need to do is work hard and you'll get your rewards that way.*'

'Well, shit, you saw right through me. Don't I feel dumb.' Adams was back in the folder. 'Now, apart from that one incident with Joseph Ajayi, aka Tag, you've a clean record in here. So what comes next? When you're out?'

If it was a choice between his old life and serving up fries for a year on a zero-hours contract so he could stand on the Mulsanne Straight, Sean knew which one he was going for. So he looked Adams in the eye. 'Back to my mates,' he said.

'Ah, yes. The Littern Guyz, right? Bit after my time, but I still know the names. Friends, loyalty, identity. That's it, isn't it?'

His voice grew unexpectedly warm and Sean cocked a suspicious eye. Adams was the first adult inside to talk about the Guyz like membership wasn't a dose of chlamydia, and that put him on his guard.

'So?'

'So I know exactly where you're coming from, which is why we're having this chat. I'm after lads with similar sets of values who might want something with all the benefits of the Guyz and none of the drawbacks. A number of other inmates have been identified as suitable and I'll also be speaking to them. At the moment it's invitation only. So . . .'

Adams opened the folder and passed a sheet of A4 paper to Sean. He took it, flipped it round, and read what was on it. Two minutes later he raised his eyes to stare at Adams.

'You're joking, right?' he said. 'You can't actually be serious.'

Adams shook his head. 'It's a new initiative,' he said, nodding towards the sheet. 'Full approval of the Ministry of Defence. The government wants to try it in a couple of places like this before rolling it out further. So it's a test case, a pilot thing. An army cadet force in a Young Offender Institution. Still a few bits and pieces to sort out, so it goes live in January.'

Sean shook his head. 'I'm not a toy soldier.' He pinched the tracksuit top he was wearing, stretching out the material. 'And I'm sick enough of wearing green. So whichever dickless politician thought this up, you can tell them I'm not interested.'

'I understand.' Adams shrugged. 'It's not for everyone. Some will always find it easier to back off from a challenge than try it out first.'

Sean didn't like the implication. 'I didn't say I wasn't up to it. I said I wasn't interested.'

'So you're happy just being a waster doing fuck all with your life?'

Sean blinked. He had never heard a member of staff say 'fuck' before. Some rule about half the inmates technically being children.

'Are you allowed to talk to me like that?'

'I can talk however I like.'

'Look, I just want to do my time,' Sean said, working hard to stay calm. 'I don't want to run around in some crap uniform, doing push-ups and star jumps. You think that's better than the Guyz? You've got no idea. No idea at all.'

Adams rolled his right sleeve up to the shoulder. Sean stared at the ink. He didn't recognize it exactly, but he knew what it was. A gang mark.

'Got that twenty years ago. My mates, my gang – they're all gone now. Dead, or gone straight, or inside. Mostly inside. Yeah, I could get it lasered off, but it's a reminder. Where I've come from, what I've done, where I am now.'

'You've been inside?' The question blurted out – Sean couldn't help it.

'Not . . . technically.' Adams let the sleeve drop back and pulled up the hem of his T-shirt. A scar stretched from his belly button diagonally across his abs – which Sean couldn't help noticing were a lot more prominent than his own, and he knew he was fit. 'I got stabbed, spent a week in a coma, five weeks after that on life support. So I got time off in lieu.'

Sean didn't move. He wanted to say something that would shut the man down for good, but he was on the back foot now. The words wouldn't come.

Adams tugged his shirt back down. 'What you have here, Harker, is a choice. Take a look around you. This could be your home on and off for the rest of your life. It's comfortable, you get fed; you're pretty safe too. Don't even have to think for yourself really, do you? Just let the state sort everything out. Did any of your schools teach you enough science to know what a parasite is?'

Sean sat up straight. 'Who you calling a parasite?'

'Or you could grow a pair and do something. Put your skills and talents to use.'

Sean laughed. 'Read the file, mate. My skills and talents are twoccing cars and getting into fights. Not saluting some bloke I've no respect for every day.'

Adams shook his head. 'First,' he said, 'the only way

you can show some bloke any respect at all is if you first learn to respect yourself. And from what I see, that's a long way off from happening. And second: Vietnam, Malaya, Oman – all military campaigns, but which is the odd one out?'

Sean stared at him. 'You what?'

'It's Vietnam. Absolute fiasco. The other two were led and won by the British Army. And the way we did it was we won the locals over to our side. Instead of bombing them into the Stone Age and expecting them to be grateful for the privilege of being on the front line, we used the skills they had in their native environments. You're a native, Harker.'

'Only problem is, we're not at war.'

'You reckon?' Suddenly the smile was still on Adams's mouth but it had left his eyes. 'We're at war right now. Just because you don't see it on CNN, don't think it isn't real. It's building on the streets, and one way or another you're going to be a street soldier – maybe in uniform, maybe not.'

Suddenly there was a screw at the door, jangling his keys to make a point. 'You've had your five minutes, Sergeant. I need to lock Harker up.'

'Coming.' Adams stood and headed for the door.

'Hey . . . Sergeant?' Sean began.

Adams paused by the screw, looked back. 'Didn't say,

did I? Yes, I'll be in charge of it.' He touched one finger to his forehead. 'Don't bother saluting. I wouldn't want you to salute some bloke you've no respect for.'

So, that was day five.

Days six and seven just sort of merged. Adams's piece of paper lay untouched on the table.

Day eight, Sean was in his own cell again.

King escorted him back. He stood in the middle of the floor and looked around. It was a strange anti-climax. It was cool to just be left there and not have the door locked behind him, but even so.

'You been re-assigned to a lesson schedule yet?' the warder asked.

'Not yet.' Again, his voice sounded unusually loud inside his skull. He thought of going to see Gaz or Copper to announce his return – but they would be at their own lessons. 'Can I have a shower, Mr King? Could do with a good hot wash.' The showers in basic were time-limited and supervised.

'Not the usual time of day, but – sure, knock yourself out.'

Sean grabbed his towel and set off.

The shower block smelled of damp and stale water, with a stronger toilet smell than usual today. Noises echoed off the tiled floors and walls, including the trickle of water from a cubicle that was already occupied. The showers were in individual cubicles; the changing area was common to everyone. Getting naked in front of other guys had been weird at first, but you got used to it.

He stripped off quickly and headed for the cubicle next to the occupied one. Taking a shower during the day was unusual, but hey, he was doing it so why shouldn't someone else?

He grinned as the hot water hit his skin. He held his head under the flow and let it wash the memories of solitary away. He was letting the water flow over the rest of him when he felt something nudge his foot. He jerked it away instinctively and looked down. Then leaped away.

'*Oh, fuck, that's disgusting!*'

All the cubicles had a common gutter, so that your neighbour's water and grime flowed along through yours and into the drain at the end. A turd, an actual lump of human shit, was bobbing along in the stream, as innocent as a scabby, flea-bitten rat turning up on the kitchen counter.

Furious, Sean rinsed his foot and wrapped the towel around his waist. He hurled himself out and hammered on the door of the occupied cubicle. 'The *fuck* do you think you're doing, you—'

The door swung open and he stared straight into the

bloated, twisted face of a lad dangling by his neck from a towel wrapped around the shower bracket.

Sean shouted, but only in surprise, because it took him a moment to realize who it was. The features were so distorted and it was the last person he expected to see. The two realizations came one after another. *This is a guy who has hanged himself who sorta looks like Gaz.* And then he clocked the Guyz tattoo, and he put two and two together, and he shouted more, and the shouts turned to screams.

He threw himself at the body. Water streamed over him as he fumbled at the knot of the towel. It was soaking, and his fingers slid off it. He tried to work them into the knot, but Gaz's weight had pulled it tight. He had to wrap his arms around Gaz's thighs and heave him up, which relieved the weight – but now he couldn't spare a hand to get at the knot.

Gaz's legs were swollen and dark and his skin was clammy to the touch, like uncooked chicken. Sean squeezed his eyes shut and fought back a heaving stomach. He fumbled for the taps and shut them off, still holding Gaz up with one hand.

He knew even then that it was too late, but he wouldn't, couldn't leave his mate to dangle. And so he screamed again as he held Gaz's weight in his arms.

'*Help me—*' He had to bite it off abruptly as his

stomach took advantage of the opening, and a column of vom shot halfway into his mouth. He swallowed, and forced it down, and screamed again with words that bounced back off the dead, flat tiles. And he kept screaming through his tears until someone came.

'*Help me! Help me!*'

Chapter 6

Sean's breath condensed in the air. It was a frosty January morning outside, and the gym hall was cold enough to double as a morgue, which was a comparison he didn't want to make. The screws had told him and a dozen other lads, all of them in their gym kit, to stand in a line. He knew them all by sight. Sean was surprised so many had turned up. There had been nods and grunts when they all set eyes on each other – the closest any of them were going to get to something like, *Hi! How are you?* There was a faint air of embarrassment hanging over them.

Time was something they all had plenty of, but Sean didn't know anyone who would spend it here without serious persuasion. He wondered if the others had been through anything like he had to motivate them.

With Sergeant Adams, apparently, it was being knifed into a coma. With Sean, it was seeing a friend dangle from a pipe. All his life Sean had made a conscious effort to be more like Gaz – and apparently being like Gaz could lead to *that*.

No. Not going to happen.

The dull *clank* of the gym door closing was followed by measured footsteps as Sergeant Adams came to stand in front of them. He was flanked by two other men, both seriously muscled. All of them wore pale green T-shirts and camo trousers, with their names marked in black on the left breast.

The sergeant's voice echoed around the gym. 'First of all, well done to all of you for turning up. This was by invitation only. Some of those invited declined the offer. That's their decision, this is yours. You've already made a change to who you are and what you're about.'

If this was just going to be a motivational chat, Sean thought, then he was going to walk.

'The fact is,' continued the sergeant, 'that an initiative like this doesn't work if people are forced to do it. The army is for volunteers only. Conscription's no good. We want to work with people who want to work with us. That way, we can achieve something, and so can you.'

Sean was getting fidgety, and he wasn't the only one.

'So if you're ready, I will hand over to Corporals Edwards and Grant.'

The bigger of the two corporals stepped forward.

His skin was as black as the other corporal's was pasty white. 'My name is Corporal Grant. You can call me Corporal.'

Sean wasn't sure if he was trying to make a joke. Regardless, no one laughed.

'For a soldier to be effective on the battlefield, he needs to be well trained and he needs to be fit. And I don't mean being able to run a couple of miles in fancy dress for charity. If you don't like to push yourself, then take the easy option and sod off right now. Because I promise you, you will be pushed – not simply to your limits, but beyond them. Understood?'

No one answered.

'And just so you know, if I ask a question, I expect an answer. And that answer is *Yes, Corporal.*'

Sean joined in as the line of inmates chorused weakly, 'Yes, Corporal.'

'What was that meant to be?' yelled Corporal Grant, stepping forward. 'You need to make yourself heard!'

Sean had seen too many war movies where the tough-as-shit drill instructor shapes an unpromising crew of cadets into killing machines, mostly by screaming at them. He had to suck his cheeks in to stop the snigger. Grant glanced sideways at him – only for half a second, but the hardness in his eye was enough to drive all the smirks right out of Sean's system.

'Again!' the corporal ordered.

The line tried again, and this time Grant seemed a little more satisfied.

'Better. Now, in a line, start jogging round the edge of the gym. And if any of you cuts a corner, you get ten push-ups. Move!'

Twenty minutes in and Sean was screwed. His legs were barely able to keep him upright, and his lungs felt close to being coughed up in a spew of blood and vomit.

'Keep going!' Corporal Edwards barked as Sean and the others switched from another dash down the hall, back to pushing themselves through a series of burpees – dropping from a standing position to the floor in a crouch, to spring out into a press-up, then back up again. 'Pain is weakness leaving the body, that's all! Do not give up! Do not quit!'

Sean felt dizzy as he staggered to the assigned spot for the next round of burpees. They were a killer. With every rep, his body seemed to get heavier and heavier, with more and more effort needed to get himself back to standing again. Down the line he saw one lad drop onto his face. Corporal Edwards was immediately next to him, yelling at him not to give up, to keep going. The lad dragged himself up, made to walk out, but the corporal followed him. Just as Sean expected to see the lad disappear through the gym doors, he turned and was back in line.

Sean focused on his own movements. Every muscle was a line of fire, running into joints which felt like they had molten lead pouring into them. He'd been chased by the police, he had run from other gangs, he had been in fights – he had even jumped a three-metre gap between roofs and hit the wall opposite – but this was way beyond all that.

So why didn't he stop? No one was making him do this. He could just walk out . . .

. . . and go back to a life of staring at walls, just waiting to return to the outside world . . . and end up like Gaz. Something was keeping him here, forcing him to push through the agony and ignore the alarms sounding in his mind to just stop.

A whistle blew.

'Right, girls, grab yourself a drink, have a breather. Well done.'

Twelve lads slumped by the wall, chests heaving, hair plastered, clothes soaked with sweat. Sean clutched his water bottle, but suddenly found he didn't have the strength to lift it to his mouth. He let it drop back on the floor. He would try again in a moment.

'Jesus.' The lad next to him forced the words out between gulps for air. Sean couldn't turn to look at him;

his head just sort of flopped round on his shoulders. The lad's face was split with a huge grin. 'I feel . . . I feel like . . . like I just had the best . . . shag . . . *ever.*'

'You . . . you're . . .' Sean had to take even bigger breaths just to get a sentence out. 'You're definitely doing it wrong, then.'

They collapsed in helpless sniggers which they didn't have the strength to stop. Then the whistle blew again.

The rest of the session raced by in a blur of sweat, pain and exhaustion. Back in his cell, it was all Sean could do to stop himself spinning down to unconsciousness on the floor. He managed to make it to his bed, limbs aching and shaking. He lay down. Passed out.

'No. Fucking. Way. You're joking.'

Sean was sitting with Copper over dinner and the conversation wasn't going well.

'No,' he said, shaking his head. 'I'm proper serious.'

Copper stopped eating, chucked his cutlery down on his tray. The knife landed in a puddle of congealing gravy. He didn't seem to care. 'You can't be,' he said. 'You hear me?'

'Well, I am,' Sean replied.

Copper shook his head, pointed a thick finger at him. 'Nah, you're not listening to me, Seany. You can't be serious. It's a statement, right? It's me telling you. So you'd better listen.'

Sean stopped eating, eased himself back on his seat, just far enough to be out of Copper's range. He didn't like the dark look in those eyes. 'It's got nothing to do with you,' he said. 'It's my life and my decision.'

Copper lowered his pointing finger, but not his stare. 'So you want to join the army.'

'Didn't say I wanted to. Just said I was thinking of it.'

It had just been there, in his head, when he woke up. He had opened his eyes and looked at the grey wall of the cell, and then there was an explosion in his brain.

It doesn't have to be like this.

He had a way out, if he wanted to take it. It was like all the physical punishment in the gym had torn something open inside him. He was thinking thoughts he would never have dared think before.

'Because what? You think that'll solve all your problems? Is that it?'

'It'd beat ending up back in here,' Sean said. 'And if I go back to what we both know, then that's what'd happen. I could do it. I could do it easy. I've got my community service after this. I can do my entrance tests while I'm doing that, then go in as soon as all this shit is over. It's a no-brainer.'

Copper laughed. It was not a sound Sean enjoyed. It had teeth and claws.

'The only no-brainer here is you, you pussy. Where's your loyalty? What about everyone else? Your friends? Think this is what Gaz would want?'

Bringing Gaz into it made Sean want to plant one right in the middle of Copper's large, angry face.

Gaz wanted to be dead. That's what Gaz wanted.

'And what about Matt? Look. Three weeks' time, I'm out of this place. You want me to go back to Matt and tell him *this*? You'll break that guy's heart, all he's done for you!'

'Didn't say I was going to,' Sean repeated, forcing himself to be calm. 'Just said I was thinking of it. Can't a guy think? And anyway, my friends is my friends, always will be. It's not like I'd turn snitch or anything like that. Give me some credit, bro.' He pulled his sleeve up to show his Guyz tattoo. Just like Adams had shown him his. 'I've got this and always will have.'

'Seany,' said Copper. 'Mate. Dude.' He took a breath. 'Bro. You join up, you're out – you know that, right?'

Sean stared. 'Why?'

Copper leaned forward to rest his arms on the table. 'You only get one family in life and it's the one you're born with. Us. Me. Matt. Against the foreigners.'

Sean looked blankly at him. 'What foreigners?'

'Oh, fer Chrissake. Haven't you noticed? There's foreigners moving in, Seany! Used to be you could walk one end of Littern Mills to the other and only see familiar faces. Now you can't step outside your flat. New people, taking over. Like that lot.'

He nodded over at the crowd of East Europeans who hung together in one corner of the canteen. Sean hadn't mixed much with them, but he respected them. They showed up at every class that Burnleigh offered and would be leaving here considerably better educated than him.

Sean shrugged. 'Everyone's new somewhere, once. Shit, my mum works in Lakhani's shop. He came here when he was a kid but he's lived here all his life. So, you calling him a foreigner?'

'Missing the point, Seany. Missing the point.' Copper gave a big theatrical sigh and a shake of the head. 'And speaking of your mum, what about her, then?'

Sean's eyes narrowed. 'And just what is that supposed to mean?'

'If you're out, who will look out for her?'

'I will, you bastard. Me. Her son.'

Copper shook his head. 'I'm just telling you how it is, Seany. If you're not around, if you're not in with the rest of us – she'll be on her own, right?'

Sean gripped the table to stop himself jumping across

it. 'I'll keep her right,' he said. 'And if anyone lays a hand on her . . .'

Copper stood up. 'You won't be able to stop them, will you, Seany, if you're off playing soldiers? And if you're not rolling with us . . . I'm not sure we'll be able to stop them either.'

'Right!' Sergeant Adams's voice echoed in the gym. He thumped one fist into the other. 'This is a controlled aggression exercise.'

The lads were sitting on benches set in a square the size of a boxing ring. Sean was standing in one corner, his gut twisting itself into knots, focusing on not being sick. In the opposite corner stood Copper.

It had been two weeks, and Sean didn't know if he was more surprised that he was still in the cadets, or that he was still alive. The fitness training was brutal, with the sergeant and the two corporals pushing him and the others beyond what any of them thought possible. Word was spreading. A few other lads had accepted Adams's invitation to join in – and Copper was one of them.

'The fuck?' That had been Sean's involuntary reaction when he saw Copper's bulk straining against his gym kit, standing in line with the rest of them. He had mostly succeeded in avoiding Copper since their argument in the canteen, and with only a week to go before Copper's sentence was up, Sean had been hoping he could make it all the way through without any more encounters.

Copper had winked. 'Someone's got to keep an eye on you, Seany.'

Now Copper was smiling. It didn't make Sean feel any better about what was about to go down. They were both wearing boxing gloves. Sean was surprised by just how heavy they were. They seemed to drag his hands towards the ground.

Adams continued to brief them.

'As soldiers, you need to be able to manage your ability to draw on something that most people cannot comprehend – to switch from calm to mental in a beat.'

Sean noticed Copper's grin get even wider. *Fuck*, he thought, *the big bastard is going to kill me* . . .

'You have a minute in the ring with your opponent. It is not a question of winning or losing. Instead, this is about not quitting. You get knocked down, you get back up and pile in. You get smashed on the nose, you retaliate, harder. Best defence is attack. You will be nervous. You will get hurt. But it's just sixty seconds. Get in there and fight. That's all there is to it.'

Sean took a slow, deep breath. The sergeant's pep talk had done nothing to make him feel any better.

'Ready?' Adams asked.

Sean nodded. Copper nodded. Of the two of them, only Copper was smiling. The sergeant bumped his fists gently together as a sign. Sean held out his gloves; Copper knocked his own gloves against them. Technically it was the same as shaking hands, but the gleam in Copper's eye was still there.

'When I give the word, you fight,' said Adams. 'Fists only. No biting, kicking, head-butting; if your man goes down, you let him get up again. Keep it clean, above the belt. And just keep going.'

He stepped back. '*Fight!*'

Copper was into him like a freight train, and Sean was barely able to get his hands up in time to block the attack. He fell back, dodging as best he could, arms in front of his face for protection. Copper was relentless. Sean knew the rest of the lads were cheering them both on, but he couldn't hear them. The only sound he was aware of was *thud-thud-thud*, Copper's fists pummelling into his arms. He had to do something, but what? He'd been in fights, but most times it was little more than a quick exchange of blows, then a lot of running away. Here, there was no escape.

Copper kept going, his fists arcing in left and right, left and right, always aiming for the face, giving Sean no opportunity to drop his guard. And that was how Sean saw his chance. There was no variety to Copper's attack.

It was just all in, no change of target or punch. No jabs, no crosses, just *bang-bang-bang*.

Sean ducked his head, and Copper's swing from the left went wide, exposing his side. It wasn't much, but it was enough, and Sean was in. He drove his right fist hard into Copper's ribs. Copper gasped and the steady rain of blows faltered. For the first time he moved his arms to protect himself, instead of just attacking, but he had worn himself out and he was slow. All Sean had done so far was protect his skull, and he was still fresh. So he pressed home with his attack, hammering in with another heavy crunch to the ribs. Copper woke up just enough to change what he was doing, but his shot went wide again, a right jab that just scraped Sean's forehead. Sean stepped in, thumped a hammer blow to Copper's stomach, then another. He kept himself coiled up, then launched an uppercut to Copper's jaw. It connected. Copper went down hard.

The sergeant blew his whistle and Sean heard something he had never expected to hear. Lads around him actually applauding and cheering his name.

'*Hark-er! Hark-er!*'

The corporals were attending to Copper, who was struggling to sit up.

Adams took hold of Sean's wrist and held it out to Copper. 'Shake, Mulroy.'

Copper looked up, dazed. The sergeant shrugged, and picked up one of his gloved hands. He bumped it against Sean's. 'There. No hard feelings.'

Yeah, like fuck, Sean thought as Adams led him over to his corner.

'Thought he was going to kill you,' the sergeant said, removing Sean's first glove. 'But when you finally switched on to what was happening, you did seriously well.'

'I was just trying to stay alive.'

'Of course.' He began to unlace Sean's other glove. 'But whether you realize it or not, you read the situation and you only attacked when you saw an opportunity. You took the fight back to your attacker, and you turned what he was doing against him.'

Sean said nothing.

'God help me, I see a soldier in you,' said the sergeant. He rapped Sean gently on the forehead with his knuckles. 'Potential for one, anyway.'

The second glove was off. All Sean wanted to do was sit and ignore just how sore everything felt.

He looked over at Copper, who was finally sitting up, bruised face bowed, resting his arms on his knees. 'OK to talk to him?' he asked.

'Of course.'

The corporals had got Copper's gloves off and had

moved on to the next pair scheduled to fight. Sean went over and crouched down in front of his opponent.

Copper looked at him with dazed, puzzled eyes. 'Fuck me, Seany.' His face was serious. 'Where did that come from? I figured smashing you up would be easy.'

'I'm joining up.' Sean looked him straight in the eye as he spoke. 'And you can tell the Guyz that if anyone, *anyone*, even *thinks* of laying a finger on my mum – I'll do to them what I just did to you.' He tapped Copper gently on the head, the way Adams had done to him, and grinned. 'Bro.'

Chapter 7

The Warrior roared and shook as it thrust its way over rutted heathland. Sweat trickled down Sean's face beneath his helmet, and the webbing of his battle kit cut into his body with every lurch. The only consolation was that the seven other soldiers he was crammed in with, all fully kitted up in light greens and browns – the multi-terrain pattern of No. 8 Temperate Combat Dress – would be feeling the same.

The Warrior wasn't built for finesse. It looked like a small tank, hurtling forward on its tracks at speeds that stopped just short of shaking its human cargo to bits. The driver, Tommy Penfold, seemed convinced that he was the very image of an action hero and was obviously doing his best to find every pothole and rut in their way.

Sean loved the machine. It looked angry from every angle. Its heavy armour was surrounded on all sides by protective grilles, like an animal carrying its own cage – one that was going to break out at any moment to chew you up into small, gristly pieces. It had the fire-power to do it too, and that didn't just include the heavily armed and seriously well-trained bastards inside. On the outside, it was armed with a 30mm autocannon, a 7.62mm chain gun, and anti-tank rockets.

But it was hot inside and it wasn't padded. The sweat mingled with the camo paint that clogged up Sean's skin. He felt like a chicken roasting in an atmosphere of engine fumes, dust and sweat, and his bones rattled with every bump and dip of the vehicle. He was only carrying battle kit, enough to get him through twenty-four hours of fighting, rather than a full Bergen, which would keep him going for about three days, but it wasn't designed for sitting down in. No position seemed comfortable.

And Sean had never been happier.

It was a muggy August day outside – almost a year since he had finished the community part of his sentence. He had been allowed to work for some basic qualifications while that was going on. He had bagged a first-aid certificate, and a few others on field craft and drill, and he had nailed the army's fitness requirements. He could never have imagined that Gaz's death, which had driven him into the gym that day, would change the course of his life so totally. Hard work had got him a life, pay, mates. For the first time ever he had plans that extended beyond the next time he could get a car, get wasted, get laid – ideally all on the same evening.

After his parole Sean had done his six-month Combat Infantryman's Course at Catterick, in Yorkshire, his first time beyond the M25. Then he had been posted with the Royal Regiment of Fusiliers, part of the 1st Armoured Infantry Brigade, based in Tidworth, on Salisbury Plain. The Fusiliers used the Warriors, and that was what had sold the regiment to him.

The time he had spent inside felt like years ago – a different life led by a different person.

He looked across at the soldier opposite him. Toni Clark. She winked at him from beneath the rim of her helmet and he smiled back. Like him, she had the tactical recognition flash of the Fusiliers on her sleeves: a square divided into two triangles, blood red on top and mustard yellow underneath.

She was a tall, well-built West Indian woman in her mid-twenties, and the moment Sean set eyes on her he had fallen in love . . . with the 2-litre 1992 Ford Escort Cosworth that she drove and spent most of her pay on. Sean was the one member of the platoon who understood half of her technical talk, and once she realized that he really was interested in the car and not just a kid trying to get into her knickers, they had bonded.

Not that he would mind getting into her knickers, if

the right time came up and they were a long, long way away from the army. It had been drilled into him, and into everyone, many times during training. Relationships between soldiers were Not Allowed.

You go into combat on the understanding that your fellow soldiers will support you equally and without bias. They need to know and trust that this will be the case in return. You will assist each other exclusively on the basis of need, not on who you happen to be shagging.

Right now, shagging was the last thing on Sean's mind.

He gripped his SA80 automatic rifle. He had got to know it well in the past year. It looked like something out of a science fiction movie, with its stubby barrel, its curved magazine behind the pistol grip, the blunt stock with all the workings crammed into it, and the ACOG – the Advanced Combat Optical Gunsight – clamped to the top, looking like a small weapon itself. Sean could strip and snap one back together again blindfolded. And he would be the first to admit that holding and firing one – loosing off NATO standard 5.56mm ammunition at over 600 rounds per minute – was nothing short of awesome.

The Warrior thundered to a halt and a voice barked through each soldier's earpiece via the PRR – the Personal Role Radio mounted in a khaki pack on every soldier's left shoulder which kept them wired into each other.

'*Move!*'

The rear door hissed open on its pistons. Curtis West and Ravi Mitra were first out, and Sean was on his feet, spilling out of the back with the others. As his boots hit the ground, he snapped his weapon up to his shoulder, scanning the ground ahead and around. Soldiers never focused on just what lay in front. They made sure they were aware of attack from all quarters and ready to respond.

Dust from the Warrior settled around them; they looked like ghosts fading under the sun. Sean dropped to the ground, one knee up, the other in the dirt, staring through the ACOG with both eyes open. It had taken him a while to get used to this – taking in the ACOG's enhanced view and the natural sight of his own eye at the same time – but now it was second nature. Closing one eye meant shutting yourself off from everything apart from what you saw through the small aperture, and that was suicide. By keeping both eyes open, a soldier stayed aware of everything around him. He got the full field of vision from both eyes, with a magnified circle showing whatever was right in front of the ACOG.

The Warrior had come to rest behind a small clump of bent trees. The sky was clouding over and a cool breeze blew, bringing a taste of rain with it. Sean had no doubt that it would hit them before the night was out. That was something else he'd learned: air smelled different according to the weather. Back in London's fumes of fast food and exhaust and warm pavements, he'd never noticed.

The voice of Corporal Josh Heaton came through on the PRR.

'Intel reports insurgents are located in the cottage at the edge of the village, five hundred metres beyond the other side of the trees. Move!'

Sean was up on his feet, weapon lowered but still in the shoulder so that he could bring it to bear quickly if they were attacked. Ahead of him was Heaton, taking point. Behind him came Toni Clark and Johnny Bright. They moved together down to the left of the trees, and the village below came into view. It looked empty, not a soul about; the buildings were battered and abandoned. They followed a small rise in the ground until they were about two hundred metres from the cottage – a small stone building, two up, two down, with an overgrown garden. Sean felt adrenaline racing through his body like high-octane fuel, scorching away any tiredness and fusing him to the moment.

Heaton came through again.

'Stenders and Clarky, take position by rock at eleven o'clock. Shitey and me will drop down at the end of the rise.

That gives us two firing positions with good cover. We pin the bastards down while US takes Kama Sutra and Chewie through the front door.'

Shitey was Bright, for reasons obvious to anyone who ever had to share an enclosed space with him. US was Lance Corporal Marshall. Kama Sutra was Ravi Mitra, and Chewie was Curtis West, nicknamed for his phenomenal ability to grow facial hair, which he tried to tame with a moustache and sideburns like a seventies porn king.

And Stenders was Sean. He had got the nickname because someone at Catterick, who had never been further south than Leeds in his life, thought he talked like a character from *EastEnders*. As far as Sean was concerned, the only people who talked like characters from *EastEnders* were characters from *EastEnders*, but it had stuck.

Heaton's battle order made strategic sense, but there was one drawback that Sean could see immediately.

'So we're at the back again,' he murmured to Clark. The corporal had a tendency to put them together, somewhere where the action wasn't. There were various reasons Sean could think of for that. For him – well, OK, he was the youngest in the platoon. For Clark – the only possibilities he could think of weren't good ones, and he didn't like them.

But if Clark was having the same thoughts, she just shrugged them off. 'We're the ones with the UGL,' she said with a smile, tapping the underslung grenade launcher bolted to her own SA80. 'So the money's on us surviving over those two bastards.'

Footsteps came up alongside, followed by the dark silhouette of Bright. 'Corp loves me more, mate, that's just all there is to it,' he said softly as he padded past. He made surprisingly little sound for a bloke who was six foot tall and, unlike Sean, had the bulk to go with it.

'Nah, he's just using you as a human shield,' Sean answered in kind. 'Me and your mum'll have a good long shag in your memory.' He grinned as he got the finger by way of reply.

Sean and Clark hurried over to the rock, rifles at the ready and scanning all the way. They dropped to the ground in its shadow, giving the enemy as small a target as possible, and brought their weapons to bear on the building. Sean focused on the target through the ACOG with the same unblinking stare which, in another life, he would have given a car that he intended to take. Now all they had to do was wait.

As it started to rain, the order came through on the PRR to attack.

Sean and Clark opened fire.

The SA80 bucked in Sean's hands as it spat out

three-round bursts. He held it firm, adjusting his aim every time he pulled the trigger. To his side, Clark did the same, and further on Heaton and Bright joined in, providing covering fire, drawing the attention of the insurgents in the building away from the rest of the section, who would come in from behind.

The attackers, led by Marshall, were a blur of movement by the garden wall. They chucked a couple of flash-bang grenades through the windows on either side of the entrance, and kicked down the front door. Bright bursts of light flashed inside the building, punctuated by sharp bursts from their own weapons.

'First floor clear . . .' A disembodied commentary came through on the PRR.

With their own people inside the building, Clark and Sean had to be more selective in their fire. They eased off, scanning windows and doors through the ACOGs for any signs of the enemy emerging, ready to open fire again at a moment's notice.

There was still firing from inside as the soldiers went from room to room, clearing each one out as they went. Sean tried to picture it in his mind from the overheard snatches.

'Take the stairs . . .'
'Grenades stand by . . .'
And then –

'*Shit! There's a hostage in here!*'

Sean and Clark looked at each other.

'Oh, crap . . .' she murmured.

'*You should have been prepared for that eventuality!*' a furious Heaton bellowed over the PRR. '*US, I will have your balls if—*'

'*Hold fire! Hold fire—*'

The PRR went ominously silent.

'*US,*' Heaton growled, '*speak to me now or so help me—*'

Marshall's voice, when he came back on, sounded very tired. '*Hostage is confirmed dead.*'

'*Shit! Right, everyone cease fire!*'

Sean groaned, and dropped his head to rest on the ground.

Chapter 8

In the distance, as the ringing of the gunshots died away, Sean heard clapping and ironic cheers. He pushed back his helmet and looked up at the ridge a quarter of a mile away. Two more Warriors were parked up there, with the rest of the platoon silhouetted against the skyline.

A fresh voice spoke in the PRR – the kind of voice Sean would have immediately labelled 'posh twat'. . . until he met its owner. Second Lieutenant Mike Franklin might have been public school educated, but he had earned his platoon's respect by being on the same page, and by sheer bloody hard work.

'Exercise over. Stand down. Corporal Heaton's section, stay where you are. Penfold, bring the Warrior over. We're coming down to join you.'

Through the trees, Sean heard the Warrior's engine roar into life. He and Clark stood up, flicking the rifles' fire selector switches to safety. They had all been firing blanks for the exercise, but even a blank discharge could cause severe injury. Together they headed down to the edge of the training village.

Imber had once been a real village, Sean understood – houses, shops, church and people. Then the Second World War happened and the locals had been turfed out to make way for the US Army to train. After the war ended the village was still considered a useful training ground, and the residents had never come back.

At the cottage, Corporal Heaton was busy tearing a strip off West, Mitra and Marshall, the three who had gone in. The hostage, very alive again now that the exercise was over, was leaning against the wall with his back to Sean and Clark, arms folded, nodding and putting in the occasional word. He wore green fatigues and a shabby, shag-order army surplus combat blouse.

Heaton glanced over the hostage's shoulder as Sean and Clark approached. He nodded briefly at Sean, without missing a single beat of the bollocking. Clark might as well have been invisible or someplace else for all the attention he paid her. She and Sean glanced at each other, and she made a show of adjusting her helmet. Only Sean could see that her thumb and forefinger were curled into an O, and she was moving it back and forth. He grinned.

The Warrior lurched through the trees and skidded to a halt under Private Penfold's unskilful guiding hand.

The hostage looked round. 'Christ, is that how he always drives?' he asked.

And Sean clocked his face properly. His mouth dropped open and a word blurted out before he could stop it. 'Sergeant!'

Sergeant Phil Adams gazed casually back, not registering any surprise. 'Well, bugger me, it's Sean Harker. Worst traumatic flashback I ever had.'

Heaton looked from one to the other. 'You know each other?' His expression suddenly changed. 'And – uh – *Sergeant*?'

Sean reckoned Heaton had known the hostage was a volunteer, but not that he was also a guy who outranked him. Minus his helmet, you could see that he was a slim, usually scowling twenty-one-year-old. He was from the same part of the world as Sean, and that was all Sean knew about him. Sean wondered if he had a gang background too. Maybe he still clung onto the old politics and couldn't bring himself to be chummy with one of the Littern Guyz.

Now, Heaton was looking at Sean with slightly narrowed eyes, like Sean had kept a deep secret from him.

'All the way back to the Why-Oh-Whys, Corporal.' Adams straightened up and began to unbutton the combat blouse.

The Why-Oh-Whys was the name that had inevitably got stuck to the YOI Cadets – probably the first time someone said the name out loud. It certainly summed up Sean's feelings after that first, intense session in the gym.

'You back with the real army, then, Sergeant?' he asked.

'Recruiting for the Why-Oh-Whys was only a brief posting while I got sorted out after Afghanistan, Harker. Yes, I'm back, for my sins.' He pulled off the blouse to reveal the standard smock of a Personal Clothing System Combat Uniform, with his three sergeant's stripes clearly visible. From his pocket he pulled a dark blue Fusiliers beret, which he set on his head with precise, millimetre accuracy. The red and white feathered hackle ruffled proudly in the breeze.

'And guess what, lads,' Adams added. 'I'm your new platoon sergeant, so it is my pleasure to be the first to tell you that what I just saw was an *absolute fucking disaster*. Lance Corporal Marshall's gorillas came into the room guns blazing. If it had been live ammo, there'd have been a neat row of holes stitched right across my chest, just prior to tearing my torso apart.' He clapped his hands together with a big smile. 'So I can see I'm going to have the time of my life setting you lot straight.'

*

The three Warriors were parked up in a half-circle around the cottage, while Franklin took them all through the exercise – what had gone right, what had gone wrong, quite apart from the small detail of having killed their hostage. A light drizzle drifted over them.

The platoon was split into three sections, each commanded by a corporal, with a lance corporal as his second in command. Above them was the sergeant, second in command of the whole platoon, and above him was Franklin – the Rupert, the officer in overall charge, with a piece of paper signed by the Queen to prove it.

In real life, Franklin would have been the one getting it in the neck from his own superiors for the hostage's death, so he was probably being nicer than anyone deserved.

'OK, so you weren't expecting a hostage. *Not important.* I didn't tell you to expect one. *Not important.* I might not have had the full gen from Intel either. Or the hostage might have been acquired more recently than the latest report. Or there might not have been a hostage at all, but there could have been valuable intelligence for the Green Slime' – he meant the Intelligence Corps – 'on planned attacks or the placement of Improvised Explosive Devices – anything that would serve the army better if it was retrieved in one piece, rather than vaporized along with the people who put it there. That was why we went in on foot in the first place, rather than just taking the place down with a Light Anti-Structures Missile. And if you were on patrol in Helmand province, or anywhere, you might get orders to go in somewhere without me or Sergeant Adams to look over your shoulder and make sure you don't spray hostages with bullets as you go into the room.'

'It's only training—' West muttered, and broke off when Adams wheeled round on him.

Franklin gave half a smile. 'Care to take this one, Sergeant?'

Adams didn't need to be asked twice. '"Only" training, did I hear you say, Private whose name I won't bother asking because I will then have you for ever pegged as Private Whoever Who Says Fuck-Stupid Things? There's no such thing as "only" training. It's only ever one step away from the real thing. You train hard to fight easy, because if you train easy, then you fight hard and you die. We're at full readiness for deployment at all times. We may have bugged out from Afghanistan, but it doesn't mean that some other pile of shite isn't going to come and land on us any time soon.'

'IS,' said someone.

'IS,' Adams agreed, 'who would just love you lot to crop up in a home movie on their Facebook feeds.

Meanwhile the Russians are getting arsy again, Christ only knows what's going on in Asia, and an Italian gave my wife a funny look the other day.' There was a ripple of slightly nervous laughter, dented by his obvious sincerity beneath the joking. 'It'll happen, lads. Attacks on the continent, foiled plots in our own country – it's just a matter of time before it all blows up in our faces.'

A silence hung over the platoon for a few seconds, before Franklin asked: 'Any other questions?' He surveyed the assembled platoon.

Mitra put a hesitant hand up as far as his shoulder, then seemed to decide *What the hell*, and thrust it into the air.

'What is it, Private Mitra?'

'Sir, can we get a cork for Private Bright's butt? Or at least make him ride up top next time?'

After the tension of getting their arses publicly torn off, it was like pricking a balloon. Everyone pissed themselves laughing.

'You love it, really, Kama Sutra,' said Bright. 'The bouquet is exquisite.'

West's hand rose. 'Sir? Shitey just said "exquisite". Isn't that a court-martial offence?'

'Only if he can spell it,' Franklin said, without missing a beat. 'Right, that's enough for today. Dismiss them, Sergeant.'

There was one more surprise that day. As the Warrior engines fired into life and the sections loaded themselves up, Heaton called, 'Stenders!'

And when Sean looked over at him, he jerked a thumb up at the turret of the Warrior that carried their section. 'Up here, with me.'

The infantry section sat in the compartment inside the rear hull. The driver had his own personal world in the front hull, and the commander and gunner took the gun turret on top. Heaton was the commander, and for the time being there was no gunner, so that space tended to be handed out on a whim.

Sean was surprised to find that it was his turn, but he wasn't going to argue. It beat squeezing in with everyone else, so he flashed a big smile at his mates and climbed up nimbly. He dropped himself into the gunner's hatch and ignored the shouts of 'Wanker!' from below. He would have done just the same in their place.

A few moments later, Heaton climbed up into his own hatch. The two of them were side by side, emerging from the waist up. Heaton pulled on his headset. 'In your own time, Penfold,' he said into the microphone.

The Warrior lurched into motion and followed the others along the rutted tank tracks that crisscrossed Salisbury Plain. This was the army's training ground in the south of England – a world within a world that civilians could only know from looking at Google Maps.

For a few minutes Heaton just leaned his hands against the coaming of the turret, looking out across the rolling grassy landscape. Then he pulled the microphone down from his mouth and put his hand over it, so that only Sean could hear him. 'You never said you were in the Why-Oh-Whys.' Somehow he made it a question.

Sean looked at him sideways and shrugged. 'You never asked.'

Technically, that was giving lip to a superior, but Sean reckoned there was enough informality around – and a small enough gap between their ranks – that he could get away with it.

Truth to tell, no, he hadn't mentioned that bit of his past. He appreciated that in the army, no one leaned on their mates to get their life stories. The Why-Oh-Whys had been his way of leaving the past behind, and that was where they belonged.

'Right . . .' Heaton said softly. His mouth twitched into a faint smile. 'So what were you in for?'

Sean drew his head back with a frown. That was a bit like asking *When did you last have a wank?* No one's business, and not something he had to answer.

'OK, I'll make it a little easier for you,' Heaton said,

maybe guessing why Sean had hesitated. 'Breaking and entering, me. Feltham. Course, we didn't have any cadets in my day. Had to work ourselves out the hard way.' His eyes and his smile had narrowed.

So Heaton had been in a YOI too. Sean still thought it was none of his business, but OK, he appreciated the confidence.

'Taking without consent,' he said. 'Burnleigh.'

'Well, ain't we a pair, then? Bad lads together, that's us.' Heaton paused, frowned. 'But the sergeant . . . ?' There was just a hint of uncertainty in his voice, and Sean burst out laughing.

'Hell, no! No way. He's straight up. Straight as they come. No, he was just in the Why-Oh-Whys for . . .' He paused. 'Well, I dunno, to tell the truth. I mean . . .'

And it was then that he remembered Adams hadn't always been as straight as they come. He had heard it from the horse's mouth and seen the evidence in his tattoos. But he wasn't going to say it. It was Adams's story to tell, not his.

However, Heaton smiled grimly. 'He said it himself. Makes jokes about traumatic flashbacks, said he was getting sorted out after Afghanistan. Reckon our sergeant has had a touch of trouble . . .' He tapped his head and whistled.

Sean scowled. The chance to ride up in the turret was getting less and less enjoyable. 'Is that important?'

'Just like to know what I'm up against.'

'Why are you up against anything?' Sean said it before he could think.

Heaton looked at him coldly, then suddenly smiled. 'You're totally right. I'm out of order. Wouldn't want anyone talking about me like that. Just old habits . . . Shit, you know what I mean. In the – let's say, in the old days, you had to know what was what out on the streets, unless you wanted to get shanked. So I basically like to know everything. What I'm getting into, who I'm with. Don't rely on anyone else to get it right, even if they have got three stripes on their arm.'

Sean didn't want to make an enemy of the corporal, and he could certainly relate to that. So he breathed out. 'Yeah. Damn right.'

'It's good to talk to someone who understands.' A pause, and then Heaton barked a harsh laugh. 'I mean, there was this time I was with this mate, Eamonn, and we accidentally wandered off our turf. And it was only the frigging Yardies on the next patch, right? Kind of sensitive about wandering white boys. I think they could see we were just kids, so they didn't take real offence, they just wanted to scare us, but they had us surrounded and they asked our names. And Eamonn was just getting them more and more pissed off every time he opened his mouth, and neither of us could understand why – until I clocked it: they thought he was taking the piss out of their accent. Every time he said his name they thought he was saying *Eh, man.*'

'Yeah?' Sean snorted and laughed. It sounded exactly like the neighbourhoods he had known – and some of the people. 'Well, you know how I got my nickname?'

Heaton was outraged when Sean told him. 'No fucking way do you sound like some ponce actor pretending to be a Cockney! Bloody yokels don't know a proper accent when they hear it. I knew this guy once . . .'

The convoy of Warriors rolled up to the depot, with Sean and Heaton laughing together like old mates.

Whatever else you did in the army – whatever else was going on, whatever other plans you had – in the absence of an all-out invasion by enemy forces, your kit came first. Your uniform had to be pressed, your boots had to be sparkling. Your weapon, your kit, yourself: that was your order of priority.

But after that, if you weren't on duty or bivvied out on the Plain, your time was your own. And that was how Sean came to be sitting behind the wheel of Clark's bright red Cosworth, parked with the bonnet up in one of the spaces outside the barracks where they both lived in Single Living Accommodation, in en suite rooms costing all of £58 per month, all bills included.

The Cosworth was hardly recognizable as the car it had once been, thanks to spray jobs, body kit, roll cage, massive performance upgrades, and a sound system that would put a nightclub to shame. Sean grasped the steering wheel in both hands and breathed in the perfume of the leather seating, while the engine throbbed gently in the background like an animal that would be severely pissed off if someone woke it up.

Gaz, mate, you should be here . . . he thought. He still sometimes – but only sometimes – thought of his old friend, and at least he could do it now without the feeling of a knife going into his heart.

'OK,' Clark called from behind the bonnet. 'Give it a tap . . .'

Sean trod gently on the accelerator. The engine's throb slid rapidly up the scale, from barely contained threat, to dangerous, to *The fuck do you think you're doing?*

Nice! It had been a long time since he'd sat behind the wheel of a car, pumped the engine, and felt the machine respond to his demands.

Once upon a time his reaction to a car like this would have been to nick it. Then he would have driven it to within an inch of its life and probably dumped it in pieces, ruined – unless of course he decided to hand it over to Gaz for stripping down.

There were moments when he wished he could go back in time to meet his younger self and smash the little prick's face in. A car like this deserved to cherished. He wondered if he would ever get the addiction to motors out of his system. Maybe when they let him drive the Warriors.

'OK!' Clark shouted. There was the tiniest change in the note of the engine. 'That's it. Thanks.'

Sean reluctantly took his foot off the pedal and the engine rumbled back down to its usual idle. He climbed out, and found to his surprise that they had an audience. Corporal Heaton, in civvies, stood a short distance away, hands thrust into his pockets.

'Nice car, Stenders.'

'Thanks, Corp,' Clark said.

'Mind if I have a word?' Heaton said. Yet again, Clark might as well not have been there, which struck Sean as bloody rude. He and Clark looked at each other, but she diplomatically rolled her eyes and buried her head in the engine again.

'Sure.' He wandered over and looked quizzically at Heaton.

The corporal looked slightly embarrassed. 'Say, this is going to sound kind of weird, but, uh . . . you got any plans for the weekend?' And then, just as Sean was asking himself in disbelief, *Is he trying to chat me up?* he burst out laughing. 'Shit, that sounded like a come-on, didn't it? Wasn't meant to. I'll try again. On the total under-standing that we're both one hundred per cent straight, have you got any plans?'

Still weird, Sean thought. And of all weekends, this wasn't the best one for Heaton to decide they were suddenly going to be mates. Sean didn't want the corporal declaring that they were going to hit the town together.

'Yeah,' he said. 'Saturday, I'm heading into London.'

'OK, that's cool. But, uh, Friday evening? Reason I'm asking – my girlfriend's coming over, and she's got a college friend staying with her, and they're both from our old neighbourhood too, and the friend's going to be at a loose end unless . . .'

Sean's eyes went wide. 'You trying to fix me up?'

'Well . . .' Heaton flashed a grin. 'Unless you've got other plans?'

Sean was still inclined to say *No, thanks*, on principle. He had never needed to be set up with a girl before and he didn't want to start now.

On the other hand . . .

Someone like Clark would only ever be a good mate, and it had been a long time – a *long* time – since Sean had got the chance to be with a girl, one to one, instead of shouting over the noise of half a dozen pissed squaddies in the pub.

'Yeah. OK then. So, how do I get to yours?'

Heaton gave his shoulder a friendly punch. 'Be at the gatehouse, eighteen hundred, Friday evening. I'll give you a lift.'

Sean went back to the car, still wearing a slightly puzzled frown.

Clark looked up at him from the air filter she was unscrewing. 'Did I just hear you get fixed up on a blind date with the corporal's girlfriend's girlfriend?'

'Uh. Yeah? I think you did.'

'Well, enjoy. And if you can't be good, be careful.'

She laughed when he gave her the finger.

Another of the many things Sean had learned from the army was to be punctual. He was at the gatehouse at 17:55, Friday. It was a modern, red-brick building with parking spaces just inside the barrier, and a large sign warning that the threat level was SEVERE. Which, Sean knew, meant that in the opinion of people cleverer than him, an attack on UK forces, somewhere, was considered highly likely.

The sentries were taking it seriously. The barrier was down; every incoming driver had to produce ID before it went up for them. Every now and then a car would be picked out at random to pull over into the spaces so that they could check under it with a mirror. Bonnet and boot would be popped, and a dog would be sent in to sniff for the chemicals associated with explosives.

Sean appreciated the effort, but right now he was wondering if he had overdone it when he gelled his hair and spritzed himself with aftershave.

Heaton was waiting for him, leaning casually against a metallic blue Subaru Impreza – 4-wheel drive, 2.2-litre engine and a hood scoop to feed its greedy oxygen habit. Sean whistled. Another car Gaz wouldn't have minded getting his hands on – though probably just to strip straight down. It had come like that out of the factory – it didn't have the hand-made artistry of the Cosworth. But still . . .

'Man, that is sweet.'

The corporal grinned. 'If you look at Debs's mate like you're looking at my car, you'll get a slap in the face, you dickhead. Get in.'

'Shit, I thought Clarky was the petrolhead!' Sean said as he secured the seat belt. 'How do you afford this? And it's new, isn't it? Fucking hell . . .'

Heaton punched the accelerator, blasting them out of the barracks and onto the road. The surge of acceleration that pushed Sean back into his seat was like a hug from an old friend.

'Clark's car is just like her,' Heaton said. 'All colour and in your face about it. Nothing on the inside.'

OK, that was *not* cool. Several responses ran through Sean's mind, but he was the guest in a sweet car, so he bit his lip and let it go. The corporal eased back on the speed, dropped a gear, and hung a right. The Impreza took the corner like it was on rails. Heaton punched it again and the roar of the exhaust made the air throb.

'You go to war,' Heaton continued, 'you've got to be united, all the guys together, heart and soul. Yeah, yeah, Clark can cut it in training and there's probably a space for her somewhere in the army. But front line, like you and me? Nah. See how long she lasts when it comes to the crunch.'

Enough was enough. Worst case scenario – Sean got chucked out of the car and never got to meet the blind date. He could live with that.

'Hang on, mate . . .' he started, anger flashing in his eyes.

'OK, OK. What I said about colour – sorry, that was out of order. It came out wrong. And she's your mate – that's cool. She'll get a chance to show what she can do soon enough.'

Sean hadn't realized quite how hyped up he was to fight until he felt it draining out of him. Heaton was saying sorry, and that was enough to let it go. So instead he picked up on the other thing the corporal was saying: Clark getting a chance to show what she could do.

'You mean, when we all ship out to wherever we're going?' he asked.

Heaton pulled a face. 'Reality lesson, Harker: we're going nowhere. Why do you think we've been kept home for so long?'

Sean shrugged. 'Because it's cheaper?'

'Because the war's coming here, mate,' Heaton said. 'Everyone knows it. All those wankers who've been heading out to the Middle East to join some group of crazies – they're coming back to spread their own twisted brand of crap. How long do you think it'll be before we get the army on the streets here, in England, like we used to in Northern Ireland? And I'll tell you frankly – it can't be soon enough, in my book.'

Sean frowned. He hadn't thought of it like that.

The corporal lived in a block of flats a five-minute drive away; it couldn't have been more than two or three years old and seemed way off limits on a corporal's salary. The large living room was full of light from the studio windows.

'Stick some music on,' Heaton said, with a vague wave at a music system in one corner. He disappeared into the kitchen area, an alcove set into one side of the main room. Sean squatted down in front of the system and whistled again. It was Bang & Olufsen, all smooth, flat surfaces that only lit up with hidden controls when you touched them. Put that with the cinema-sized TV, and Sean was pretty sure it would cost more than everything he had ever nicked in his life, all added together.

He pressed a button at random. Music began to play from hidden speakers – quadrophonic, around the room. 'Smooth . . .' he murmured.

Heaton popped his head out of the kitchen and grinned. 'Want to see something else? See what that remote does.' He pointed at a small unit on the table. It wasn't as sleek as a shop-bought device – in fact, Sean suspected as he picked it up that it might be homemade. Instead of buttons it had sliders. He experimentally moved a slider from top to bottom.

That was how he found out that it controlled the flat's hidden lighting. Turn it up, turn it down, even change the colours and synchronize it to the music.

'Yup,' Heaton said proudly. 'I wired it all up myself. Did an electronics course at Feltham – about the only good thing I got out of it. Get you a beer?' He pulled open the door of a well-stocked fridge.

'Uh – sure.' Sean caught the can Heaton chucked at him. 'But how the fuck do you afford all this?'

He still wasn't one hundred per cent certain that the story of the girlfriends wasn't a con. On the other hand, there was no doubt that this flat was a first-class shagpad. He took a quick scan around as he pulled the tab on the can. He wasn't an expert on the brand names of kitchen appliances or furniture, but he knew what looked good. Shit, this was impressive.

'Meh. I inherited some money a couple of years ago – seemed like an investment.'

And five minutes later the girls showed up, dropped off by a taxi. A dyed blonde and a redhead – natural, at least so far as Sean could see.

'Right!' Heaton clapped his hands and rubbed them together. 'Remind me, which of you two is Debs?'

'Oh, ha fucking hilarious.'

The blonde opened her arms up to him. He walked straight into them and the two locked lips for so long that Sean and the redhead started to feel self-conscious, hanging in the background behind their respective friends.

Sean caught her eye. 'Uh – get you a beer?' he offered.

After that things became less awkward. In fact, a whole lot less, even though it turned out she wasn't from East London. Her name was Rachel, she was from Lancashire and she was going back on Sunday, not knowing when she would be down again. But she was really grateful to Sean for showing up, she said. She hadn't looked forward to being the odd girl out.

All this came out in chat while they knocked back their beers and waited for the pizzas to arrive. They ate their slices and Heaton kept the drinks coming while they squeezed onto the sofa to play games and watch all the crap TV he had stored on the TiVo. It was good fun, lubricated by booze and music and good company. After a while it seemed only natural for Sean to put his arm around Rachel. She seemed to appreciate it, if the snuggling close and head resting on his shoulder were anything to go by.

It was all pretty sedate compared to the chemistry blazing away at the other end of the sofa. It was fairly obvious how Heaton and Debs intended the evening to end, at least for them. Heaton would not be calling a return taxi for Debs that night.

After a couple of hours they disappeared into Heaton's room, and everyone knew they weren't coming out again.

Which meant it was crunch time. Sean wasn't quite sure how far his duties as Rachel's escort extended, or how she felt about it. It wasn't a question he had ever had to ask before. Rachel was a nice girl, but he hadn't really been expecting . . . Had she been expecting . . . ?

Just taking a taxi back to barracks and leaving her wouldn't be very friendly, and he was too tall to sleep on the sofa comfortably. But then she draped her arms around his neck and looked into his eyes, and pointed out that the spare bed was a double . . . and the problem kind of solved itself.

Chapter 9

'Sit in the front, you twat,' said Heaton.

'Nah,' Sean said with a grin. 'This way I get to pretend you're my taxi.'

He had climbed into the back seat of the Impreza and spread his arms over the rests. Heaton rolled his eyes, but he gunned the engine and the car pulled away.

Heaton had dropped the girls off at Andover station – Rachel had a train to catch, and Debs was seeing her up to London. Then he had run Sean back to barracks to get his overnight kit, and now they were heading back to the station again so that Sean could head into London himself.

Sean and Rachel had exchanged a heavy goodbye kiss and a 'See you, then,' both knowing full well that they wouldn't. They had both known it was for one night only, but a bloody good one. Sean knew for a fact that he had had the best night of his life since getting out of Burnleigh.

'So what you getting up to in town?' Heaton called over his shoulder. He wasn't exactly breaking any speed limits, but the Impreza didn't hang about. It gripped the road like the tyres were glued to it. 'Seeing your old crew?'

'Doubt it,' said Sean. 'Just checking up on my mum, that's all.'

For the first time since he had left her, a year ago . . .

Of course, she hadn't made his passing-out parade, though she had said she would, and Sean hadn't been back to Littern Mills since he got shipped off to Burnleigh. The parole service had thought it was best he was relocated to a new estate, away from his old haunts, which had suited him fine. It had already stopped feeling like home. His name would have been mud with Copper and Matt – he remembered everything Copper had said back in the prison, and he just couldn't be arsed with the hassle. And of course there would be the gaping hole left by Gaz. Cutting himself off had been a big deal, and he'd done his best to make sure he did it properly.

It had helped that PJ had been one of his mum's longer-term boyfriends. It had sounded like he was looking after her, so Sean hadn't needed to head back and check up. The occasional phone call was all he needed. Only PJ had finally gone the way they all did.

So he thought it was about time he paid a visit. Make sure the silly cow was doing all right.

'Good man. But it's always handy to keep the old contacts alive, right? Never know when they could come in useful.'

Sean laughed. 'Yeah, because they'd be well useful in a firefight!'

Heaton shrugged, then grinned. 'So what'd you think of the pad?'

'Fucking A,' Sean said sincerely. 'Still can't believe it.' He wondered if Heaton was on the lookout for a lodger in the spare room . . . No. That really would be weird. And unless Debs brought a friend along every time she stayed over, Sean would be the odd one out on other occasions. He had his pride.

Heaton laughed. 'Thing is,' he continued as he shifted gear, 'maybe I wasn't one hundred per cent truthful about my, uh, inheritance. It's the easy answer I give when I don't know someone that well. It's what I tell the neighbours.'

'So – how . . . ?'

'I worked for that place, Stenders. I earned every penny.'

Sean was all ears. Heaton earned *that*, on a corporal's pay? No.

Heaton went on. 'You have to make the army work

for you too, right? So that's what I've done. Army pay only goes so far, so you have to use your head a little, know what I mean? And that's how I have this.' Heaton tapped the dashboard like he was giving an affectionate pat to a pet.

'Then whatever it is you're doing, I want in!' Sean joked. 'I haven't even got a car!'

He knew a few other lads who had sidelines to their regular jobs. The army gave you skills that civvies were always on the lookout for. Some worked occasional nights as doormen in Andover or Salisbury. Nightclubs were always happy to bump up security with a soldier or two. Others bought and sold cars, upgrading each time so that they eventually ended up with a decent motor – though nothing like what Heaton was riding around in.

'I might take you up on that,' said Heaton. He looked at Sean in the mirror; he was smiling, but his eyes were serious. 'Could always use a little help. Assuming you're the right person for the job, of course. All kinds of perks. Cash, mostly, but also payment in kind.'

Sean grinned. 'It's the cash I'm after.'

'Whatever.' Heaton leaned forward, keeping one hand on the wheel and fumbling beneath the driver's seat with the other. He pulled out a flat box and passed it back. 'What do you think of this?'

Sean took the box in both hands. It was heavy. The

photo on the lid showed the smoothly curving, dark lines of a Glock 17 Gen 4 pistol. It was the one pistol Sean could have identified immediately, since it was issued as standard to the British Army and he had just finished a training course on it. It could hold seventeen rounds compared with the thirteen of the Browning that it had replaced. It was also considerably lighter than the old Browning, because its frame, magazine body and components were built from a nylon-based polymer that was pretty much bombproof. It was a state-of-the-art, space-age weapon.

'You're kidding!'

But it wasn't the picture of the Glock that surprised him – it was the logo next to it. A silhouetted figure of a huntsman with a rifle, and the word AIRSOFT. Sean had heard of Airsoft, never seen it. Grown men running around in woods in camo, playing soldiers with replica weapons – identical to the real thing on the outside but modified inside to fire off plastic pellets with compressed gas or springs. To Sean, who handled a real-life SA80 every day, it was laughable.

'You mean, you run around with real weapons during the week, and then you dick around with wannabe Rambos at the weekend too?'

He opened the box out of curiosity, and whistled. Inside, as the box had told him, was a replica Glock. A very accurate replica, right down to the wear and tear detail on the moulded matt surface.

'Give it a feel,' said Heaton. 'Only don't wave it around. Police don't like seeing blokes in cars waving guns about. It's political correctness gone mad, but what can you do?'

'So what? It's still a fake.'

But Sean picked it up, as invited. It sat comfortably in his hand with just the right weight and balance. The NSPs – the Normal Safety Precautions – that had been drilled into him meant he automatically pulled back on the slide to reveal the chamber, and peered into it to check for rounds. It was the first thing any trained soldier did when picking up a fresh gun, to ensure they knew what state it was in.

And suddenly, with a feeling like cold water trickling through his body, he knew that this wasn't a fake. This thing didn't fire bits of plastic. He was looking into a chamber that was precision engineered to take standard NATO 9mm Parabellum rounds. This was real. Empty, but real.

'Uh . . . Corp . . .'

In the mirror, Heaton's eyes were cold. 'No one wants to be the next target, right? I'm just being pre-emptive. It saves time and bother if you keep it in a box that says it's not real, you know?'

'So . . .' Sean struggled to think this through. 'You've got a real Glock just knocking around in your car?'

'It's all legal and licensed and signed for. Trust your corporal. And put it back in the box.'

Sean did as he was told, quickly.

Club bouncer? No. Whatever it was Heaton was doing, if it required his very own Glock, then he was into something way heavier than that. And Sean was pretty sure Heaton was winding him up, deliberately being mysterious until Sean just *had* to ask what was going on. And then he would be in whether he liked it or not.

Sean didn't appreciate dancing to other people's tunes. If Heaton wanted him, Heaton could tell him. In his own time. Badgering him would just sound desperate.

And then they were at the station. Heaton pulled into the drop-off zone. 'Have a good weekend.' He held out his hand.

Sean, surprised, reached over and shook it. 'Will do. And thanks for the ride.' He pushed the matter of the gun to the back of his mind and took one last look around as he climbed out. 'Shit, I seriously need this car.'

Heaton winked. 'Well, maybe we can do something about that, eh?'

Chapter 10

All the familiar smells of home, thought Sean. *Damp concrete, frying stuff – and do I detect the faintest aroma of stale piss? I believe I do.*

God, I used to live here.

He'd got into London at lunch time, and then spent a few hours knocking around the West End before heading east. Part of it was just practical – his mum had told him not to turn up before she ended her shift at the shop. And part of it . . .

Part of it, he had to admit, was that he hadn't been sure if he would still recognize the place.

He got off the Tube for the familiar five-minute walk to Littern Mills. The estate was basically three large squares, each one surrounded by four tower blocks. The ground level of each block was a row of shops set behind concrete pillars. Above them were levels and levels of open-air balconies, and the front doors of the inhabitants.

The sun was halfway to setting and the tower blocks

cast long shadows over the square where his mum lived. He scanned the shops at the bottom of his block as he slouched his way over, bag slung over his shoulder. They seemed pretty much the same. The laundrette and the chippy – both doing good business on a Saturday evening. Lakhani's, the small general store where his mum had stacked shelves for as long as he could remember. It was closed, with a metal shutter pulled down over the plate-glass windows. Cool – she would be home.

For some reason he remembered Copper's dire warnings, eighteen months ago, about the estate. *There's foreigners moving in, Seany!* Which basically meant *strangers.* Well, Sean didn't recognize any of the kids clustered around the dry fountain in the middle of the square, knocking back tins of stuff they were way too young for. But he was prepared to be friendly, so he gave the hand sign that identified the Guyz – thumb, forefinger and little finger pressed together, other two fingers outstretched, hand held across his chest. It was meant to be something that could be used anywhere – it could look like a deliberate signal or it could look like you were just scratching your shoulder.

'Hi, guys.'

Three of them gave him the finger, two of them sniggered, one just rolled his eyes in disgust.

'Fuck off, pig.'

'*Pig?*' Sean exclaimed, half laughing, half horrified. They thought he looked like a cop? Maybe he was just too smartly turned out. Shit. 'No, mate, you got it all wrong. I was just on my way to shag your mum so I thought I'd be friendly.'

That got their attention. They stood up, and two of them blocked his way.

'You got a problem?' the pig boy asked.

'Nah.' Sean took the smile off his face and looked at him the same way he looked through an ACOG at something he was about to shoot. He also didn't break step. 'You?'

He saw their shoulders square up, their jaws go firm . . . and then give, as it dawned on them that they might match him in height but there was no way they matched him in build or confidence. They stepped aside and he walked between them, shoulders bumping.

'Twat,' one of the boys muttered. Sean held a finger up over his shoulder to say goodbye as he walked away.

Now, that was interesting. A bunch of kids who obviously weren't Guyz, acting like they owned the place. OK.

He didn't bother to see if the lift was working. Even if it had been, Sean knew from experience that the piss smell would be strongest inside it. He took the steps up to the fourth level two at a time, long legs falling automatically into the old rhythm that had always helped him keep in trim, even before the army. At least the graffiti was the same – the usual riotous swirl of colours, tags, slogans and misspelled obscenities. He swung onto level four and a grin appeared on his face as the stylized G that had always dominated the far wall came into view.

But the grin stopped, and then faded, as he saw more of it. Only half the G was visible. The rest was covered over. He was pretty sure that at least two of the symbols and glyphs that had replaced it were gang logos, but he didn't recognize either of them. There were slogans in English, and something foreign with letters he could at least read, and something even more foreign in squiggles that he had no clue about.

OK . . .

The balcony was worn and chipped, with graffiti on the bare concrete. He walked along to the third door and raised his hand to knock. And hesitated, millimetres from the scuffed paint of the door.

Come on. Just knock. Get it done.

He gave the number a last check – like there was any doubt about it being the right one – and knocked a quick rhythm against the wood. Then he stood back and waited.

On the other side, he heard a door open, then footsteps shuffling closer. Sean checked to make sure he looked smart, presentable. He wanted his mum to see that her son was doing OK.

The door opened.

'Hello, love . . .'

She seemed to say it to his shoulder. She couldn't lift her head any higher. He stared down at her. He still towered over her, of course. Janice Harker was thirty-three years old, sixteen years older than him, but looked fifty, and the dye didn't hide the grey. She'd done her hair and put on her best clothes for him – a fading blue dress over an appallingly thin figure. Eh? He had always thought of her as a soppy fat cow. Now she was anything but fat.

And she had clearly spent some time on her make-up, but he didn't know if that was to impress him, or to hide the bruises on her face. They weren't visible, but the swelling was.

Sean didn't wait to be invited in. He stepped into the flat and gently pulled her along with him, shutting the door behind them. He dropped his bag on the floor. 'Shit, what happened, Mum? Was it PJ?'

'Oh, don't you worry about that.' She waved her hands vaguely in front of her face. 'Just a little accident, that's all. PJ never laid a finger on me. Not that way, anyway. Now, a cup of tea? And I bought your favourite – that syrup cake you love!'

Sean wasn't listening. 'An accident? Don't play me, Mum. Who did it?'

She eased out of his grip and slipped into the tiny kitchen that led off the hallway. He followed her, past the doorway to the lounge. Then he did a double take and shot a look into the other room. Two chairs and a TV, sitting on the floor.

'Mum . . .' He ducked into the kitchen and took it in with one glance. The counters were bare. The cooker was scabby with old food but obviously hadn't been used for a long time.

'Do you still have one sugar or have you given that up? I mean, you're all healthy now, aren't you? All that running and army fun. Oh, Sean, look at you!' Her eyes actually lingered in his direction, though they still couldn't quite get as high as his face. 'You got so big and handsome! You got a girlfriend? I'd love to meet her.'

'You need to tell me what happened, Mum.' Sean dropped down to a crouch and opened the fridge. Empty shelves stared back. Without a word, he stood up, checked a few cupboards. A couple of tins of sardines, a stale loaf of bread, and some own-brand tea bags. That was it.

She flicked the kettle on and dropped a tea bag into a mug as it began to warm up. 'There won't be any milk, I'm afraid—'

'No milk?' said Sean. 'Mum, there's no food anywhere!'

'That's because I'm waiting for my delivery, love. It's due later today, I promise.'

'Delivery?' Sean said in disbelief. 'You mean you have food delivered?'

His mum nodded.

'So you ordered it, right? Through a website?'

She nodded again, smiled.

'Even though you haven't got a computer or a smartphone?'

Her face flickered as she sought for an explanation. 'I used their computer next door,' she said. 'You remember Lisa and John? Yes, that's what I did.'

Sean shook his head, fighting his temper. He should have known it would come to this. Spend a year away from her, and he worried about her. Thirty seconds back in her company and she was pissing him off again.

'Mum, just tell me—'

'Let's talk in the lounge,' she said. 'It's more comfy in there.'

Sean stood his ground. 'Mum. You need to talk to

me. I can see you're not spending it on food or booze or smokes or drugs, so where—?'

The flat shook to the sound of a knock on the front door, angry and demanding. Something like a stab of pain shot across his mum's face.

'Who's that?'

'It's no one. Please, love, go to the lounge and I'll send him away.'

'Him? Who's *him*?'

Maybe there was another man in her life, PJ's replacement – but that hadn't sounded like a guy coming to meet his girlfriend. Oh shit, she wasn't getting beaten up again, was she?

She pushed past him, holding her hands to her chest like she didn't even want to touch him. But it wasn't that. He could see that her fingers were wrapped around something, trying to hide it from view. He reached out and blocked the door with one arm, stopping her from getting any further. Then, gently, he took her hand in his and opened it, ignoring her weak struggle. Staring back at him was a roll of £10 notes.

'Mum . . .'

'It's nothing,' she said. 'I just need to—'

Sean took the money as another knock shook the door. 'Stay here.' He eased his mum gently back into the kitchen. 'Let me sort this.' She started to cry. 'No. Stay,' he repeated.

Sean closed the kitchen door and took the three steps to the front of the flat.

The door shook again, even more violently.

'Oh no, Sean, don't, please . . .' His mum's voice rose in a wail of sheer terror.

He pulled the door open.

Chapter 11

Sean found himself staring at a white guy a few years older than him, maybe Heaton's age, fist clenched and raised to deliver another hammer blow. The guy caught himself just in time, and let his hand down slowly. His skinny frame was bulked out by a massive white shell suit. A gold chain and a baseball cap completed the look.

'Yes?' Sean said, staring coldly at the guy.

'Who the fuck are you?'

'I was going to ask the same question. I mean, I can see you're some pranny with his dick where his face ought to be, but that doesn't tell me *who* you are.'

The guy's eyes narrowed and his head tilted slightly. 'Tell Janice Ricky's here. Collecting her monthlies.'

'And what exactly are they?'

'Look, just send her out, will you, bro? I've got other people to see, know what I'm saying?'

Sean stepped out through the front door, closing it

behind him. 'No, I don't know what Pricky's saying. So why doesn't Pricky explain?'

Ricky looked at him appraisingly for a moment. Then he slipped a packet of cigarettes from a pocket and offered Sean one. Sean just stared at him, so he popped it into his own mouth and lit up.

'New kid on the block? OK, quick update for future reference. Janice makes a monthly payment that guarantees safety—'

'Thought it was the Littern Guyz who took care of all that.'

Ricky smiled around the end of the cigarette. 'We got arrangements with the Guyz.'

You say? Sean thought. Cool fury began to smoulder deep inside him. 'How did she get the bruises?'

Ricky took a deep draw on the cigarette. 'The what?'

'The bruises on her face. Where did she get them?'

A shrug. Another deep draw. 'Fell over. You know how it is.'

'So in fact you're pretty shit at guaranteeing safety.'

'Like I say, if she don't pay dues . . . What can you do? Shit happens.'

'Yeah, it does. In fact . . .' Sean snatched the cigarette from Ricky's mouth and flicked it onto the floor. He crushed it beneath his foot. 'I squeezed one out this morning looked just like you.'

Ricky stared down at the butt. Then his face twisted into a snarl as he looked up at Sean, and his mouth opened. Sean cupped his hand and slapped the guy hard across the right ear, faster than Ricky could react. Ricky's scream echoed along the landing. He staggered back and dropped to the floor like his legs had snapped.

Sean crouched down. 'That's a ruptured eardrum,' he said. 'Don't worry. It'll heal in – oh, three months, max. And you've got another one.' He cupped his hand again and made as if to hit the other ear. Ricky recoiled. 'But I want you to hear me clear so I won't do that one too, unless you ask real nice.'

Ricky attempted to get up onto his knees, but Sean pushed him back onto his arse.

'I'm Janice's son,' he said. 'Didn't she mention me? Aw, now I'm all hurt as well as angry. Doesn't matter really. What does is that you will never visit her again. Understand?'

'Piece of shit,' Ricky hissed through the pain.

Sean smiled. What he wanted to do was beat the slimy wanker into a pulp. He had no doubt that Ricky was the one responsible for his mum's bruises. But he was almost as angry with himself as he was with the shit stain lying in front of him. If he'd stayed at home, not joined up, this wouldn't have happened. He could have protected his mum, looked after her. He remembered what Copper had said, back when he first decided to join up. The bastard had been right.

And so Sean kept smiling, and heaved Ricky to his feet.

'Seems to me my mum's entitled to a refund. So I'll take it now.' He held out his hand. Ricky glared hate at him, but reached into his pocket. And suddenly Sean found himself staring down the barrel of a revolver. It was pointing directly at his face, and it was loaded. Sean could see the ends of the rounds sitting in their chambers.

Ricky's hand was shaking. Whether it was from the slap, or because he wasn't used to the weight of a pistol, Sean couldn't be sure. It didn't make him feel any easier about what was going down.

'Right, then, you shit,' Ricky said. 'Back off and get your bitch of a mother out here now!'

Sean raised his hands – not right in the air, just either side of his face. 'Hey, you don't need that, bro.' He had to work to keep his voice calm, low. 'We can discuss this.'

'Shut up!' Ricky screamed. 'What? You think you can come back here and tell me what to do? You think?'

Sean focused on the weapon, taking in how Ricky was holding it – sideways, like an American gangster, trying hard to be cool. All that meant was that he was twice as likely to miss. When he fired, the gun would recoil, and the way Ricky was holding it, the shot could go anywhere. And even if he'd been using it properly, it was one-handed, the end of the barrel waving around all over the place. He didn't know squat about handling a weapon.

If he had been only a few metres away, Sean would have felt pretty confident, because what with the shaking hand and the recoil, Ricky would almost certainly miss him. But this close, even for a novice, missing him would be a lot harder.

'Now, get your mum out here! Ricky's waiting!'

'Pricky can go fuck his own.'

Ricky raised the gun a bit higher – and Sean moved.

He hadn't officially done the unarmed combat course, but he had practised with mates who had. Speed, aggression, surprise – that's what you needed.

Ricky was holding the gun in his right hand. Sean darted to his left, Ricky's right: his mates had said it was harder for a guy holding a gun in one hand to move it quickly in that direction. He wrapped the fingers of his right hand around the barrel and brought the heel of his left hand up under the hammer, and in one swift movement he had levered the gun out of Ricky's grip. It was a textbook move. Ricky's finger was still inside the trigger guard and it nearly came with it. He howled as Sean heard the snap.

With the same movement, Sean chucked the gun

away down the passage and threw his whole body forward into the guy, piling in with his right fist, smashing it hard and fast into Ricky's face. Ricky's nose gave way under a barrage of blows, blood bursting out across his cheeks. Sean drove on, pushing into him, punching, punching, punching, right arm pistoning into the guy's head. Ricky collapsed in a shrieking, weeping, quivering heap. Sean stepped back and picked up the gun. Then, slowly, deliberately, he levelled it at his assailant. For the first time in his life, after all that training, he was holding a live weapon aimed at another human being. It was a strange feeling. And he held it properly, two hands on the grip, feet apart, arms straight, staring straight down the barrel at his target. Ricky stared at his finger, which hung down uselessly. Then he screamed again.

'We were discussing a refund for my mum,' Sean said. The skin on his knuckles had split and his hand throbbed, but he held the gun steady.

Ricky opened his mouth, and Sean thumbed the hammer back with a loud *click*. He had no intention of pulling the trigger, but Ricky wasn't to know that. He fumbled inside his top and pulled out a thick wallet, which he threw down on the floor by Sean's feet. Weapon still trained on him, Sean knelt on one knee to pick it up. He opened it with one hand and looked down at a thick wad of tens and twenties. Taking hold of the wad with thumb and forefinger, he lifted it out so that the wallet fell away. Then he kicked the wallet back to its owner and stuffed the money into his own pocket.

'Your refund is accepted. Now do us both a favour and fuck off already.'

Ricky was clutching his hand with tears in his eyes. His face was a volatile mix of rage, agony and confusion as he clambered to his feet. 'You're fucking dead. Your bitch of a mum owes me. Now you do too.'

Sean walked backwards to the flat and pushed the door open with his shoulders and arse, without bringing the gun down.

'You can't protect her all the time, soldier boy.' Ricky spat blood, hunched over to protect his hand, while tears of pain ran down his spattered face. 'I'll be back. Those bruises I give her the first time? They won't be nothing on what's coming if she don't pay up, and this time I don't care how many extra shags I get out of her.'

Sean paused, halfway into the flat. Then he crossed the threshold again and approached Ricky with steady, measured steps, tapping the gun against his thigh. 'Oh, Pricky,' he said softly.

He had cut off Ricky's escape, which Ricky suddenly realized – about the same time as he realized he should maybe have kept his mouth shut about the extra shags.

'No . . . no, wait . . . please . . .'

He cowered back into a corner.

Sean feinted, pretending to drive his knee into Ricky's groin. Ricky shrieked and bent double to protect his balls, which meant that Sean could grab the back of his neck and drive his knee in hard, for real. Sean let go and Ricky dropped to the floor. He retched a couple of times, then spewed vomit and blood over the passage.

Sean crouched down nearby, just out of range of the pool of vom. 'You've got arrangements with the Guyz? I'm one of the Guyz and let's just say your arrangement is over.' He went back into the flat and shut the door.

He didn't look at his mum as he worked out how to break the gun open. He dropped the bullets into his hand, then stuffed rounds and weapon into different pockets.

On the other side of the door, Sean heard Ricky call him a 'dead man' and a 'fucking bastard' as he retreated, stumbling down the landing towards the stairs. Then silence.

He stared hard at his mum. She looked back at him the way he had looked at her the one and only time she had caught him in bed with a girl.

'Why didn't you tell me, you dozy cow?' he asked softly.

Her face seemed to crumple. 'Because if I did, I knew you'd come and sort it out.'

'And that's a bad thing?'

'Yes! You went through so much to get away from this place . . . I'd die if you got nicked again. I'd die.' Her eyes were like a rabbit's caught in the headlights, just before the Land Rover splatted over it.

Sean thought for a moment, then pulled her into a gentle hug. He gave her a kiss on the cheek and then rested his chin on the top of her head. 'What happened?'

Finally she started to cry. 'When PJ went . . . he took everything. Said he'd paid for it so it was his. And . . . and he cleared out the account because most of it was his money . . . and I didn't feel safe without him and without you, so—'

'So you started paying Pricky. Fucking hell.' Sean closed his eyes, shook his head. 'From now on you tell me everything, right? Everything.'

He gently pushed her away and clapped his hands together like nothing had happened. 'So!' He winced. Shit, his hand hurt. He flexed his fingers slowly to keep the blood flowing and stop them swelling up. 'Cup of tea, you were saying?'

He would give it a couple of minutes before letting her know that he had to go out again. Unexpected business to attend to.

Chapter 12

Sean leaned against the concrete wall outside the flat and gazed into the night, at the lights from curtained windows. He stared at one particular set of curtains while he finished off his can of lager. Then he set it on the edge of the balcony, pulled out his phone and punched in the number. It was a new phone since he got nicked, new number, but he had copied over the contacts.

The sound of distant ringing went on too long. He was about to hang up when someone picked up at the other end.

'Yeah?'

'Matt?'

'Nah, you've reached Justin Bieber's private line. Course it's Matt! Who's this?'

Sean laughed. 'Sean, mate. It's Sean.'

Silence. Then, 'Get out of here! Sean? Mate, where you been? How long's it been since you joined up? You come to your senses finally?'

'You around?' Sean asked.

'Why, you want to link up? That'd be sweet. Where are you now?'

'I'm outside my mum's.'

There was a pause, and then the curtains Sean was looking at were pulled aside. He gave a single wave with one hand; the figure in the window lifted a hesitant hand in return.

'Sure, mate. Come on over.'

'On my way,' said Sean. 'You decent?'

Matt laughed. 'Yeah, I'll make sure me and – uh – the wifey are dressed.'

Sean grinned. 'Don't know her name, do you?'

Matt had always made it a point never to have the same girl in his bed twice. 'Just get yerself over here, you prick. Bring your balls, if you can remember where you left them.'

Two hours later, Sean found he had lost the power to say 'Hectic.'

'Het – hetci—'

He hadn't got truly smashed since he joined up. He was out of practice and didn't particularly want to get back in.

But that wasn't washing with the people h
right now. His return home – because th

saw it – had quickly turned into an excuse for a massive party. Booze was flowing, music was pounding, and a gentle haze of weed hung in the air, though so far Sean had successfully avoided having a spliff pressed into his hands. His arms and ribs ached from having his hand shaken and being pulled into hugs by people he knew, and a fair few he didn't but who were drunk enough to think they did.

He had kind of hoped Curly might be there. No such luck. Curly had hit the big one – seven years for armed robbery, which kind of sucked for his pregnant girlfriend.

'Hectic, mate.' He had finally nailed it. He popped the ring on the can, took a sip. 'Love it.'

He and Matt were crammed into a corner of the kitchen, which seemed to be the designated serious conversation zone. No one bothered them there. Matt had asked how the army was working out while he sank a deep glug fr⸺ own can. 'Pissed a lot of folk off,' he said, 'y⸺ ⸺s.'

⸺id immediately.

⸺e sees it.'

⸺on?' Sean gestured at the ⸺ing, laughing, talking.

⸺ne, right?' Matt said. ⸺ on Sean's leg. '*I've*

missed you, mate. Like a brother. After Gaz – that was fucking tragic; did you hear his old man died a few months ago, inside? Broken fucking heart. After Gaz, and Copper – well, he's still around, but he's got, let's say, side projects – after Gaz, and Copper, there was . . . you. But the way you disappeared? That was shit of you. Well shit.'

'I'm back now, aren't I?' Sean pointed out.

'I'm serious,' Matt said. 'For some folk, you know, this is everything, isn't it? We're like family to each other. You leave, you cut ties, that hurts people. Unavoidable.'

Sean took a breath. He wasn't pissed enough to forget the reason for coming over. 'Like my mum?'

'What do you mean by that?'

Sean told Matt what had happened. 'And this guy says they've got an "arrangement" with the Guyz. An *arrangement*? Are we, like, hiring out now?'

Matt picked up his drink, but he didn't take his eyes off Sean. 'Interesting use of the word "we" there, Sean mate. *We* are the guys who hung around to look after things. *You* are the guy who pissed off.'

'Except you ain't looking after things,' Sean said levelly, 'if you're letting pricks with guns from other outfits cruise the estate, beat up the people who live here and take their money. What's going on?'

'What's going on, Sean, is that life is more complicated than it was when we was kids. You hang around, you grow up here, you realize it. But you didn't hang around, you sodded off to be a soldier boy, so all this has kind of passed you by. I can see it's a leap to catch up, but you'll have to make it. You get out what you put in. And your mum – shit, she's a sweet lady, Sean, we all know that, but she don't exactly put much in, do she? So she gets messed around, and there's nothing to make it worth our while looking out for her. OK, OK.' He held up a hand as Sean took a deep breath. 'This guy was well out of order. We shall have words. But apart from that – well, she don't look out for herself and you're not exactly paying your dues.'

Sean slowly let the breath out again and stared at Matt, who was innocently downing the rest of his can. He had once looked up to Matt like any boy looks up to a hero. Now he was a stranger.

'Fuck, you sound like Copper,' he muttered.

Matt lowered his can. 'Now, he's one of those who thinks you bailed on us.'

'Guessed that,' Sean said. 'But it's nearly a year and a half since I last saw him. Surely the big tosser's got over it by now.'

'You can ask him that yourself,' Matt told him. 'He'll be here in about ten minutes.'

Sean stopped his lager can halfway to his mouth. 'You serious?'

Matt nodded. 'Don't worry though. He's mellowed about it now. Sounded well excited when I told him you were here.'

'You told him? Why didn't you tell me you'd told him?'

'Didn't know I had to,' Matt said. 'Chill, all right? Copper and you go way back.'

'Last time I saw him, I'd just smashed his face in.'

Matt stared and was actually silent for a second or two. Then he laughed. 'Funny, he never mentioned that. But he'll be over it now. It was a long time ago.'

Sean raised his can the rest of the way, drained it. He wasn't so sure, but there was nothing he could do. Walking out right now wasn't an option. He'd never live it down, and he probably wouldn't make it to the door anyway. Best just to sit it out and wait.

He didn't have to wait long.

Copper's arrival was announced with cheers. He'd always been popular but it had obviously gone up some since they'd last hung out together.

The crowd parted and the big man himself walked over. The look on his face was all bulldog. No warmth, just an animal snarl.

'Seany.'

'Copper.'

For a moment they stared each other out. Sean didn't

know whether to get ready to defend himself, or to just cut to the chase and get in with a pre-emptive strike.

Then, amazingly, Copper's snarl vanished and a grin appeared. 'Come here then, you bastard!'

Sean was helpless as Copper wrapped his massive arms around him and lifted him off the ground. 'Good to see you too,' he said, squeezing the words out of squashed lungs.

Copper dropped Sean back onto his feet and ruffled his hair. 'That fuck awful haircut says you're still in the army.'

Sean nodded. 'That a problem?'

'Only if you want it to be.' Copper took a can from Matt's offering hand.

Ah, thought Sean. He heard the edge to Copper's voice. Despite the outward show of everything's-all-right-now, it wasn't.

'So, what you been up to?' Sean asked, deliberately changing the subject.

'Did my time, got released, come back home,' Copper said. 'Life's good, ain't that right, Matt?'

Matt reached over, bumped fists with him.

'So, what brings you back now?' Copper asked.

'Misses us, I reckon,' Matt said.

'Something like that.' Sean attempted a smile.

'Not sure I believe that,' Copper said. 'Eighteen

months is a long time to miss a guy without, you know, doing something the fuck about it.'

'It's Mum,' Sean said. 'She needs someone to keep an eye on her.' He looked from Copper to Matt, then back to Copper again. He finished his beer.

'You want us to watch out for her, is that it?' Copper asked.

'Yeah,' Sean said. 'Look, I know it's asking a slot . . . I mean, a lot . . .' Oh, shit – great time to be pissed. If he'd known he would be tangling with Copper, he'd have stuck to the soft stuff. 'But she already had some twat beat her up, and he was armed too.' He took a breath and ran on with the sentence in his head, before he lost the power of speech altogether. 'I'd just rest easier knowing you had your eye on her. 'Cos, face it, Copper' – he saw no harm in a little flattery, and anyway, it was true – 'they know you're on her case, no one's going to mess with her.'

Copper stared at Sean over his beer can, sinking great gulps until it was finished. Then he crushed it and chucked it into a corner of the room. 'So you think you're still one of us?' he asked. 'Even with all that soldiering shite?'

'I'm still *me*, Copper,' Sean said. 'You know that.'

Copper was silent, his eyes never leaving Sean. Then he said, 'Remains to be seen, don't it?'

'And what's that supposed to mean?'

'Means it's a long time since you brought anything into the Guyz. And I've got a short memory.'

Their eyes locked together, neither of them giving an inch.

Matt broke the deadlock. 'Fr'instance, Sean, from what you were telling me, there's now a surplus gun on the estate . . . Where did that get to? Seems to me the Guyz could use something like that.'

Sean slowly turned his head to glower at his old mate. 'I dealt with it.'

One thing he was absolutely sure of was that the Guyz did not need a gun. God knew what they would do with it. A year ago he would have handed it over without question. Now he had a professional's pride when it came to weaponry, and he knew what guns could do in the hands of amateurs. He had wiped it for prints – he presumed his were still on file, and it would be a *really* bad idea for former car thief Private Harker's prints to turn up on a hooky gun – and then chucked it into the recycling. Let the council work out where it came from, if they ever found it.

Copper came up real close to Sean. 'Army turned you soft?'

Sean made to push past. Copper didn't budge.

'Soft, and a chicken too? Well, fuck me, Seany, what's happened to you?'

Sean pushed again, and this time Copper let him past.

Matt called after him. 'Come on Sean, mate. Copper's only joshing with you . . . Aren't you, Copper? Right?'

Sean caught the look in Copper's eyes. 'I don't need to prove myself, Copper. All I'm asking is a favour!'

'And all I'm asking is a little proof. It isn't much, Seany, you know that. But keeping an eye on your mum – that's work. It takes time that we could be using for something more profitable. It *costs*, Seany. So if you can show you're still a part of the family – if you keep on paying your dues and don't just want to sponge off us – then I guarantee your mum will be safe. My word.'

Sean was out of the flat, down the short flight of stairs and outside before he either had the chance to respond, or punched someone.

Fuck this! He had to *prove* himself to fucking Copper?

After everything he had achieved in the last year, Sean felt no need to prove himself to anyone ever again. He knew who and what he was. And Copper just shat all over that and counted it for nothing.

What did Copper know, anyway? Nothing, that's what.

He shouldn't have bothered. Should have just taken his mum and got her out of there, put her up in a flat away from the estate, let her start again, like he had.

His phone rang. He snatched it from his pocket,

expecting to see Matt's number come up. But it wasn't Matt.

'Mum?' Sean heard crying down the line. 'Mum! What's happened? What's wrong?'

The sobbing continued for a while longer until at last words came: 'Sean, I got worried – you went out and you didn't come back . . . Suppose Ricky comes back? He will, Sean—'

'He won't, Mum,' he said automatically. 'I'm talking to some guys about it.'

More sobbing. 'I miss you, love, and I get so scared when I'm on my own . . . Didn't used to be like this, not when you were around . . .'

Sean closed his eyes and groaned. *Not you too, Mum!*

That was what it came down to. As a kid he had thought the Guyz were family. They looked out for each other because that was what families did. But no, apparently he had got it wrong. The Guyz looked out for the people it was useful to look out for.

He had to make himself useful again.

'I'm going to sort it out, OK, Mum? I'm going to sort it out right now. I promise. Just hang tight. Can you do that for me?'

'Yes, love, of course I can.'

'Good,' said Sean. He jabbed at the off key and the line went dead.

He knew exactly what he had to do. It had nothing to do with proving himself to Copper. It had everything to do with family. His own, and the gang.

He walked for twenty minutes to get safely away from the estate. The old rule about not shitting in your own bed still applied. Then he quickly took a left off the high street, dropping down into a small side road. It was lined with parked cars. Staying alert for passers-by, he walked along, testing doors. It had never ceased to amaze him how many people left their cars unlocked. All it took was a moment of forgetfulness – and, yep, just as Sean had expected, an open door. It was a Ford Orion, an old model but in good condition. That meant two things: easy to wire and easy to flog.

He slipped into the driver's seat and his fingers felt expertly in the dark for the ridges of the plastic cover beneath the steering wheel. He pulled the panel free and chucked it onto the passenger seat. Next his fingertips worked over the clusters of wiring until he had the bundle that was the battery, ignition and starter wire. He pulled it free and delved into his pocket for his penknife, then stripped an inch of insulation off the battery wires and twisted them together.

Now the car had power, and if all he wanted to do was listen to the radio, he was sorted.

Instead he went on to join the ignition wire to the

battery wire. The dashboard panel came alight. Last of all he wrapped his fingers in his hanky for insulation and stripped half an inch of insulation off the starter wire. A spark flew when the metal blade touched the live wire and Sean hissed through his teeth as it stung him through the cloth. But now the wire was bare. He touched it to the connected battery wires and the Orion choked into life. He quickly revved the engine, but it was in good condition. It only needed that fleeting touch to get it going. After that, the engine ran itself.

'Still got it,' he murmured as he eased the vehicle out into the street. 'Even when I'm pissed.'

He didn't speed off. He didn't want to draw attention to himself: he was taking without consent *and* way over the limit. At the back of his mind was the knowledge of just how much trouble he would be in if he got caught. With the police, with the army. But he didn't need treacherous little voices whispering good sense to him, so he told it to shut the fuck up as he made a call with his phone on hands-free.

'Matt? Yeah, it's Sean. Put Copper on. I've got something for him. Call it a down payment for services.'

Chapter 13

'You really want to watch us strip?' asked Bright.

A ripple of laughter ran down the rank. The platoon stood at ease at the end of the firing range, feet apart and hands behind their backs, while Sergeant Adams paced to and fro in front of them.

'Correct. Today isn't just about sending a few thousand rounds down the range, it's about me making sure you lot know what you're doing from the moment you pick up a weapon, right through to when you hand it back in. No one is firing off a round till you've all stripped and rebuilt your weapon. And that goes for every single one you use today, from your SA80 to the GPMG and your side arm. Or, if you prefer, we can spend the day doing PT. I really don't mind.' He got out his watch. 'So, platoon. Take up your weapons and . . . begin.'

At that, the platoon dropped to the ground to sit cross-legged or on their knees, and everyone got on with pulling apart the SA80 in their laps.

Undo the clips on the stock and remove the firing mechanism. Remove spring, cocking handle and bolt. *Click, click, snap, click.* Unlatch the handguard over the barrel, remove the gas adjuster . . .

There was a soothing rhythm to the lightly oiled, precision-engineered pieces of metal sliding together exactly as designed. Not too much force, not too little, and the gun responded in your hands like a trained pet. It didn't take long for Sean to have his weapon in pieces and laid out on the cloth in front of him. Muzzle, flash eliminator, trigger, trigger housing . . .

He was grateful to be focusing on something he could do with ease. It was Tuesday and his weekend was long behind him, though not long enough.

Sorting his mum out, a scrap with a loan shark, and twoccing a car were all things that hadn't been on his to-do list. Yet done them he had, and somehow got away with it all. Copper had come through for him too, shifting the car within hours. Minus his commission, he had handed Sean a good roll of notes. Five hundred quid – most of which Sean had then had to hand straight back. Protection money for his own mum.

No, he kept reminding himself, not protection money, just his dues. Sean had made a contribution to the Guyz so that it would still be worth their while to keep an eye on her. That was OK? Wasn't it?

But. He couldn't keep popping up to town and supplying Copper with a car whenever funds were low. And he had to keep the Guyz settled, somehow. His idea of getting his mum off the estate had evaporated in the cold, sober light of day, the moment he checked his bank balance.

He had met guys who weren't paid much more than him but had thirty or forty grand put away. A couple of tours in Afghanistan, with nothing to spend your dosh on, would do that for you. But he had yet to earn a full year's salary off the army, and while his income was way higher than his expenditure on Single Living Accommodation, his balance would take one look at a London rent and vanish.

If the soppy cow was going to be looked after full time, he needed a more steady way of paying his dues. And his regular salary was never going to be enough.

Adams checked the platoon's work, and announced himself satisfied. They moved onto the range proper and stood on the firing line. Sean clamped the ear defenders to his head, though not yet fully over his ears so that he could hear the sergeant's orders. In front of him, stretching out from approximately fifty metres to a maximum range of three hundred metres, were a number of Figure II targets attached to plywood boards – man-sized images showing a helmeted soldier charging towards you with a bayonet fixed. The end of the range was marked by a huge, steep bank of soil covered in patches of grass and weeds.

'Best part of the job, this!' It was Heaton, standing alongside him.

Sean nodded in agreement, with a big grin. Legally firing off guns was the next best thing to driving a fast car.

And what had Heaton said in the car? *Could always use a little help* . . . That sounded a lot like an offer. How serious had it been? He gave the corporal a sideways glance and wondered if now was the moment to bring it up.

But then the order came through from Sergeant Adams to prepare to fire.

Sean was in standing position, his weight already forward on his left foot, ready to fire. He pulled his weapon up and into the shoulder, staring down through the ACOG, which drew the targets in close and clear.

'Single shots, in your own time,' Adams said. 'Have it, then!'

Sean squeezed the trigger. The crack of the round was followed by the thump of it slamming home down range. He fired off single shots, lowering his weapon between each one to adjust his aim and stop his arms fatiguing, breathing, staying calm. He knew why they were on single shots rather than the usual three-round bursts – this was all about nailing their accuracy and marksmanship. And fully automatic was, as every soldier knew, a last resort. If you were down to that, odds were that things had really gone to shit.

For the rest of the day the platoon cycled through a range of weaponry, honing their skills so that they could use each gun efficiently and with deadly accuracy. Last item of the day was their Glock pistols, firing 9mm rounds down range. Which made Sean think of Heaton again. He took up the position, feet apart, hands together on the grip, sighting along the barrel at the target, a black silhouette of an attacking soldier. And he couldn't help thinking back just a few days to when he had been sighting like this for real, on a cowering, pimply loan shark he had just beaten up. How many of the lads around him could say the same?

His lips curled into a grim smile and he opened fire. Steady shots, relaxing into the kick from the weapon, adjusting his aim each time to ensure accuracy. Despite what you saw in the movies, hitting anything accurately with a pistol at a distance beyond twenty metres was not easy. In fact, it was basically a miracle. But that wasn't what these weapons were designed for. They were for close quarter combat, and that meant around five metres or less, or as backup – which meant that everything had gone to shit even more than putting your rifle on fully automatic. The Glock was your last resort.

Eventually the day came to an end and Sergeant Adams gathered everyone around him.

'Not bad,' he said. 'Not brilliant, but not bad. I'll be putting in for a few more days like this. Can't have you lot becoming slack with your marksmanship. Check your weapons and piss off. Harker, you have the lovely job of helping Corporal Heaton clear up and sign this lot back in.'

There were worse jobs. After a day on the range, while everyone else was hitting the pub, someone always had to spend a while checking the area for any live rounds, clearing up, then lugging stuff back to the quartermaster department. They all ended up doing it at some point. Today was Sean's turn.

As the rest of the section piled into the back of a Land Rover Wolf, he stood there with Heaton.

'Done this before? No? Doesn't take long,' the corporal said. 'All the weapons are already checked through and clear, so we just need to load those up, bag up the brass' – he meant the expended rounds – 'check the area, and we're done.'

'What about the rounds left over?' Sean asked.

'No problem. I'll deal with them, you get the weapons sorted, right?'

Sean nodded, and for the next half-hour loaded up the SA80s, side arms and GPMG into the Wolf.

Finally Heaton came over. 'Done?'

'All in and accounted for. You?'

The corporal nodded. He had stacked up the ammo crates that had accompanied them for the day on the range.

'I'll give you a hand,' Sean offered.

'No need,' he said. 'You can drive.'

Something else the army had done for Sean was get him through his driving test. His HGV licence was the next target on the radar. He went round to the driver's door and clambered in. A couple of minutes later, Heaton got in beside him. Sean sparked the engine into life and spun the Wolf round to head off back to barracks.

'Your mate Clark was on good form today,' Heaton said. 'Nice to see a woman can aim and fire at the same time.'

Sean bit his lip and several angry responses ran through his mind but he'd had practice in this kind of thing, with Copper. You didn't get offended by Copper being a jerk – just like you didn't blame a dog for yapping: it was what they did. So all he did was mutter, 'Leave it out,' and they drove in silence for a few moments.

'Good weekend, then?' Heaton asked.

Sean grunted. 'I've had better.' He subconsciously

flexed the fingers of his right hand again. Shit, they were stiff. The split skin had scabbed over and the bruises were fading, but it had never taken that long before. He really must have pounded that bastard Ricky.

Heaton saw the movement, then leaned closer. He whistled. 'OK, so things kind of went downhill after Friday. What was that? A bust-up for old times' sake?'

'Something like that.'

Sean was happy to let Heaton think whatever he wanted – telling an NCO he'd stolen a car was probably not his best plan. Especially not when he wanted to get into the NCO's good books. He took a breath to raise the subject of extra work, but Heaton got in first.

'Do you miss it?'

'What? London? Nah, not at all really.'

'That's not what I meant,' Heaton said. 'Your old mates, all that . . . The lifestyle.'

Sean shook his head.

'Not very convincing,' Heaton noted.

'Lifestyle got me banged up,' Sean said. 'Never again.'

He wasn't sure what else he could say. He didn't miss it, but at the same time . . . There was no question about it. Grabbing that car had felt good. It had scratched an itch he hadn't known he had, and it meant his mum was safe.

And there was still the issue of money.

'I . . .' he began.

Heaton looked at him expectantly as he pulled the Wolf off the ranges track and onto a metalled road.

Sean looked straight ahead. 'I could really do with some extra cash. Like you were saying.'

Heaton glanced sideways at him. 'Oh yeah?'

'Yeah. It's just that—' Sean paused, bit his lip. Heaton didn't need to know why he needed the money and he wasn't going to start blurting out his mum's problems. 'Yeah. Stuff at home . . . It'd come in handy.'

For the next few minutes neither spoke. Sean drove on, his right arm resting out of the open window, his left making sure the Wolf stayed in a straight line.

Heaton cut the silence. 'I think I can help you out there.'

'Yeah?'

'Yeah. It's easy work. Just delivering stuff for me, that's all. Would give me time on some other projects. Cash in hand and we'll split anything I use you for sixty–forty. How does that sound?'

'Sounds sweet,' Sean said. 'What's the money like?'

'Depends,' Heaton told him. 'Sixty–forty would get you . . . a few hundred extra a month. Say, half a grand.'

Sean glanced at him. Alarm bells were going off in his head. 'For delivering stuff? What stuff?'

'Supplies,' Heaton said. Sean kept looking at him and

he shrugged. 'Reassigned stuff. Stuff we get for free but' – he gave a laugh – 'some freaks will pay big time for it. And you're about to hit that lamppost.'

Sean looked back at the road, just in time to pull the Wolf back within the white lines.

'You mean you steal from the quartermaster? Are you fucking mental?' The last thing he needed was to get nabbed by the army and thrown back inside, this time in a military prison.

'I said *reassigned*,' said Heaton. 'Damaged, out-of-date kit – the MoD doesn't want it. They'd only destroy it. I just cover with a bit of paperwork and it's done. Anything from a sleeping bag and a stove to ration packs and magazines. I just siphon it off.'

'Sleeping bags,' Sean said sceptically. He thought back to Heaton's flat. It would take a lot of hooky sleeping bags to pay for that. But he had learned long ago not to ask too much unless you knew for a fact that you would like the answer. What you didn't know couldn't implicate you. And he really needed some way of earning more money.

Heaton laughed. 'OK. Let's just say that what the MoD doesn't need, I make use of, and leave it at that. It's in that strange grey area between black market and eBay. So, you free Saturday evening? I got a new contact placed an order. Small delivery to sound me out, potential to go mega.'

Sean looked stonily at the road ahead. The gatehouse was approaching and he shifted down a gear. To tell the truth, Saturday night he'd been kind of hoping to hit the town with some of the lads from the platoon. Beer, dancing and a distinct possibility of pulling . . .

But five hundred quid for a few nights' work was five hundred quid more than he would get any other way. And he might be back in time for the night out.

'Sure,' he said. 'Saturday.'

Chapter 14

Sean had kind of hoped he would get the loan of the Impreza to make the drop. No such luck. Heaton also had a battered blue Daewoo Matiz for these occasions. It had about as much street cred as leg warmers and a perm, and he had to put the seat as far back as it would go to get his long legs in. But the radio worked, so he just settled back and followed the satnav directions, thumping out the beat from a CD of old-school rock hits on the steering wheel.

The route took him out over Salisbury Plain, on well-maintained civilian roads rather than the rutted army tracks he had got used to. It was getting on for sunset on a late summer evening, so the sun was low and the rolling landscape was bathed in orange light. Sean wondered how it was that civvy and military roads apparently had different weather systems. Whenever he was out on exercise it seemed to be raining.

But now the weather was good, the roads smooth,

and he found himself simply enjoying being out and about – until the satnav told him where to go.

'Your destination is on your right.'

It was a rutted track, overlooked by trees. Sean squinted doubtfully down it.

He had kind of assumed they would meet in a layby or something and do a simple switch. Still plenty of daylight for everyone to see something perfectly innocent going on. Other cars passing by. No one watching would think there was anything funny happening.

But off the road, in an out-of-the-way place like this? And if things went south, he was hardly in the world's greatest getaway car.

That thought made him laugh. It also eased his nerves. He had met people who tried to go back on deals. Take the goods, refuse the payment. The ones who survived the reminders soon went out of business for the simple reason that no one would trust them again. A successful operation was based on trust – and Sean had seen with his own eyes that Heaton was successful. He wasn't being set up.

He put the car into gear and headed down the lane.

The trees blocked out enough light for the car's headlights to come on automatically. The smell of stale manure started to drift in through the car vents and he wrinkled his nose. Country smells had been a brand-new experience during training; he had been quite revolted to learn that cows and sheep could just crap in the field and no one picked it up. He had seen more of the countryside in the last year than he had in his first sixteen, and he still didn't like it.

At the end of the track he drove into a small yard surrounded on three sides by old farm buildings. The skeletal remains of a tractor were rusting in a far corner. He checked his watch – early by five minutes. He turned off the engine and stepped out.

Car headlights swung off the road in the distance and disappeared into the tree tunnel. The lights strobed through the trees as the car drew near. Then it was out of the tunnel and rumbling towards Sean. He recognized the silhouette as a Range Rover. He propped himself against the Matiz and tried very hard to look cool.

The driver's window slid down smoothly. 'So where's the package?'

The voice was one of those accent-less ones. Well-spoken but difficult to trace, giving no real hint of being from any particular part of the country.

'In the boot.'

'Well, it's not doing much good to either of us there, is it?'

Sean shrugged and made his way round to the back

of his car to pop the boot. He hadn't asked Heaton what the package was, and Heaton probably wouldn't have told him if he had – they both appreciated the need for plausible deniability. It was barely the size of a weekend suitcase, so whatever it was, it definitely wasn't sleeping bags. It could be ration packs, he thought; medical kit maybe. Wasn't his problem.

He reached in and lifted the box. And almost fell into the boot. 'Shit . . .' He hadn't expected it to be so heavy. He had to use both hands to haul it out.

The man climbed down out of the Range Rover and went to open the rear door. 'You OK with that?'

'Yeah, no problem . . .' Sean carried it over.

'Just drop it in here.'

Now Sean could get a better look at him. He was dressed in dark jeans and shirt. Hair short, age about thirty. He was shorter than Sean; Sean guessed he could take him in a fight, if the guy tried to stiff him for the payment. Sean had enforced a few debts in his time, and he had never enjoyed it.

'Thank you,' the man said as Sean swung the package into the back of the vehicle. 'And this is yours, I believe.' He held out a brown envelope.

'Yeah, cheers,' said Sean. As per orders, he opened it and ran his finger over a large wad of notes. The man snorted but waited with exaggerated patience.

It was all twenties, all used, and fifty of them. So, yes, a thousand quid.

'That would all seem to be in order,' Sean allowed. Then, as the man shut the rear door, he couldn't resist adding, 'Never realized there was such a market for army surplus.'

'Army surplus?' The man laughed. 'Whatever. Give me five minutes. I don't want to feel I'm being followed.'

So Sean watched him drive off before returning to the Matiz. It seemed even smaller now, even more pathetic, having sat in the shadow of the Range Rover.

He chucked the money on the passenger seat and squeezed himself in after it. Then he paused, and picked up the envelope again. Flicked thoughtfully through the notes.

Since leaving Burnleigh he had been clean – until this week – and now he had broken the law twice. The first time could have just been a relapse – old, buried habits unburying themselves. But this? He hadn't just broken the law – he was getting paid for it too. That made him a pro.

Heaton had said that it wasn't *exactly* illegal, more a sort of grey area. Like shit. Legal stuff did not go down in deserted farmyards in the arse end of nowhere.

Sean tucked the envelope into a pocket, still

thoughtful. Clean sheet, to amateur, to professional, all in one week. What lay at the end of that particular path?

But he was no longer some hot-headed kid, doing it for the rush. This was grown up. He needed the money for a good reason, and so he was earning it. The risk was low compared to some of the stuff he'd done in the past, and no one was getting hurt.

Sean smiled as he eased the Matiz off the track and out onto the road. Perhaps he could have it both ways. The proper job, all above board, with pay and everything else that came with life as a soldier: excitement, adventure, awesome kit to play with. And alongside it a little bit of lawbreaking that wasn't going to harm anybody. Why not? He felt the pocket that bulged with the envelope inside it. *Yes, why not?*

A week later, Saturday afternoon, he was on his way again, working for Heaton, pushing the Matiz up the M3 and onto the M25, then hooking onto the Great North Road and into London.

The week in between had been a real ball-ache, thanks to Sergeant Adams, filled with relentless PT and checks, right down to kit inspection, all rounded off with a night attack exercise. Now Sean badly needed to spend some time sorting out all the stuff Adams had found wrong with his kit. But that, as Heaton had pointed out on Thursday night when he made the offer, wouldn't take all weekend. And it was an easy journey – he almost knew the way blindfold. Right next to Walthamstow.

With the Matiz in second gear – first was not just painfully slow, it made the engine squeal like a pig caught in a trap – Sean threaded his way off a main road into a small side street. It was lined with derelict warehouses, blank walls rising up high – old mills waiting in line for some developer to come along and turn them into expensive flats to be sold to celebrities.

The street came to a T-junction. Sean turned left and rolled on until he came to what Heaton had described as *a door the colour of shit.* He climbed out of the Matiz and knocked on the door with the delivery under his arm. It was slightly larger than a shoebox, heavier, but nowhere near as heavy as the box a week ago.

Footsteps, then a bolt shifting.

The door opened and Sean found himself looking – staring – up at Copper.

'It's the delivery lad!' Copper's face was one huge grin. 'How's it hanging, Seany?'

Sean finally found words. 'What you doing here?'

'Waiting for you, you twat.' Copper glanced over Sean's shoulder at the Matiz and smirked.

'Don't say a word,' Sean warned.

'Suits you,' said Copper. 'Come on.'

Sean followed him inside.

'I'm guessing Josh Heaton didn't tell you I was the customer, then?' Copper said cheerfully.

'No, he didn't! And how the fuck do you know Heaton, anyway? And how did he know we know each other?'

Copper led him down a passage with a scuffed carpet and scabby wallpaper. 'How do I know him? Mutual acquaintances. How does he know about us? He asked me if I knew a lad who looked like a daddy longlegs that can't get laid. I said, sounds like Sean Harker. He said, that's him!'

Sean seethed. 'How long have you known him for?'

'Mm. Dunno. A year, maybe?'

A year . . . Sean thought. That was considerably longer than he had known Heaton. Had Heaton made the connection between Sean and Copper the moment he joined the platoon?

So all that 'you never said you were in the Why-Oh-Whys' bollocks was . . . well, bollocks. A way of opening the conversation, that was all. Heaton must have intended to recruit him from the start. The wanker.

Sean couldn't deny he appreciated the money. He did not appreciate being played.

They had come to a small room filled with boxes.

Another door led off on the opposite side, to the back of the building.

'The owner lets us store a few things here,' Copper said. 'And in exchange we throw a few things his way, if you know what I mean.'

Another of those times Sean was deliberately not going to ask for details. He passed the package across and Copper carried it over to a bench.

'Just need to check the goods, mate, OK?'

Sean held out his hand. 'As long as you don't mind me doing some checking of my own?'

Copper grinned and pulled an envelope out of his coat. He placed it in Sean's hand with exaggerated care. 'Go wild.'

Sean went to lean against a wall and shuffled quickly through the notes while Copper opened the box up on the other side of the room. Sean had just got to the eight hundreds when he was suddenly distracted by a sound he both recognized and couldn't understand. The smooth metallic slick-and-click of a pistol being readied.

He looked over at Copper with wide eyes. The big lad was hunched over the box and the sound had come from him, Sean was sure of it. But he must have been mistaken. Heaton hadn't said anything about guns. And he, Matt and Copper – they never used to have guns.

Then the sound came again, and when Copper raised

his right hand, Sean immediately recognized the silhouette of what he was holding. And he wished to God that he didn't.

Copper was holding a Glock 17 Gen 4 pistol. And it was Sean who had put it in his hand.

Chapter 15

Sean was across the room in a beat. 'The *fuck* are you doing?'

'Like it?' Copper asked, turning his hand to get a good look at the pistol. 'Here, have a go yourself if you want.'

Sean didn't. He'd used one just like it many times. He could strip it down in seconds.

And now Copper was holding one.

'I asked you a question,' he said.

'Relax.' Copper put the weapon back into the box, and Sean saw that it had come with a pancake holster, designed to fit on his belt and hold the gun concealed close to his kidneys. 'Money well spent, right?'

Sean didn't give a shit about the money. 'I have to take it back,' he said. 'Must be a mistake. No way should that be there.'

But the brutal reality now facing him was creeping into the corner of Sean's mind. Heaton had said he sold off surplus stuff – kit the stores wouldn't miss. But guns were not surplus – they were active or they were put beyond use, and there was no middle ground. Heaton supplied stolen weapons, and had lied to him.

Copper rested a hand on Sean's left shoulder; it was heavy, like a large joint of ham. 'I'm guessing,' he said, 'that Josh hasn't told you the whole truth.'

Heaton wouldn't be such an idiot, Sean thought. You couldn't just nick weapons from the MoD. There were procedures. This shit was traceable!

'Unlike you,' Copper said, his voice slow and quiet, as though explaining something to a child, 'Josh kept in touch with his old life, old contacts, mates. Smart lad, if you ask me.'

'I'm going to kill him.'

Copper closed the box. 'It's not like it used to be,' he said. 'Life is different now. Things have changed. We have to keep up, make sure we're safe, look after our own. You've seen it for yourself, right? That guy coming after your mum?'

'That's bollocks and you know it!' Sean kept a lid on the volume, forcing it down from a shout. 'That was just some lone tosser. It's not like everyone's getting tooled up!'

Copper nodded towards the door. 'You've done your job, Seany. Take the money, forget it. Best way, right?'

He tucked the box under one arm and headed for the

exit that led out the back. 'See you around, Seany,' he said. 'Pull the door to when you go.'

Sean sat in the Matiz, his whole body shaking. He was beyond anger and into a whole new kind of rage. Then he roared, hammered his fists into the dashboard.

Heaton had lied to him. Sleeping bags? Ration packs? It was all bollocks and Sean felt sick at the way he'd been taken in. He should have realized. The money should have given it away. No way was any of that other stuff worth what was being paid.

Then he remembered the day on the ranges. He'd helped clear up and Heaton had insisted on sorting out the spent and unused rounds himself. Even when Sean had offered to help, he had kept him away. Was that what he had delivered to the bloke in the Range Rover? Sean wondered. A box of full metal jacket ammunition, picked up from the range?

And the Glock in Heaton's car . . . That couldn't be his own property at all. It was another stolen weapon.

Nausea and anger swept through Sean, making his stomach churn, bringing a metallic taste to his mouth. But he kept a hold of himself and didn't puke.

He slipped the keys into the ignition. He needed to have a talk with Heaton. A serious talk.

*

PLEASE NOTE WE ARE UNABLE TO SERVE YOU IF YOU
ARE UNDER 18 . . .

Sean hadn't touched his pint – which the barman
had served him without question, despite that smug little
notice pinned up above the till. He couldn't remember
the last time he had been age checked. Whenever he hit
the pub nowadays it was with a bunch of squaddies, and
he was usually the tallest, even if he was also the youngest.
No one ever bothered with ID.

And the minor illegality of drinking underage was
like ant's piss in the huge great puddle of gun-running.

The pint sat in front of him on a small round table in
a shadowy corner of the pub. The Monty – the
Montgomery of Alamein, officially – was a popular
watering hole with soldiers and it would be full of them
that evening. It was early enough to be mostly empty,
but he still didn't want any mates coming in and clocking
him the moment they were through the door.

He had arrived ten minutes ago. Heaton would be
here any time . . .

Sean still hadn't worked out exactly what he was
going to say. He'd decided to meet Heaton in the bar
because, he reasoned to himself, there was less chance of
him decking the bloke in full public view. But the pub
was quiet. The only person likely to complain about a
scuffle, other than the chubby barman with sweat stains

spreading out from under his arms, was the small white dog at the opposite end of the room. The dog's owner was asleep.

The door opened. Sean reached for his pint to calm his nerves and two girls walked in. He watched them scan the room, including him. They clocked his expression, which was not exactly welcoming, and pulled a face at each other, and then left, giggling. He put down his glass just as the door swung open again. Heaton strolled in and headed for the bar, bought a pint, looked around, spotted Sean. With a wave, he came over to join him.

'Told you it would be easy—' he started, but Sean cut him short.

'Why the fuck didn't you tell me what you were actually selling?'

Heaton sipped his pint. Didn't react, almost like he'd expected the question. And, of course, he had, Sean realized. Copper had been in touch. Which made him even more mad. He wanted to smack the bastard in the teeth.

'Insurance,' said Heaton. 'And if I'd told you from the off, you wouldn't have got involved, right?'

'You said it was stuff the quartermaster wouldn't miss,' Sean said.

'And he won't,' Heaton replied.

'What do you mean by *insurance?*'

'Come on, Sean, you're not stupid! You delivered the stuff. You can't turn me in without screwing yourself. See? Insurance.'

'You. Bastard,' replied Sean, the words barely audible through his clenched teeth. 'What have you got me involved in? No, don't answer that. Because I'm not involved. Not any more. I'm out. Here. Keep the lot.' He pulled the envelope from an inside pocket and chucked it at Heaton, then stood up.

'No you're not,' said Heaton. 'And you know it. Now sit down.'

Sean hesitated.

'Seriously. Just sit down.'

He sank back onto his stool.

'First, you need to calm down,' Heaton told him. 'Second, you need to listen.'

Sean leaned forward, folding his arms and resting them on the table. 'I'll take orders from you when I have to,' he said. 'But here? I don't have to, do I?'

Heaton took a long, slow gulp from his glass, his eyes on Sean. 'The stuff I've supplied, it's for protection,' he said. 'You've seen the news, right? Terrorists coming home to bring the war back here? People attacking and killing soldiers? Going after our lads with machetes?' He leaned closer. 'How long do you think some fundie nutcase with a machete is going to last against a trained soldier with a Glock?'

Sean shook his head in disbelief. 'You really are full of shit, aren't you . . .'

'I'm serious,' Heaton said. 'Next time you see Copper, speak to him. Ask him about the threats he's had from idiots talking about IS!'

'I don't have to listen to this.' Sean made to leave.

The corporal reached out and pulled him back down onto his stool. 'Gangs aren't fighting each other any more, Harker,' he said. 'They're protecting themselves from what's spilling out onto the streets here, just the same way as it has in Syria and Libya! There's a war coming. We need to be ready for it.'

Sean rolled his eyes. 'You really expect me to believe any of this? Islamic State are setting up shop over here?' He laughed, shook his head. 'You should hear the shit you're spouting.'

'And you need to wake up,' Heaton said. 'Next time you speak to Copper, ask him about some of the other tossers he's been dealing with. Morons patrolling the streets to enforce bullshit religious rules. Shops firebombed because they sold the wrong kind of meat. Girls with acid in the face for fancying the wrong bloke.'

Sean stared at him. 'Mate.' He took a deep breath.

'Mate. You're missing one thing.' He leaned closer. 'This isn't fucking Syria. It's fucking England!'

Slowly, deliberately, he pushed the envelope back towards Heaton. 'I have never grassed a mate and I'm never going to,' he said slowly. He looked Heaton in the eye and didn't blink. 'So, if you think your little operation is in the tiniest bit of danger from me, then you and me can step outside right now and sort it out. But, mate, I am walking. End of.'

He saw something change in Heaton's eyes as he stood up. Disappointment? Well, why should he care?

'I'll see you at work, *Corporal Heaton*,' he said sarcastically.

Heaton made a strange movement with his head – something between a shrug of acceptance and a shake. He held up the envelope. 'I'll hold onto your share!' he called as Sean walked out into the night.

Chapter 16

'Now, there's a pair who will soon be begging for mercy,' Toni Clark said with a grin as she passed through. Sean looked up and grunted, and went back to polishing the boot with renewed aggression.

He was with Shitey Bright and Chewie West, in the common area outside their rooms in barracks, cleaning kit. It was good aggression therapy.

It was Tuesday, three days after his formal resignation from Heaton's little operation. He had just about come down from his fury. Unfortunately it returned a little whenever he saw the corporal – which, as they were in the same platoon, was several times a day. Meanwhile Heaton just ignored him, like he used to, so you could say their relationship was back to what it used to be.

And Sean still had the five hundred from the first drop safely in the bank. Shit, sometimes you just had to know when a deal was done and walk away. He hadn't lied to Heaton – he had never grassed and he didn't intend to start now. His only problem now was finding another source of cash.

But still, being monumentally pissed off does not just go away, and being stuck in Heaton's company for most of the afternoon hadn't helped. He had been for a good long run when he got off duty, booted feet pounding the perimeter road until he was hot and sweaty and exhausted. Still in the same T-shirt and MTP trousers, he had hurled himself into the next essential task before he allowed himself the luxury of relaxation. And that was kit maintenance.

After that first day of agony, back in the gym at Burnleigh, Sean had gone back for more without a second's thought. But the bullshit of cleaning kit once he got to Catterick had almost been enough to make him walk. Wasn't he there to shoot guns at the nation's enemies? Did it matter what state his uniform was in? You what? But my boots *are* polished. Sorry? You want me to pick the *dirt* out of the *tread* with *tweezers* and . . . You're pissing me, right? . . . Oh, shit, you're serious . . .

But it had got into him, soaking in like polish into leather. You didn't do this because some twat of a Rupert just out of public school told you to – though that seemed to be a pretty good reason to some of the real twats. You did it out of respect for your regiment, for your colleagues, for yourself. If you couldn't keep your kit serviceable in camp, then once you were in the field you wouldn't able to function.

He went back to his boots. Two brushes – one to put polish on, one to take it off. For the polish itself, black Kiwi – accept no substitutes. For bulling the leather, a yellow duster that had been washed and tumbled a few times. For getting rid of the dirt first, an old toothbrush. He knew the ritual off by heart. Keep it all in a drawstring bag so you've always got it to hand. And to keep the polish off the floor, an old newspaper. The *Sun* could always be relied on to give you something decent to look at while you worked.

'So, after all that cleaning, how do you fancy getting a bit dirty?'

Sean looked up at her from under his eyebrows, ignoring the way West was doing pelvic thrusts under the table. He wasn't remotely taken in by the innuendo – not with the big grin on Clark's face. And he was pretty sure he hadn't totally misunderstood their relationship.

'How dirty?' he asked carefully.

'Dirty as in you and me getting under the bonnet of the Cosworth? It's still pinking between sixty and sixty-five and I can't shake it. I just got it back from the garage, but no joy. So I'd appreciate your input. And this time you actually get a ride. You look as though you could do with cheering up.'

Despite his determination to hang onto his foul temper, Sean couldn't help grinning. Shit, he had a good mate in Toni Clark. Maybe it was time to put Heaton down to experience and get on with the rest of his life.

'Shit, yeah!'

She grinned and ruffled his hair. She was the one member of the platoon who could get away with it.

'Cool. I've got some things to do first – meet at twenty hundred? I'll be at the gatehouse.' She gave him a wink as she left.

'Hey, Stenders!' West called across the table. 'You'll let us know how many *rides* you get in the Cosworth, right?' He and Bright bumped fists at the joke.

Sean rolled his eyes. 'Guys, a car is seriously uncomfortable unless you've totally got nowhere else to go. The seats are so narrow you're afraid of falling off, and it's so cramped, one of you's going to bang your head on the roof or a window whatever happens.'

He went back to his polishing, innocently not meeting their looks, fully aware that they were staring at him.

'Experience?' Bright asked eventually.

Sean let it hang for a couple more seconds, before modestly admitting, 'Experience.'

'Nice one, Stenders!' West shouted. 'And you owe me a fiver,' he added to Bright.

*

Sean left barracks at 19:55 with a spring in his step. It was a warm, sunny August evening. His good mood was only dented a little when he noticed Heaton coming down the pavement towards him. The corporal had his eyes glued to the screen of his phone.

'Harker,' he grunted as they passed.

'Corp,' Sean acknowledged, and Heaton walked on.

The gatehouse was ahead. He could see the red splash of the Cosworth parked outside, next to the SEVERE warning. Toni was leaning against it, chatting to a guard. She saw him coming and gave him a wave.

The barrier was up to let a small convoy of military vehicles through. At the front was a Foxhound, a truck only slightly less fuck-off-now than the Warrior, designed for Afghanistan – apparently by getting a Land Rover and a Humvee to screw and then rolling the baby in armour plating: Gaz would have sold his soul to get his hands on one. Behind it were a couple of troop carriers, the trusty 4x4 Leyland four-tonners. The canvas hoods in the rear were open, and each truck was loaded with getting on for twenty soldiers and all their kit. Probably coming back off exercise, knackered, dirty and starving, Sean thought, happy at that moment that he wasn't one of them. He broke into a jog to catch up with Clark.

Just in time to see the explosion that ripped through the guardhouse and enveloped the convoy in flames.

Chapter 17

Sean felt it like a hammer blow. He couldn't remember being knocked backwards – he just knew that his head was splitting, and there was grit embedded in his hands where they had broken his fall, and his mind was screaming that something terrible had just happened.

And then he staggered to his feet again, and broke into a run, all on autopilot, still only vaguely aware of what the fuck was happening; he just knew that something was, and he needed to be there. He stumbled towards the flames and the smoke and the wrecked vehicles and bodies. There was no sound. He wasn't sure if he was deaf or if his brain was just refusing to process the information, denying what he knew had just happened.

A bomb – in camp.

His hearing came back as his boots pounded on the pavement.

A haze hung in the air, and the chemical smell of

scorched metal came down on the breeze. The Foxhound had been knocked to one side, but its hull was designed to take blasts and it was relatively undamaged. The lads inside were already clambering out.

It was a different story for the four-tonners.

The first had been blown off its wheels and was on its side. Fire was spreading from the cabin and across the rest of the vehicle. The other had jumped off the road and smashed into the gatehouse. Black, oily smoke belched out of the truck and the building.

A Wolf was parked unattended in one of the spaces there, dented by the blast but still upright. Sean yanked the door open, grabbed the medical kit that was standard issue to all army vehicles, and ran to help however he could.

Soldiers were tumbling out of the back of the four-tonner that had hit the gatehouse. Some seemed fine, some were half stunned and shaky on their legs.

But Sean saw that there were bodies scattered around the Leyland that lay on its side, some moving, some not. The canvas hood was gone – shreds of charred material hung from the hoops.

For a moment he didn't know where to go, who to attend to. Everywhere he looked he saw someone injured, someone bleeding, someone dead.

Blood had been sprayed everywhere – across the road

and the remains of the gatehouse walls – like some kid had come along with a high-powered water pistol filled with red paint. The ground was covered in shattered wreckage, bits of vehicles . . . bits of humans. Some were stuck to torn pieces of cloth, the camouflage pattern just visible through the blood. Others were on fire, burning brightly as the fat melted in the heat. The air was thick with smells that reminded Sean of a barbecue – the sickly sweet tang of burned meat mixing with lighter fuel. Through the smoky, eye-stinging haze that hung over everything came the sounds of groans, cries.

Sean had dealt with injuries before. Like every soldier in the British Army, he was a competent field medic. Fully trained medics were assigned to platoons, but when you were out on a four-man patrol, more often than not it was just down to the training you'd received. And that meant being able to deal with anything and everything, usually in the middle of a firefight, right up to stabilizing a seriously wounded mate while securing an area to allow them to be medevacked.

In training they used real amputees to make it realistic – men who had done all the screaming and yelling for real. Fake blood and horror make-up ensured that it was as close to being there as the army could get. This was different. In every possible way.

'Harker!' Sean's head snapped up. Heaton was there

too, running past him, also with one of the kits. 'Help anyone you can. Stabilize them.'

'What about Clarky?' Sean yelled back. She had been waiting by the gate with the Cosworth. She could help out too. 'Where the—?'

Then he saw it. The Cosworth. Or what was left of it.

It was on the other side of the road, hidden behind one of the four-tonners. The entire front section had been blasted to nothing. The rest of it was an inferno. It was the source of most of the smoke and flames.

Sean started to run towards it, but another yell from Heaton pulled him up sharp.

'The wounded, Harker! Clark doesn't matter! Stabilize!'

Clark didn't matter? What the fuck was that about? Sean thought. Yeah, she and Heaton didn't get on, but she'd just been blown to pieces!

But he also knew what Heaton meant. You concentrated on need, not on who your mates were. A complete stranger dying at your feet took priority over your mucker who was dying somewhere over there.

Sean forced himself to turn away from the wreckage of the Cosworth and dropped down beside the soldier nearest to him. The guy had been thrown clear of one of the four-tonners and was just coming round.

'OK, mate,' Sean said, quickly, efficiently, calmly. 'I need to check you over, OK? Just lie as still as you can.'

The soldier moaned, sliding in and out of consciousness. Sean checked him over for broken bones and puncture wounds by sight and by feel.

'The medics are on their way,' he said, more in hope than conviction. He had found nothing broken, but there was a deep laceration in the soldier's leg. He quickly applied a high-pressure dressing – a wad of sterile, absorbent padding, held in place by a couple of strips of bandage, tied into position with a swiftly efficient knot.

'You need to apply pressure,' he said, guiding the guy's hands to the wound. 'Hold this. You're fine, OK? Just stay with it.' If the soldier had a job to do, there was more chance he would stay alert.

'I've done the fucking training too,' the lad muttered, but he did as he was told.

Other soldiers were arriving, running towards the scene as fast as they could. Sean moved on to the next casualty, a woman who was sitting, dazed, among shards of broken glass and shattered metal. She was staring into the distance, rocking back and forth. She didn't seem to notice the compound fracture in her arm. Bone jutted out above her elbow and blood pulsed out onto her combat shirt.

'Hey, hey . . .' Sean got her attention by clicking his fingers in front of her eyes, bringing her back to the here and now. He had nothing to splint the break with, but he wrapped it tight in another bandage. Then he guided her good hand over to hold her damaged arm.

'Just hold it straight. Steady. Right?' He cocked his head. He could hear sirens, still distant. 'They'll be with you in a minute, OK?'

He moved on again. 'Oh – fuck – me . . .' he whispered.

The next casualty was Clark.

His friend was alive, just. Sean only knew this when he saw something bubbling between her lips. She was one charred mess, from her face down to her knees. It was hard to tell where her skin ended and her clothing began. After the knees, there wasn't anything. Her legs ended in ragged stumps that were slowly weeping fluid.

For a moment it sounded like Clark was weeping herself. She wasn't. There was a long-drawn-out, high-pitched sound which Sean realized was her breathing.

Where to start? He was trained for bullet wounds and fractures. Not this.

Keep them warm. That was it. Part of it. A burns victim would go into shock; core body temperature would drop dramatically.

Sean pulled off his shirt and draped it over her. 'Clarky. Mate.' His voice shook. 'Let's have a look at you . . .'

He gazed helplessly at the remains of Clark's legs. She

could haemorrhage if they were left like that. He fumbled in the bag. 'Gonna need a couple of tourniquets here . . .'

A hand touched his shoulder, gentle but firm. 'We'll take it from here, soldier.'

And then two paramedics were there, crouched over Clark's still form, not even looking at Sean. They tossed his shirt over to one side. Sean slowly picked it up, shrugged it back on, and tore his eyes away from Clark to look around.

Several ambulances had turned up, civvy and military. The paramedic crews were at work among the dead and dying soldiers. A fire engine had arrived and its crew were spraying foam on the wrecked vehicles. It looked like a war zone.

Sean spent the next half-hour helping load casualties into the ambulances that kept on arriving. Adrenaline had him wired. He couldn't stop moving. If he stopped, then his body started shaking. It needed to be occupied.

That was until he bent down to pick up another stretcher, and realized it was Clark, and she had a sheet over her face – which meant only one thing. And then his body froze. His knees shook and his eyes filled with tears and he *couldn't move*.

'Take a rest, soldier.' The voice in his ear was gentle but firm. He blinked and focused on a Rupert, but a medical Rupert. The guy put out both hands to turn him gently away and propel him in the direction of the barracks. 'That's an order.'

Sean nodded dumbly and stumbled away while they loaded his friend into the meat wagon.

Later he sat down away from the destruction, hugging his knees, his back against the high fence that surrounded the barracks, utterly exhausted. His clothes were covered in blood. His nostrils were thick with the reek of what had happened. The smell seemed to have crept down his nose and into his skull. He wondered if he would ever get rid of it.

Slowly, deliberately, Sean clenched his right hand into a fist and pushed it into the ground, twisting as it went, keeping it going even when the pain set in. The healed skin split open and his body asked him what the fuck he thought he was doing to it. It *hurt*.

Good. He wanted it to hurt. He wanted to keep his mind fresh. Back in his old life he had seen lads just seize up like rabbits when it all got too much, when shit started going wrong, and next thing the cops had them. He wasn't going to do that. He had a vague sense that something had just changed, big time, in his life. Fine. He would rise to meet it.

And so he made himself study the scene in front of

him, committing it to memory. His first time on the receiving end of enemy action.

The bombed area had been taped off. Figures in pristine white suits moved amongst the wreckage, like aliens from another world. The scene was smeared with blood and oil and foam. The bodies were all gone, but nothing else could be touched. It was a job for the civilian police now.

The bastards. *The bastards!* So this was what it felt like to have a war on your own turf, in your own country. *The bastards!*

Sean kept a lid on his anger, holding it down with both hands. He was used to being mightily pissed off, but this was different to anything that had ever happened to him. This wasn't like someone treading on the Guyz' turf. It wasn't like that Pricky screwing over his mum, or him getting nicked. This went deep and personal. Friends had been killed. It was a new type of anger and he needed to come to terms with it. If he let it all out in one blast, then it would consume him.

Heaton wandered over, dropped down next to him. 'You OK?'

'Oh, yeah. I'm absolutely fine and fucking dandy, mate. Thanks for asking.'

They sat silently. Heaton pulled out a pack of cigarettes

and offered one to Sean. Sean declined with an angry shake of the head, so he lit up on his own.

Sean broke the silence at last. He felt his voice shake. 'Who would put a bomb in a soldier's car?'

'It's a long list,' Heaton said. 'They keep sending us to places we're not meant to be . . . Guess what? We make enemies.'

Sean shook his head. 'I didn't sign up for this,' he said. 'This isn't right.'

'Oh Christ, here we go,' Heaton breathed. *'I didn't sign up for this. Poor Sean.'* Sean stared hatred at him. Heaton stared back, his lip curled. 'So what *did* you sign up for, Harker? Being served cups of tea by grateful old ladies? Playing with guns as a dick substitute? Or was it just your get-out-of-jail-free card?' He prodded Sean in the chest with a finger, while Sean mentally weighed up the pros and cons of decking an NCO. 'You sign up, you're prepared to *fight*. You put that uniform on, you turn up for duty, it sends a statement: *I am ready to go to war.'*

He got up again. 'I'm gonna catch a shower. See you around, Harker.'

The anger was still there when Heaton had gone. For a long time Sean simply sat there and let it swirl around inside his head. He didn't trust himself to move until he had dealt with it. Because, right now, for the first time in his life, Sean felt like killing someone.

Chapter 18

The briefing room had been quiet. Even after nearly a week, no one was in the mood for chat or joshing. The platoon silently came to attention as Franklin and a uniformed woman Sean hadn't seen before entered. Adams followed behind and shut the door, then took up position there.

The woman was an attractive blonde, probably in her thirties. The three pips on her front said she was a captain, and Sean took a moment to run the tactical recognition flash on her arm through his memory. A square with its two halves divided into dark blue and yellow. That was . . . Arse, he knew this. Dark blue and yellow was . . .

'At ease. Sit down,' Franklin instructed curtly. The platoon plonked their arses on the faded brown plastic chairs, which reminded Sean of the thing he'd sat on in the custody van on his way to prison, except perhaps even more uncomfortable. One of the most technologically advanced armies in the world could never quite find the time to bring its buildings into the twenty-first century.

Dark blue and yellow was . . .

'This is Captain Fitzallen of the Royal Logistics Corps.'

Logistics Corps. Yeah, I totally knew that.

'Captain Fitzallen specializes in explosive ordnance disposal. Captain.'

'Thank you, Lieutenant.' An attractive woman and a bomb expert – she had the undivided attention of every man in the room.

A laptop and computer projector had been set up at the front of the room, looking almost futuristic compared to the massive cork boards covered with A4-sized notices that lined the walls. She touched a key and the laptop whirred into life, displaying the gold badge of the Corps.

'First, the forensics report, which will be made public this afternoon. As her mates, you deserve to know first: we can confirm that the bomb which killed Private Clark and four other soldiers was a fertilizer-based explosive planted under the driver's seat of her car.'

The picture changed to the charred wreck of the Cosworth. It was an image that would be burned into Sean's mind for ever. He glared his hate at it, wishing that somehow, telepathically, it would link to the bastard who had planted the bomb and do something useful like fry their brains.

'The sad fact is that this bomb could probably have been detected if Private Clark had thought to look for it. And with that in mind, it's been decided that all units are to receive a refresher course in bomb awareness. So, here goes . . .'

She took the platoon through the details with brisk efficiency, illustrating it with images of actual bomb parts as she went.

'Any bomb needs a detonator, and explosives . . .'

Sean sat back and rested the side of his head on his fist as she talked. Some of it he could already have told her, some was new.

'. . . The Omagh bombing of 1998 used about two hundred kilograms of explosive and killed thirty people. Deaths were mostly caused by the supersonic shockwave of the blast, and the distribution of shrapnel. But think about two hundred kilos of explosive . . . That's two hundred bags of sugar. The Omagh bomb was planted in a stolen car, but for a bomb to be planted in *your* car – well, you'd notice something that big, wouldn't you? So it's much more likely to be a few kilograms – but still something that should be visible if you take the time to look. Now, what haven't I mentioned?'

There was a pause until someone put a hand up.

'The trigger.'

'Exactly. What sets the bomb off in the first place? A pressure device hidden in your car; a timer device; a radio-controlled detonator.' More images were shown on the projector. 'The bottom line is, *someone got into your vehicle*. There will be signs, if you only take the time to notice. Which brings us on to security – how to leave your car to reduce the chances of someone breaking in, and how to check it before you get in. These habits should be routine for as long as the threat level is SEVERE, as it currently is . . .'

The talk went on. Sean mostly paid little attention. He didn't have a car, after all. He could spend the time wondering how Clark's bomb had been planted in the first place, and how it had been set off. Was it coincidence or deliberate that it had been outside the gatehouse as a convoy was coming through? If it was deliberate, then that would have been difficult to fine-tune with a timer, so had it been a remote detonation?

But someone would have thought of this. The security people would have gone through the CCTV images with a fine-tooth comb, looking for anyone hanging around with line of sight of the gatehouse. There was no talk of any leads so it couldn't have been anyone obvious.

Clark's death had brought home something Sean had always known but never really appreciated. Terrorists wouldn't be out of the ordinary. They would look so normal that they were basically invisible. They could be the person right next to you.

Shit.

The talk was over. The platoon came to attention again and Fitzallen left the room.

Franklin stood at the front and surveyed them. 'Corporal Heaton's section – you all have extra duties to perform. You're dismissed to go and get ready. I'll see you this afternoon. Do her proud, lads.'

And so it was that four hours later, Sean was in his No. 2 Service Dress, the smartest gear he owned – khaki tunic and trousers, with creases ironed to razor sharpness; shirt and tie, precisely knotted; white belt, with buckle badge gleaming – stony-faced, solemnly helping bear Clark's coffin into St Michael's Garrison Church. They formed pairs in order of height to carry the coffin: Marshall and Penfold, Mitra and West, Bright and Sean, with Heaton walking behind. The coffin was covered with the Union Jack, with a wreath and Clark's beret resting on top.

TV news crews milled about outside, on the far side of the road, anxious to catch the first of the Tidworth bomb's five funerals. Inside, the church was full of similar uniforms, the only exception being Clark's family, just as smartly turned out in dark civvy suits and dresses: a mature West Indian couple, dignified in their grief, and a gaggle of brothers and sisters, some with kids of their own.

From a soldier's point of view it was all too formal for tears – though Sean could feel them pricking at the backs of his eyes – and the extra responsibility of being a coffin bearer meant that he stayed dry-eyed. It was the first funeral he had been to – he hadn't been allowed to go to Gaz's – and he would have been determined to do it properly even without the added duty. He and the lads were synchronized to the nearest millimetre, to the nearest split second. It was their final tribute to a fallen comrade, giving her the respect she deserved.

The service passed in a blur. The company major delivered a tribute to Clark, which sounded good to anyone who didn't realize that he had barely known her. The padre made a better job of it, in Sean's opinion. He pointed out that St Michael's Church was named for the warrior archangel, the leader of the armies of heaven that would defeat the forces of evil. Still all bollocks, as far as Sean could tell, but he liked the idea. If you had to die, then you might as well be on St Michael's side when you did it. Fighting evil, whatever form it took.

The pallbearers sat in the choir stalls, sideways on to everyone else, ready to take the coffin out again. It gave Sean a good view of Clark's family, nodding quietly during the eulogies, singing the hymns with gusto. Sometimes the mother dabbed her eyes with a hanky; apart from that, her restraint and the way she held herself somehow communicated a far deeper loss than if she had been howling or wailing.

We let you down, Sean thought, looking at Mrs Clark. She chose that precise moment to glance up, and their eyes met. He quickly looked away again, but then stole another sideways glance. Her face was kind, and Sean thought he saw her give him a brief nod before turning her attention back to the padre.

And what the fuck had that meant? *Yes, I know*? Or, *I forgive you*? Or, *Wasn't your fault*?

Sean knew what he would be saying in her place, and it wasn't any of those. If he was a civvy who had just lost a loved one, he would want to scream: *If you lot can't protect yourselves, how can you protect us?*

And then they were outside again, ranks of soldiers standing at attention while the coffin was loaded into a hearse. They saluted as the hearse moved off and a small fleet of black limos carried the Clark family after it for the private cremation.

'Fall out!'

And the funeral was over.

'Well, fuck me,' said a familiar voice. 'I could very easily never have to do that again.'

199

Milling around outside the church with the other soldiers, Sean found he was standing next to Heaton. The events of the last few days had drained him of emotion and he just felt tired. They had also made him re-evaluate the reason why they had fallen out. The thoughts he had been having in the church hadn't helped.

Heaton offered him an open cigarette packet, then began to pull it away. 'No – you don't, do you . . . ?'

'Cheers,' Sean said, and took one before they were gone.

Heaton's eyebrows went up. 'Filthy habit, Harker.' He flicked the lighter on and held it out. 'Could get you killed.'

'Ha. Funny.' Sean drew in a breath. No, it wasn't really his thing, but he wanted an excuse to keep talking. 'Mind if I have a word?'

The eyebrows went up again, but Heaton nodded his head slightly down the road. They started to walk.

'Clark should have checked her car more,' Sean began. 'I know that. Doesn't mean that what happened was her fault.'

'Never said it was, mate.'

'We're the best fucking army in the world. Maybe not the biggest, but the best. And we couldn't stop one of our own mates being blown up. So how the fuck are we supposed to protect anyone else?'

He waved a hand in the general direction of the perimeter fence. 'They're defenceless, out there. We've got all the guns in here, but . . . the army can't be everywhere. It isn't allowed to be. And we've got Rules of Engagement. So in all those places where we can't be, people have to be able to look out for themselves. Stands to reason.'

Heaton looked at him strangely. 'That is the weirdest echo I ever heard. Could have sworn I said all that back in the pub. The time you – uh, let's say – resigned.'

'Yeah. Well. About that . . .'

Heaton looked up at him coolly, one eyebrow raised.

OK, you bastard, Sean thought. *You're going to make me say it, aren't you?* He swallowed. 'That thing you've got going . . .'

'Yeah?'

Oh, crap, this is going to be such a bad idea but I don't know what else to do . . . 'Tell me how it works.'

Chapter 19

Sean sat opposite Heaton at the small kitchen table in the corporal's flat. Between them was a teapot, two half-full mugs, an opened packet of ginger nut biscuits, an envelope full of money, and the main focus of their discussion: two Glocks.

Heaton grabbed his mug and took a gulp. 'So, pop quiz, hot shot. Which one's real?'

Sean stared at the pistols. 'They're identical.'

'Without doing the NSPs, pick them up,' Heaton suggested.

He did exactly that. The weight was the same, the serial numbers were there. Even the number written by the quartermaster on the hand grip. They were identical. 'I don't understand. They're both real, right?'

Heaton placed his mug on the table, picked up the weapon on Sean's right. He pulled back the slide so that Sean could see the spring mechanism inside. It was never going to fire real bullets.

'As long as no one cocks it, no one will ever know. It's really too easy. All I do is get the fake, knock it around to give it that worn-in look, sort out the serial number and the number from the quartermaster's records. And no' – he cut off Sean's question – 'the quartermaster isn't in on this. Anyone can look up the records. Then I replace the Airsoft magazine with the real thing – they're dead easy to get hold of – and there you go.'

Sean sat back and remembered the briefing on how the arms kote – the secure armoury where the weapons were stored – worked. It was next to the guardroom, which was permanently manned by armed soldiers. It had a permanent storeman, a veteran sergeant who had lost a leg in Afghanistan and was medically unfit for ops. Not a man who would easily be fooled. He was responsible for ensuring that all the weapons were present and secured by chains. Each one was individually checked out and signed for, and then checked back against the arms book, which listed every number. The book was seen daily by the duty officer, who would also count the weapons, and the RQMS – the Regimental Quartermaster Sergeant – checked the armoury at irregular intervals too. Any missing weapon would soon be found.

'So . . .' he said, thinking this through. Heaton gave him an encouraging nod to go on. It was all falling into place. 'You get the number of the real gun . . . but then you've got to get the number onto the fake . . . They're not just written on. They're engraved. So . . . you get the number one day, out on the ranges, and then the *next* time you're on the ranges, you've got the fake all prepared. The real gun comes out to the ranges, the fake goes back . . .'

'Give the boy a GCSE,' Heaton said admiringly. 'You got it.'

'How do you know who's got the gun you want to swap?'

'I'm the corporal, remember? I've got every reason to check the records. I just look up which private has the weapon I'm after. Then, at the end of the day, when all firing is done, I make an excuse – a snap inspection – to check his weapon. And I make the switch.'

'Bloody hell.' Despite everything he had been feeling about supplying stolen weapons to people like Copper, Sean felt a grudging glow of admiration. Heaton was to guns what Sean had been to cars. It was a whole new area of lawbreaking, and any kind of expert had to be respected. 'That's brilliant.' Then he shook his head to clear it and let reality back in. 'But someone's gonna want to fire the fake at some point in the future . . .'

Heaton grinned. 'There's more guns than there are soldiers. The storemaster rotates the collection and I know the pattern. I always take a weapon that's about to be rotated out of use. After a couple of months, sure, gun number 12345 is going to come back into circulation, the fake will be discovered and this little earner is going to come to an end. But until then' – he tapped the envelope – 'money, money, money. So far I've lifted four Glocks and I'll get a few more in. Plus there's plans for other stuff.'

'It'll do more than end. It'll be a fucking hurricane-force shitstorm.'

'And not one speck of it will hit yours truly.' Heaton flashed Sean a complacent smile. 'Or you.' The smile seemed to slip off his face and just hang there like it had snagged on something. It was technically a smile but there wasn't an ounce of humour in it. 'I've got a long memory, and let's just say I have my fall guys lined up to take the rap.'

The smile reminded Sean just a bit too much of Copper. It reminded him that however much he might admire the heist, he wasn't in this for fun. This was to protect people. Heaton had lied too many times for Sean to think of him as a friend now.

But everything he was saying had the ring of truth about it. All the lies had been things Sean wanted to hear. He didn't particularly want to hear this.

Even so, he had to ask: 'Suppose you need to supply, uh, a bulk order?'

He got another of those complacent smiles. 'Baby steps, Harker, baby steps. I'll let you in further when I'm confident you're not going to wuss out on me again. Let's just agree that I have other little side operations going on, and leave it at that.'

Sean flushed – he had not wussed out, he had been fucking livid about being played and used – but he had other priorities now. He sat back, thrust his hands into his pockets, gazed at the two pistols that were lying side by side in front of him. The blaze of admiration for a stroke of sheer lawbreaking genius was being pissed on by the one fact that he was truly unhappy about.

'We're still getting firepower into the hands of civilians. People like Copper.'

Heaton sighed. 'People like Copper have come to the same conclusion as people like you and me. There is a problem. This is the solution. This stuff isn't for robbing banks or doing houses over or scaring people. It's for use against the enemy. And face it, you know the enemy when you see them.'

Sean thought again, for the thousandth time, of Clark's bomber. Oh yes, he knew the enemy.

He sighed and bit his lip. And looked up at Heaton from under his brows. 'OK. OK, you got me. I'm in.'

Heaton grinned. 'I knew you'd see it made sense. You're not stupid. OK. First things first.' He opened the

envelope and peeled off twenty-five £20 notes. Sean
didn't reach out to take them. Heaton folded the notes,
reached over and tucked them into Sean's breast pocket.
Then he leaned back in his chair and rested his hands
behind his head.

'And you're just in time to help me with the next job.
This is something else – bigger than the armoury scam.
I can put a Glock in my coat, but these . . . not so much.'

'What?' Sean asked. 'What's the something else?'

Heaton got up, walked over to a cupboard and pulled
out a long box with an Airsoft logo at one end which he
laid on the table. Sean saw the picture on the top and felt
his heart stop. He didn't need Heaton to open it up, but
he did anyway.

'SA8os,' Heaton said. He lifted the weapon out and
laid it on the table with the Glocks. 'You were asking
about bulk orders. This is the fake. We need the real deal.
Times six.'

Chapter 20

Rain.

Well, what had he expected? Sean pulled the collar of his army-issue Gore-Tex jacket a little tighter around his neck, under the rim of his helmet.

He lay on his front next to Heaton in the OP, the observation point the two of them had established beneath a gorse bush in the middle of Salisbury Plain, while Heaton scanned the area ahead and below with the night-vision binos.

'Here,' said Heaton, breaking into Sean's thoughts. He passed the binos over. 'Have a goose at that.'

The bush clung to the top of a rise looking down into a long shallow valley. Sean took the binoculars and jammed them hard against his eye sockets to stop the rain running into them.

They had left the Matiz – the Impreza would have been far too memorable for other drivers – parked off the road between Tilshead and Chitterne. Then they had yomped the rest of the way on foot, which meant they were now about as far from the civilian world as it is possible to be in the south of England. That was where the army liked to hold its exercises.

If it had been a CQR, a Close Quarter Recce, they'd have dug out a hole deep enough to hide them and their kit completely. But Heaton didn't want to leave any trace of where they were hiding or where the weapons would eventually be stashed, and the scattering of soil might attract attention. So, instead of digging, they had spent a couple of hours before the Army Reserve arrived carefully carving out a hollow in the centre of the gorse bush, and camouflaging it. The stuff was a bitch to work with, carving out a thousand little pricks and cuts in your hands and wrists, but when they were done, the only way you would know anyone was hiding there was if you were the person doing the hiding, or happened to stand on them by accident.

But it wasn't waterproof. They didn't even have a basha – a piece of waterproof material stretched above them by clever use of bungees, paracord and a few well-placed sticks. It could still be seen, and it was one more thing to risk leaving behind. So tonight they had to accept that Gore-Tex clothing on top of the normal kit was the only protection.

Sean was already freezing and it was only ten p.m.

They would be here for a good few hours more. He was already fantasizing about long hot showers – never mind what the rest of the platoon was getting up to that night. They were just getting back on track after Clark's death, and many of the lads had been planning a night on the town to over-compensate. Sean knew where he would rather be.

'What do you see?' Heaton asked.

'Rain,' said Sean. 'No . . . wait a minute . . . over there on the right . . . Yep, more rain. Fuck me, mate – I think it's raining.'

'Don't be a dick.'

Sean kept staring through the binoculars. The thing they were looking at was a fair distance away, about a kilometre, but there was enough movement to make it visible even through the rain. Despite the relentless downpour, moonlight was streaming across the land. Somehow the moon had positioned itself in the one clear area of sky. It gave the evening an odd feel. The rain came down in stair rods, almost glowing under the lunar gaze. And beneath it all, small figures were moving.

'They're in for a properly shit weekend,' Sean said. He watched the Reservists busying themselves with trench-digging, and even though these were the guys they were going to rip off, he let himself feel a little sorry for them.

Heaton had deliberately targeted an Army Reserve

exercise for newbies. 'No live ammo, so they'll never get to shoot their guns, and they'll all be knackered,' he had said, back in his kitchen two weeks earlier. 'And they'll be new to all this. No ex-professionals among them, other than a few of the NCOs and officers. Once they're dug in, we'll move out. The trenches won't be more than deep scrapes. They'll be working in pairs. One will be grabbing kip and the other will technically be on watch, but even he'll be half out of it. All we have to do is crawl up to some of the ones on the outside, bag our SA80s, then disappear.'

Sean, like any soldier, had respect for the Army Reserve. Sure, he knew the jokes – *I've been in the Reservists for ten years, so in real life I just passed basic* – but they were good-natured. The Reservists made up a huge proportion of the armed forces. Even the SAS had two Army Reserve regiments, 21 and 23 SAS. And those who joined from civvy street worked their arses off to match the standards expected, and often exceeded them.

But that came later, as the Reservists settled into their role. The newbies down the hill might still think Army Reserve life was all weekend soldiering and a bit of pocket money. In a way, Sean reckoned he was doing them a favour. They were going to learn the hard way that someone could infiltrate them. It could get them killed, one day. They wouldn't make the same mistake again.

So for the next couple of hours Sean and Heaton took turns on the binoculars while the other tried to rest as best he could. They were cammed up like Arnie in *Commando*, in the same kit as the Reservists, so even if they got pinged, they could try and play like they were on the exercise too.

Finally, with midnight slipping past and the rain easing, Heaton made his decision. 'OK, let's get us some guns.'

As he'd been keen to point out to Sean, he had 'invested' in half a dozen Airsoft SA80s, and they were with them now in the OP. They'd cost him just a shade over two hundred quid each. Usually they would be more than that, but these ones had . . . well, not exactly fallen off the back of a lorry – just not got all the way from the supplier to the shop that had ordered them. And these were the ones they would swap for the real weapons. When the job was discovered, Sunday evening or Monday morning, all eyes would be focused on the stores that had supplied the weapons for the exercise.

It was, Sean had to admit, just a little bit genius, but he wasn't going to say so to Heaton.

Heaton gave his orders, directing unnecessarily with his hands. 'You go left' – gesture – 'I'll go right' – gesture – 'then, when you've swapped your three out, we meet back here' – gesture.

'So hang on . . .' Sean said. 'I go left?' He pointed right.

Heaton scowled. 'Just go in the opposite direction to the hand you wank with.'

'Aw, now I'm really confused.'

'Oh, piss off.'

Heaton took three of the rifles and slipped out of the back of the OP, snaking through the gorse and bracken. Sean followed directly behind him with the rest. At the edge, they gave each other a final look. Heaton made a wanking gesture with finger and thumb, and slid off to the right. From that point on, Sean focused on his own movements. Heaton was of no interest.

Move fast, stay low, Sean told himself silently. He got behind a low rise, then was up on his feet and running at a crouch. The *thump-thump, thump-thump* of his feet sounded loud enough to wake the dead. But when the rise came to an end, and he slipped back down onto his front, he was still safe. No one was alerted to his presence. Yet.

Now he was within a couple of hundred metres of his targets, each scrape about fifty metres apart, and he could barely see them. The clouds had finally caught up with the moon. They were full and thick, and only the dimmest glow came through – just enough to enable Sean to navigate through the darkness.

He edged forward, leopard crawl, the three Airsoft SA80s clamped to his chest. Cold, wet grass brushed against his face, and the smell of damp vegetation was strong in his nostrils. The first trench came up fast and Sean paused. The sentry, the waking half of the pair, was sitting at the far end, hunched up, looking the other way and clearly not enjoying life. From his low position, Sean couldn't see into the trench – couldn't see what the other guy was doing. But he could hear gentle snores coming from ahead. He aimed his body in that direction and began to crawl again—

Then a flare went off: a *hiss-s-s* as it fired into the sky, and a sharp *crack* as it exploded, flooding the small valley with white light as bright as day.

Chapter 21

'*Shitshitshitshitshit!*'

Sean flattened himself belly down under the glaring light, for all the good it would do. He might as well just walk up to them and pretend to be invisible.

The trenches were in chaos. Shouting. Lots of it. Action. Figures moving. What the fuck was going on?

More shouting. The trenches were emptying. Not in an orderly fashion either. The Reservists were up and out of them like rabbits from a warren.

An order disguised as a yell rolled across to him: 'Get back in your trenches now! Move! *Get in there!*'

This was quickly followed by a shout of, 'Who the *crap* let off that bastard flare?'

Whoever it was, Sean guessed, wasn't going to own up. Because whoever it was knew he would be getting a royal kick up the arse.

And then came a shout which Sean thought at first must be directed at him: 'You! Soldier!'

He gritted his teeth and looked up. Time to bluff his arse off.

'What the *fuck* are you doing without your rifle?'

So, obviously not at him. He blinked into the light and studied the panicking Reservists more closely. Sure enough, he could count one, two . . . considerably more than six without their weapons. Their guns must still be in their trenches, alone and abandoned.

This was his chance.

He leaped up, and forward. The flare was dying and would soon hit the deck. There was still monumental confusion all around, and the trenches were empty.

He was in and out of the first in a heartbeat, one SA80 swapped. He scooted across to another trench, ducked in, bagged what he was after; same again at the third trench. And then he was out of there and into the dark before he'd even had a chance to think about what he'd just done. Several of the guys running around like headless chickens must have seen him, but he was dragged up like they were and no one saw anything unusual. The flare faded into nothing and he legged it without looking back, crouched all the way, until he got to the OP.

He dropped to the ground and spilled the weapons onto the dirt. Then he realized one flaw in the plan, which was that the entrance into the bush was too well hidden. He couldn't find it in the dark. OK, so he could wait for Heaton and they could do it together.

He stayed still, listening for any sign of someone coming after him. But there was only one noise – the sound of someone else breathing nearby. It turned into a low chuckle.

'The flare worked a treat, didn't it?'

Sean swung round in the dark. 'You are shitting me!' he gasped between breaths. 'That was you? Why the fuck didn't you warn me? I was out in the open! I could have been spotted!'

'I was thinking on my feet,' Heaton said. He emerged from the shadow, a dark shape splitting from a dark shape, and squatted next to Sean. 'One of the Reservists must have dropped a flare. I found it. *Boom!* And look what it got us.'

They both looked down at what was lying between them. Six SA80s. And somewhere out in the dark, six unsuspecting Reservists were at some point this weekend about to experience a whole world of confusion.

'Have we really just done that?' Sean felt himself start to grin. He was still mighty pissed off with Heaton – but hey, he might have done the same thing if the opportunity had come up. And between them they had pulled off one cool heist.

'Yeah,' said Heaton. 'A rush or what?' He didn't give

Sean a chance to reply. 'We move now,' he said. 'Get these covered and let's get out.'

That had been the final stroke of genius in the plan. The corporal didn't want half a dozen semi-automatic rifles knocking around in the back of his car or stuffed away in a cupboard back at his flat. So they would stash them there on the Plain. It was the last place anyone would look, because no one in their right mind would leave stolen weapons in the place they actually stole them.

Sean didn't need telling twice.

A sunny Sunday afternoon, the wet Saturday night well and truly gone, and Sean was back in the Monty. They had got back to Tidworth in the small hours and he had crashed in Heaton's spare room, then back to barracks for a good long hot shower. His muckers naturally assumed he'd pulled the previous night, and he saw no reason to deny it.

Heaton came in, a huge grin on his face, and headed straight over without a detour to the bar.

'Well?' Sean asked.

'We did it!' Heaton said, a grin creasing his mouth. 'We only did it! Christ, mate, this is the stuff of legend!' He slid an envelope across the table. 'Your cut of the fee. The goods have already been collected.'

Sean looked at him sharply. They were meant to be going back the next weekend, once any fuss about the guns had died down, to retrieve them. 'Whoa! But I thought—'

'Buyer agreed to collect. I just gave the coordinates. All sorted.'

Sean glanced inside the envelope. It was stuffed with notes and his heart beat a little faster.

'That's two grand, mate,' Heaton said. 'Not bad for a night's work.'

'Uh-huh . . .'

OK, so he wasn't doing this for the money. That was what he told himself. He was doing this to get weapons into the hands of people who could fight back where the army couldn't. But – like the drop he'd made in the farmyard – he couldn't deny there was a rush that came with it, and handling money only made it better. Old habits were too ingrained to die.

But if this was going to go on, something had to change.

'Jeez, don't sound too happy about it or people will stare,' Heaton said.

Sean looked him in the eye. 'Mate, you've got to start playing straight with me.'

Heaton put on a puzzled frown. 'Meaning?'

'Meaning, you didn't say anything about the buyer

collecting. Meaning, you didn't tell me about Copper. Meaning, you didn't let on what I was supplying. Meaning, you keep telling me one thing and then I find it's something else, and it's pissing me off and it makes it hard to fucking trust you.'

They stared hard at each other, unblinking.

Heaton was the first to look away. 'OK. Maybe . . . maybe I'm just too used to being a one-man show. Maybe I could learn to let you in a bit more. Shit, mate, I don't want you not to trust me. So I'm sorry, OK?'

Sean grumpily allowed himself a smile. 'Had to be said, mate.'

'Course it did. And we've been invited to a party. The buyer wants to show his gratitude.'

Sean's rising spirits came crashing very quickly back down. He shook his head firmly. 'Nuh-uh. If it's all the same to you, I'll give it a miss. You don't mix business and pleasure.'

Heaton frowned. 'Doesn't matter if it's all the same to me. It's not all the same to him, and I've already accepted on your behalf. They want to meet us, discuss possible further business.'

'There isn't going to be any further business,' Sean snapped. 'Not for bloody ages anyway. We can't just go out shopping at the quartermaster stores twenty-four/seven, can we? You said yourself – it's time limited. And we're not going to bag another handful of SA8os any time soon. You can only be lucky for so long . . .'

Heaton just looked impassive and twirled a finger, waiting for Sean to get to the end of his spiel.

Sean sighed. 'When is it?'

'We can be there in an hour,' Heaton said. 'Drink up.'

Chapter 22

'OK,' Sean said as the Impreza rolled up a gravel drive, small stones popping and crunching beneath the tyres, and the house loomed at the end. 'He's rich.'

The place was all old wood and red brick, with a stunningly landscaped garden behind it. There were discreet cameras at the corners – not big enough to spoil the looks, but enough to be noticed.

All Sean knew was that they were somewhere near Guildford, which automatically meant money. The house, the grounds and the collection of cars parked outside – Jags, BMWs, wanky sports cars – meant lots of it.

Heaton hadn't gone into any detail about their mysterious host, despite repeated questions as they made their way up the M3 and round the M25. Now, for some reason, he laughed. 'Yeah. He's Rich.'

'Why's that funny?'

'Because he's *Rich*, you prick. That's his name.'

'Oh, for fuck's sake.'

'He's . . .' Heaton drummed his fingers on the wheel as he found a spot between the swishmobiles. The Impreza could hold its own there. The Matiz would have crept away behind the nearest tree and quietly shot itself. 'He's one of those guys who knows people. Lots of people. And he's best mates with every one of them. He wants something, he can grease it so it happens. You learn not to say no.'

'So we're going to be best mates too?'

'Shit, no.' Another laugh, this time more of a bark. 'We're the workforce. But fuck that. He treats us decent and, above all, he's the customer. Got that?'

'Got it.'

They climbed out and Sean gave the house another appraising look. He didn't know what Heaton made from their deals, but even at two grand a pop it would take a lot of illicit hauls on Salisbury Plain to pay for this place. It was way out of his league. 'I'm gonna guess the, uh, merchandise isn't here.'

'Only illegal thing here is your haircut, mate. C'mon.'

Heaton led him up brick steps to the front door. It opened at his third knock to reveal what Sean could really only describe as a hard bastard.

The man wasn't particularly tall – probably around five foot nine, so Sean had a couple of inches on him. He wasn't particularly heavily built, either, not like some nightclub bruiser pumped full of steroids. He wore a nice suit that was probably tailored.

But the eyes that flitted across Sean's face were dead. Not a flicker of curiosity, or any kind of emotion. This guy, Sean knew with a certainty based on two seconds' acquaintance, would squish him without thought or care if he had to.

'Josh Heaton and Sean Harker,' said Heaton, 'as ordered.'

The man stepped back to let them enter, then closed the door behind them. 'This way,' he said, in a strangely soft voice – which made it sound all the more sinister.

The hallway was thickly carpeted, with wood panels on the walls. Now they were inside, Sean could hear the muffled sound of polite conversation dusted over with a sprinkling of laughter. The hard bastard led them through to a large room dotted with comfortable chairs and sofas, the walls covered in what Sean guessed was expensive artwork. A fire was burning in the ornate fireplace, even though it was the middle of a warm September, filling the air with a faint sweet smell of wood smoke. There were around twenty or thirty people there, all well dressed, all smiling, none looking in any way criminal.

A tall man, late forties or early fifties, tailored suit, sauntered over, holding out a hand. 'Josh!' he intoned in a deep, resonant voice. Then he turned to Sean. 'And you must be the rather excellent young man who works with him. Sean, yes?'

Sean nodded, didn't speak. Thirty seconds earlier he had felt comfortably clean and well dressed in his usual civvy gear of jeans and T-shirt and leather jacket, but right now he was feeling like some homeless guy they had dragged in off the street to have a laugh at.

'A drink?' the man said, and gestured to a young woman circling the room with a silver tray and a number of filled fluted glasses.

Condensation on the sides was slick beneath Sean's fingers as he took one, and he suppressed the urge to hold it up to the light and watch the little trails of bubbles as they streamed up from nowhere. He guessed that for the first time in his life he was holding a glass of champagne.

Shit, I'm turning into a real nob. Crime really *did* pay, if you did it right.

'There's plenty of food,' the man continued. 'Just help yourselves.' He nodded to a far wall, where a long oak table was piled high with nosh in silver dishes. Sean took a sip from the glass and sneezed as the bubbles found their way up his nose. People drank this for pleasure?

But still, champagne . . .

The nosh was bloody decent too, especially the

lobster. The only seafood Sean had ever eaten before was fried in batter, with a side order of chips. This was ten times richer, buttery and with a whole range of flavours, none of them bad.

About an hour and several more glasses of champagne later, Sean was onto his third plate of food and having the time of his life. Free food, head pleasantly tingly from the bubbly, and everyone treating him with respect. The one downside was that apart from Heaton he was half the age of anyone else in the room. And there were no birds – no women at all, apart from the one serving the drinks – which seemed a bit lame . . . but hey, it wasn't his party. The man who had shaken his hand was the perfect host. Insisting that Sean call him Rich, instead of Richard – 'because I don't enjoy formality in a relationship like this, do you?' – he had taken him around the room, introducing him to everyone. One of them asked suspiciously if he was Irish, but relaxed when he said he had got his name because his mum fancied Sean Bean.

'You make it sound so easy,' Rich said as Sean finished telling, for the benefit of yet another interested party, the tale of how he and Heaton had scrumped the SA8os. 'Which is actually rather shocking, wouldn't you agree?'

Sean shrugged. 'Not saying it was' – he fought down a hiccup – '*easy.*' He had a reputation to keep up. Easy?

He'd like to see any of this lot try it. 'I mean, we planned it, y'know? 'Cos we got' – another hiccup, and he bit back a laugh – 'skills. We recce'd the place first, sorted a hideout . . .'

'Using your army skills to look after number one,' said another man, this one middle-aged and a little portly. 'Something I approve of utterly. After all, it's not as though this bloody useless government of ours is going to, is it?'

There was a murmur of approval from around Sean. It was the first time since they'd arrived that he had heard anything other than general cordiality.

'We need more people like you,' the man went on, turning to point at Sean. 'People with the balls to stand up and take control and actually do something about what's happening in this country.'

Sean wasn't sure where the conversation was going. One minute he was bragging about nicking weaponry; now he was in the middle of some kind of angry political discussion.

'It's not all that bad,' he said, looking for the woman with the silver tray.

'The biggest problem we have facing us today,' continued the fat man, ignoring Sean, 'isn't unemployment. It's worse than the financial crisis, or immigration, or family breakdown or even gay marriage.'

The fuck's gay marriage got to do with it? Sean thought. He looked around for tray girl and stumbled because only one of his feet felt like moving.

But the line about immigration made him look around again – and notice something he hadn't clocked earlier because it hadn't seemed like a big deal. Everyone here was white. He had spent a year in a multi-ethnic world and suddenly it seemed weird.

'What it is,' the fat man barked, 'is those *traitors*, those so-called British citizens, who grow up here, living off the state, using our hospitals and doctors and benefits and God knows what else – then have the audacity to claim the right to act as they like on our sovereign soil and kill our people! It's outrageous!'

All the politely swish, upper-class, rah-rah bollocks seemed to have evaporated.

'Terrorists are shits,' Sean agreed. Tray girl appeared in the corner of his eye and he swagged another glass, even though Heaton tried to take it off him.

'The Tidworth bomb . . .' said a younger man with a moustache. 'Five brave soldiers dead. You'd think that would be enough of a wake-up call, but no! The government tackles the problem by cutting back on the armed forces even further. What is it going to take for them to open their eyes?'

The fury that had never quite gone away came surging

up from inside. Sean drained his glass in one go. 'Me and Heaton – Josh – we were there. Our mate got blown up.' He burped out some bubbles and tried to force his muzzy brain to come up with the right word. For some reason it wasn't as easy as usual. 'F-wank-stards.'

'They should be hanged,' said the older man. 'Summary courts – no clever lawyers to get them off to reoffend.'

'It was a car bomb, wasn't it?' said the man with the moustache. 'Inside the camp. Which means the terrorists probably had an inside man.'

Sean snapped round at this. 'Hey, that was the mate I was talking about! It was her car!'

'Sorry,' said the man, raising a hand in defence, 'but I'm just saying what I heard. You never know, do you? They're everywhere, these people. Like a bloody rash.'

'Clarky wasn't a fucking terrorist, mate,' Sean said.

The man with the moustache narrowed his eyes at him. 'I'm not your mate,' he said. 'And all I'm saying is that we need to be careful. Vigilant. They could be anywhere, couldn't they? They've infiltrated the Iraqi army, so why not ours?'

'Because our soldiers aren't terrorists,' Sean said. 'They're the bravest bunch of bastards I've ever met!'

Moustache man laughed then, his voice like a dagger of ice. 'Wake up!' he said. 'They're everywhere! For all we know, you're one!' He laughed again, clearly enjoying his joke.

But Sean wasn't laughing. Him, a terrorist? Who did this posh twat think he was? The bastard! The utter, wanking bastard!

He gave no warning. One moment he was calmly resting his empty champagne glass back on the silver platter. The next, he'd nutted the moustachioed bastard in the face to split his nose, and now, with him floundering on the floor, was going in for more.

'So I'm a terrorist, am I?' he yelled. 'Is that what you think? Fuck do you know, you twat? Nothing, that's what! Hanging out with all your wanker pals, talking bollocks about what's going on, when what do you actually know? Fuck all, is what. Fuck all!'

He was reaching down to drag the man back to his feet, just so he could have another go, when something like steel pincers grabbed his left arm and jammed it up into the centre of his back. He tried to stand up straight, and white-hot agony fizzed along his arm through the champagne bubbles. His arm was held at an angle which made it plain that bones would snap unless he moved exactly as directed. His eyes focused on the mirror across the room. He could see himself bent forward with the hard bastard right behind him, and the guy's eyes were deader than ever.

Heaton ignored the sight of a comrade being attacked and made a beeline for their host. 'Rich, I'm so sorry,' he said. 'Look, I mean he's a good lad – he's just not used to—'

'Oh, go fuck yourself,' Sean shouted. Somewhere in the haze of champagne bubbles in his head was the vague idea that this was not good, but screw that. 'Tash-twat reckons I'm a terrorist, and Clarky was in on it and blew herself up!'

The man with the moustache was now back on his feet, nursing his face with a napkin.

'Harker, you're pissed!' Heaton shouted back.

'Can't be pissed,' Sean protested indignantly. 'It's only champagne, for Chrissake.' He tried to move, and pain shot through his hand and arm again. 'And get your fucking Doberman off me!'

'Doberman!' laughed Rich. 'I rather like that. What do you think, Malcolm?'

Despite the pain, Sean laughed. 'Malcolm? You're kidding!'

Another twist. More pain. Sean doubted his arm would go much further before giving way completely. He had to shut up.

Rich turned to Heaton. 'What an entertaining young man he is, this partner of yours.'

'That's one way to look at it,' Heaton replied, and Sean caught the sharp glance he shot at him.

'I think I'm going to like him,' Rich said, 'as long as he sticks to the soft stuff.'

Heaton agreed, with another dagger glare at Sean.

The pain in Sean's arm was penetrating the anaesthetic effect of the champagne. 'Look,' he said, calming a little. He tried to match Rich's rah-rah voice. 'Would you mind calling Malcolm off? I didn't mean to lose it.'

'Let him go, Malcolm.'

The pain and the pincer grip vanished immediately. Sean staggered free and stood up straight.

'Sometimes,' Rich said, turning to him, 'actions speak louder than words, wouldn't you agree?'

Sean said nothing. He focused on Rich and bit back on a vom-flavoured burp as his host continued.

'Sometimes,' he said, 'no matter how loudly you shout, how clearly you put across your point of view, no one takes the blindest bit of notice. It is then, as you just demonstrated, Sean, that you have to act to make someone listen. And sometimes that involves doing things you wouldn't normally do or indeed approve of. Don't worry about the law. Just get above it.'

Sean had no idea what Rich was on about. Didn't care. Wanted to get back to barracks. The room was boiling hot and he was sweating freely.

In fact, he realized suddenly, getting out of this room

and into the toilet in the next thirty seconds would be a really good idea.

Rich walked up to Sean, leaned in close. Sean had given up on trying to focus. Rich was a man-shaped blur.

'I like you,' Rich told him. 'I like your . . . verve? Yes, that will do I think. Verve. Now— Oh, Christ! Josh! Get him out of here!'

Sean dropped to his hands and knees as his guts heaved, and seven glasses' worth of champagne and a lot of chewed-up lobster spewed out over Rich's thick, expensive and very absorbent rug.

The journey back to barracks was silent.

Chapter 23

'Fuck me, Stenders, what happened to you?'

Shitey Bright had been posted outside the briefing room to guide the platoon in. Sean came shambling down the corridor towards him, pain lancing through his head like someone had wired electrodes to his temples, his stomach still churning. He had forced a piece of toast down for breakfast, and now even that felt like it might be going the same way as the lobsters.

At zero eight thirty on a Monday morning the platoon was meant to be doing PT. When Sean clocked the notice that they were to report to the briefing room instead, he began to think there really might be a God.

'What's going on?'

Bright shrugged. 'Change of orders. And, mate, if you don't mind me saying, you look like something that fell out of my arse last night. Only worse. And that was saying something. I mean, I had this mega-hot curry, right? Cut through me like a welding torch!'

Weeks after Clark's death, the platoon's banter levels were approaching normal again, and Sean would usually have given as good as he got. Now his stomach twisted at the thought, but he seemed to have done most of his throwing up.

'Met this total div at the weekend,' he muttered. 'Thought champagne was basically fizzy wine. Didn't realize it's twice as strong, and the bubbles mean the alcohol gets absorbed into the system double quick.'

'Champagne, eh?' Bright grinned. 'Sounds like your mate ought to stick to his type of people. Only wankers drink champagne for pleasure.'

'The real wank de la wank,' Sean agreed.

Bright sniffed. 'And then, by the smell of it, your mate slept with his mouth open and the cat used it for a litter tray. Here.' He handed Sean a packet of extra-strong mints. 'Eat the pack. Sergeant gets a whiff of that, you'll be right in the shit.'

Sean took the mints, dropped four into his mouth and crunched. Then he went on through to the briefing room.

Five minutes later the door opened, and Lieutenant Franklin and Sergeant Adams bowled in. The room came to attention. Sean was pleased that he could still do that and not hurl or fall over.

'Sit,' Franklin ordered curtly. He stood at ease, feet

apart, hands behind his back, and surveyed the room. Adams stood behind him, silent and impassive. 'You'll be wondering why you're all in here, and not out getting your arses worn into the ground by some psycho PT instructor.'

Sean squeezed his eyes shut, hoping to push some of the hangover out. It didn't work.

'Over the weekend, during an Army Reserve exercise up on Salisbury Plain, it was discovered that a number of SA80s had gone missing.'

Sean heard gasps. If he'd been more alert, he would probably have reacted. In his current state, it was all he could do to stop himself chucking up.

But the gasps were more amused, not dismayed. It was the first good laugh the platoon had had in a long time.

'The daft bastards left them out there?' said Mitra. 'And now we have to go and find them – is that it, sir?'

'No, that is not it.' Adams took over, no hint of amusement in his words or tone. 'Now, from time to time we've all heard about some daft twat who hasn't quite clocked the harsh realities of life and decides to take his gun home as a souvenir. The army catches up with him and that's the end of that. But this was not some daft twat taking his gun home.'

'Correct,' said Franklin. 'This was half a dozen automatic rifles, swapped for fakes. Wherever the real ones are now, that's a small arms cache – enough to ambush an army unit with . . . enough for a major terrorist incident.'

The smirks around the room were disappearing fast as the reality sank in. With everything that had happened in the last month, the words *major terrorist incident* had a way of hanging in the air and sucking the last shreds of humour out of the situation.

It was just a shame, Sean thought, that he wasn't able to reassure them; that he couldn't tell anyone, *No, lads, the point is, we're preventing another one . . .*

He wondered how Heaton was taking the news. The corporal was sitting at the back of the room so Sean couldn't see him.

'There's a full and immediate investigation into what happened,' Sergeant Adams said. 'Every unit based on Salisbury Plain – and I mean *everyone* – is going to be interviewed. Starting now.'

'Why, sir?' asked West. 'Weapons got nicked and they think it's an inside job? That's bollocks. No one would be that stupid. Swiping that many SA80s? That's organized crime stuff, that.'

Franklin said, 'The point is, West, no one knows who did it, or why, or even how. Hence the interviews.'

'But, sir, it's not like they can actually send out the Redcaps and interview every one of us, is it?'

The sergeant shook his head. 'No, they can't. Which is why it'll be me and Mr Franklin.'

For a second or two it was clear no one believed him. Then everyone did, mainly because Adams's face had grown even darker.

'We will interview you all this morning,' Franklin explained, 'and then we will be interviewed ourselves by Special Branch to report on the results. Men, I don't expect any of you to have any idea about what happened, but that doesn't mean I don't expect you to take it seriously. You will.'

'Because if you don't,' Adams added, 'it'll be a boot up the arse followed by the shittest week you can imagine. And don't think, based on everything that's happened recently, that I can't make it shittier – because I promise you, I can.'

No one doubted it.

Oh . . . shit.

Sean closed his eyes for a moment, then forced them open again in case anyone thought he was dropping off.

He had never lied to Sergeant Adams. He had never tried, or wanted to. He had too much respect for the man. And the sergeant was the kind of guy who forced you to tell the truth just by sheer will power. So how was he going to get through an interview and not get pinged?

By being ready, he told himself. *That's how.* He had been questioned by men in uniform before, even before the one time he got nicked. They had always had to release him. Just say 'yes' and 'no', don't rise to the bait, don't try to fill any silences.

So he had practice. But what had seemed like an easy job was now turning into a serious ball ache.

Adams was speaking. 'This won't take all day. Interviews will be held in the room across the hall, and we will start with . . .' He paused and glanced around his soldiers.

Sean stared into the middle distance, avoiding the sergeant's eye, trying to appear relaxed – anything to avoid being picked first.

'Let's have Shitey first, I think,' Adams said.

'Ah, bollocks,' said Bright. 'Now?'

'Unless you have any other pressing appointments, Private,' Franklin said.

Sean watched as Bright followed the sergeant and the lieutenant out of the room and across the hall. Now all he had to do was sit and wait.

Someone tapped his shoulder. He turned to find Heaton staring at him.

'What kind of prick nicks weapons, then?' the corporal asked.

'One with no brains and massive balls,' Penfold offered from behind them both.

'Well, it's not Shitey,' Mitra said. 'Can't be. They'd have caught him by now, just by following the stink from the crime scene to his man-cave.'

Sean laughed, hoped he didn't sound nervous. Then he said, 'And Penfold's out. Too fucking clumsy. They'd have been able to follow the trail of broken weapons parts.'

More laughter.

A few minutes later Bright came back and nodded at Penfold. And that was how the rest of the morning panned out. One would leave, have a chat, then come back and send in the next. No one who had been questioned was allowed to talk to anyone who hadn't been, apart from sending them in.

At first Sean hadn't wanted to be picked first, but he soon realized that waiting was a hell of a lot worse. He had longer to think, longer to work on his innocent face, longer to go through every possible scenario that might play out if the sergeant suspected anything.

He and Heaton could really do with a cover story for that night. They could just say they had been doing completely separate things – why not? But if Heaton said he had been at the movies, say, with Sean . . . Oh shit, would he? Did he have the sense to leave Sean out of it? He wished he could have even thirty seconds to discuss it, but there was no privacy in that room with the dwindling numbers of the platoon.

And so, at last, he entered the interview room. It was very simply laid out – a table in the middle, Franklin and Adams on one side, an empty seat on the other. There were the usual notices on the walls, chairs round the sides, and a second door which was shut.

'Sit,' Adams said. It wasn't polite and neither was it rude. It was just an order.

Sean obeyed. He spent a few moments trying to get comfortable without giving the impression that he wasn't – because, he was sure, that would make him look like he had something to hide. Then he worried he was breathing too loudly and tried to control it – except that now he sounded out of breath. Next it was his heart he noticed, the *thump-thump, thump-thump* of it surely visible through his clothes. Surely both men could see, he thought. Yes, that was why they were making him wait so long, wasn't it? They knew he was guilty. Oh, fucking hell . . .

'Right, Harker,' Franklin began. 'Before we begin, you need to know that this conversation is completely confidential. Sergeant Adams will be taking notes and you will be given a copy if you want one. Also, it's not so much an interview, more a conversation. We're just going to chat through what we know and go from there. Understand?'

Sean nodded, realizing for the first time that he had been too busy worrying about what Heaton might say to think up a cover story for himself. The lads thought he had spent the night with a girl. Oh shit, if they pressed him for details, then he was going to have to get creative on the spot, and that was how they always found the loopholes . . .

'What do you know about what happened?' Franklin asked.

Sean shrugged. 'Only what you just told us, sir, which isn't much.'

'That's because not much is known,' the lieutenant agreed with a tight smile. 'Have you got any idea how someone could swap real for fake weapons?'

'No, sir,' said Sean. 'We have to sign everything in and out.'

'Exactly,' agreed Adams. 'The missing weapons are not traceable to anyone. In fact, no one can actually work out how this was done at all. Whoever did it really knew what they were doing.'

Sean wasn't so sure. 'So why are we being interviewed, sir?'

He bit his lip. *Arsehole! Shut up! Don't engage!*

'I wasn't exaggerating when I said the missing rifles were enough for a terrorist incident. It is Special Branch's belief that this is exactly why they were stolen.' Franklin looked at him impassively – though his face was a naked mass of emotion compared to Adams's rock-like blankness. 'Does that bother you, Private?'

'Course it does,' Sean said indignantly, and remembered to add, 'sir. What soldier would give guns to terrorists? That's just . . . crazy.'

'So is stealing weapons in the first place,' said Adams.

'Yeah, but none of our lot would steal weapons for terrorists.'

'So you think they would steal them for other reasons?'

'That's not what I said,' Sean said, suddenly feeling cold.

'So what are you saying?'

Sean stopped talking. He was digging himself into a hole. The sergeant was just trying to push his buttons, had probably done the same with everyone else. It was his job to be absolutely sure, after all, wasn't it? Make sure his lads had no involvement?

'What about your own past?' Adams asked. 'It's not like a bit of theft is beyond you, is it, Harker?'

Sean's face blazed red. That was a low blow, even if

it was absolutely true. 'Sergeant, I would never give weapons to terrorists,' he said tightly.

He thought back to the people he had met the last night. Rich and his types were dodgy, yes, but they weren't radicalized teenagers. *That* was terrorists. Rich and his fellow tossers were white Brits, and proud of it. Posh gits with slightly weird political views, sure, but there was no way they were terrorists. And the point – he reminded himself yet again – was that they were *protecting* people.

Adams and Franklin looked at each other, and some signal seemed to pass between them. The sergeant slowly rose to his feet and walked over to the second door. He stood at ease next to it and gazed at Sean. Sean nervously returned the look. It reminded him of . . .

It reminded him of the very first time they had met, in his solitary cell back at Burnleigh. Adams had had the same expression in his eyes then: a confident, I'm-going-to-have-you look.

Only that time, Adams had also been smiling. He wasn't smiling now.

Sean looked back at the table, where Adams had left his jotter. He hadn't written down any notes at all. Not one.

'Private Harker,' Franklin said. Sean swung his eyes round. 'The questions we have asked you so far are the questions we have asked everyone, so you will all have something to chat about when you compare notes afterwards. Now we are going to ask you some questions that are just for you.' He nodded at Adams.

The sergeant came to attention, then turned to open the door. He stepped back to allow a pair of civilians, a man and a woman, to enter the room. They looked like any pair of off-duty Ruperts – a Rupert and a Rupertess. The woman wore a light summer dress. The man—

Oh, fuck!

Sean could swear his heart stopped.

The man wore a sports jacket with an open collar. Not what he had been wearing the last time they met, but what the hell.

'These . . . individuals,' said Franklin, 'are from MI5. They have asked specifically to meet you.'

He pushed back his chair and went to stand beside Adams, feet apart, arms crossed. The two civvies took the two seats opposite Sean. Adams closed the door again but remained standing.

And Sean's stomach heaved as he looked at the man. He wanted to throw up his guts over the table. This was a million times worse than getting nicked. The last time he had seen this guy, this MI5 spook, he had seemed so . . . *harmless.*

'Hello again, Private,' the man said. 'A couple of weeks ago we met in a farmyard and you gave me a package full of illicit unfired ammunition. The package had your fingerprints and DNA all over the outside. Both of these are of course on the National Criminal Database due to your past. And I have just visually ID'd you – so I hope it's fairly clear that any kind of denial will get you nowhere. So why not tell us about these missing rifles?'

Chapter 24

'He's in shock,' said the spook woman when Sean hadn't spoken for a few seconds.

The fact was, he couldn't speak. His mouth was desert dry.

'Take as much time as you need, Private.' She looked up at Franklin. 'There's no need for you or the sergeant to remain.'

It was a clear dismissal. Adams didn't budge, merely glanced at the lieutenant. Franklin's crossed arms might have crossed a little more tightly. 'That's kind of you, but we'll stay.'

Her mouth tightened. 'It wasn't a request.'

'Then I have nothing to decline.'

'I could make it an order.'

'You could. And if it came to me via a superior officer who you could actually persuade to order me to abandon one of my men, I would have no choice but to obey.'

Oh, go on, just piss off! Sean thought bitterly. He didn't want any more witnesses to his humiliation than strictly necessary. Least of all Adams.

Because he was screwed, and he knew it. If he had thought a few months in prison were bad, what would he get now?

And it was his fault. Totally, utterly his own stupid fault. He could have walked when he found out the truth, but no. He'd stayed.

You stupid, stupid idiot, Harker. You've done this to yourself.

The woman dismissed the point with a slight nod, and turned her attention back to Sean, one eyebrow raised a little as she waited for him to speak.

'I . . . I . . . I don't know anything,' he said. He could hear how pathetic the bluster sounded, but then he remembered the one thing he had left. *Yeah*, he thought fiercely. *Pride. I'm not just a crook. I was doing this to protect people. Where were you when Clarky got slotted?*

The man spook folded his fingers together and regarded Sean over the top of them. 'If we wanted to arrest you, Private, we wouldn't be bothering with this talk. As I said, your prints were on the *outside* of the package. That means you had nothing to do with wrapping the goods. The fingerprints inside belong to one Joshua Heaton, now a corporal in your unit, sent down when he was a teenager, five years ago, for breaking and entering, also with a record of aggravated assault and inciting racial hatred.'

Sean fought to keep his face impassive as a chill spread down his spine. Heaton had only admitted to one of those three crimes.

'When we met, you were driving a Daewoo Matiz with fake plates, but the colour and model match a car previously registered to one Mrs Daphne Heaton of Leyton. Corporal Heaton's mother. Do you see how things are falling into place?'

Sean forced his breathing to steady. 'Why aren't you asking Corporal Heaton all this?' he said.

The man's gaze was unblinking. 'Because we're asking you.'

Still Sean kept quiet. He hadn't lied when he told Heaton he'd never grassed, and he wasn't going to start now.

'You're a loyal friend, Private Harker. Do you think Corporal Heaton will repay this loyalty? That he'll go down without dragging you with him?'

'Of course, he's been a good friend to you too, hasn't he?' the woman said softly. 'He's shown you the time of your life. He's given you tasters – just tasters – of a life you could never afford on your salary. Cool gear. Fast car. Nice digs. Did you enjoy your night with the girl?'

Shit – how long had these people been watching him?

249

She had exactly described what happened. Had they even had a camera in Heaton's spare room?

'You already know so much,' he said bitterly, 'you don't need me to tell you anything.'

'We didn't know.'

Sean frowned, despite himself. 'Then how—?'

'The word is "grooming", Private. It's not just something paedophiles do on social media. And yours is a textbook case.'

Sean snorted. 'That's bollocks. OK, yeah, I stayed over at Corporal Heaton's, and there was a girl. She was his girlfriend's mate and I was invited along for company.'

'His girlfriend's mate,' the man repeated with a faint smile. 'So the corporal has a girlfriend. Talks about her all the time, I bet. Sees her every weekend. Never off the phone to her. Tell me, is there a single picture of her anywhere in his flat? Anywhere at all?'

It had never occurred to Sean to check, but now the man mentioned it . . . No. He couldn't remember a photo anywhere.

'We have access to his phone records, you know. I can confirm that the only woman he has dialled on a private number in the last month was his mother. However, a week before you and I first met, he dialled an escort agency in Andover that specializes in . . . well, escorts with added duties. We've checked their rates, and the amount that appears on his credit card after that call matches what would be needed for a double hiring.'

Sean didn't blink, but it was hitting him like a very slow thump in the guts – one that just kept on coming. Oh. My. God.

Groomed.

The . . . bastard!

Heaton had even asked which one was Debs. Sean had assumed it was a joke . . .

Sean would kill him. Sean would walk out of this room right now and actually kill him. He felt sick.

And he knew his mask had slipped. The hate that churned inside him right now was impossible to put a blank face on, and they had clocked it. He had as good as confessed, without saying a word.

'I . . .' He had to force his dry mouth to say the words. 'I think I need a lawyer.'

The woman spook winced as if he had farted in polite company. 'I really don't think you do. A lawyer will force us to do this by the book, which will inevitably end in your conviction and imprisonment in a place where you'll have quite a reputation as the man who helped supply terrorists with weapons.'

Sean shot her a sharp glance when she said 'terrorists', but he kept quiet and she kept going.

'Not one I'd like myself, but there you go. It will be

something to keep you warm and happy for the next thirty years.'

'Whereas,' the man contributed, 'doing without the lawyer and cooperating with us, using the skills and training you already have as a soldier will possibly – *possibly* – mean no prison at all.'

Sean dragged his eyes away from him for a moment, stared at the wall, the ceiling, out of the window. He couldn't run. So it was either get a lawyer or work against Heaton. Of course, he didn't actually have the money for a lawyer. But would that matter?

He glared at them from under his brows, but it was merely a mask to disguise the feeling of all hope draining away. Whatever happened, he wasn't going to leave this room a free man. Face it, they knew about the rifles; they weren't going to let that go.

He switched his gaze to the floor. 'It . . . it wasn't to supply terrorists,' he muttered. That was the one shred of comfort he could hold onto. And maybe a good brief in court could get him less than thirty years if he stuck to it.

'And of all the lies Corporal Heaton has told you, that's the one true thing, is it?'

Sean stared at him. 'Yes. Course it's true. He's a serving soldier, for fucksake! What would he be doing with terrorists?'

'Just tell us where the rifles are, Private.'

The final shreds of Sean's pride crept away to die. 'He said the client had collected them,' he muttered, still looking at the floor. He was now officially grassing, and he couldn't find a single toss to give. 'I can tell you where they were. If that helps.'

'Go on.'

And so Sean described how the op had gone down: the observation, switching rifles with dummies, hiding them under the bush. The spooks remained expressionless while he spilled. Sean didn't dare turn his head to meet the glare coming from Adams. He could feel it frying the side of his face.

'Quite the criminal mastermind, is Corporal Heaton,' the man murmured when he had finished.

'So . . . you going to pull him in?' Sean asked hopefully.

But the spook just looked at his watch. 'Any more and we'll be over-running.'

The woman looked at her own watch and concurred. Then back at Sean. 'The sole reason for this entire charade, Private Harker, all the interviewing-the-platoon claptrap, was to let us spend time with you alone. There was no other way we could do that on base without being observed. And if we spend any more time now, the others will start to wonder why your interview is taking so long.

So here is what you will do – and remember, you are still cooperating. This evening you will find a reason to go into town. You will tell your friends you are calling a taxi. You will leave the base at precisely nineteen hundred hours . . .'

The gatehouse was still festooned with warning tape, somewhere between the end of demolition and the start of rebuilding. It had double the number of armed guards, and a hand-operated traffic barrier. Sean stepped through the pedestrian barrier, and out of the camp, dead on 19:00.

Oh, arsing hell, be on time, don't make me have to talk to people . . .

The excuse had been easy – his mum's birthday was coming up, shit, he was always forgetting . . . He had done his bit. Now they just had to do theirs.

At 19:00 and ten seconds a hybrid Prius swished up, with the name of a taxi firm displayed by a light on the roof. The driver wore a flat cap and a casual pea jacket. 'Ride for name of Harker?' he called, not to Sean but to the guards, in an accent that was pure Wiltshire.

The guards merely indicated where Sean waited, in civvies, hunched up and trying to be invisible to anyone who might want a friendly chat. Like any muckers who suddenly thought it was a good idea to share a ride into town.

Sean trotted over to the taxi and climbed in the back. The driver eased the car away from the kerb to head into town. Sean hadn't been in an electric car before, and even now he took time to think that it sucked. At slow speeds the Prius ran off its battery and barely made a sound.

'Hello, Private.' The voice was now accentless – as posh as it had been before. The man didn't turn round, but their eyes met briefly in the rear-view mirror, before he looked back at the road to concentrate on steering.

'Where we going?' Sean asked.

The driver signalled to turn onto the main road. The engine cut in as the car picked up speed. 'To carry on where we left off,' he said.

The last instruction the spooks had given Franklin was to issue Sean with duties that kept him well away from Heaton for the rest of the day. Which unfortunately meant that Sean had to work under Adams's gaze instead. To everyone else, Adams was his usual self – an affable tower of integrity and discipline. But Sean was aware that whenever the sergeant's eyes rested on him, they were dark and blank, and he was definitely excluded from the banter.

The feeling of isolation continued in the taxi. Apart from the opening words when he'd got in, the spook said nothing.

They headed along back roads into Andover, where they pulled up in a small car park beneath some trees, next to a much more respectable Audi saloon. The other driver's window whirred down as they drew up. The woman spook behind the wheel gave Sean a cool nod. The man spook twisted round in his seat so that he could see both of them, and pressed buttons to make the taxi's passenger side windows slide down. Now the three of them could have a conversation.

'First,' the woman said, as though the intervening hours hadn't happened and they were just continuing where they had left off, 'let us tell you why we're not immediately picking up Corporal Heaton. If all we wanted was to clamp down on his operation, we could do it in five minutes. But Heaton has the same flaw as most criminal masterminds, which is that he actually isn't one. He'll sell to anyone. He sold to us, and that is how we found you. But there is an even bigger fish who we suspect is Heaton's main customer. This individual plus the equipment provided by Heaton could lead to big, big trouble. That's who we're looking to stop – and if we shut Heaton down, our man will just go somewhere else for the goods.'

The man opened up the glove compartment and slid a photo out of a folder, which he passed to Sean. Sean glanced down, and there was Rich. The shot must have

256

been captured by a hidden camera. He was looking off to one side with no idea he was being snapped, and there was a blurred crowd all around him.

They looked at him expectantly.

'Yeah, calls himself Rich,' Sean said. 'Who is he?'

'His name is unimportant,' the woman told him, 'and if you knew it, there's a danger you would inadvertently use it in his or Heaton's hearing. Rich will do. And just in case you continue to harbour delusions that he is some harmless eccentric with a few right-wing views – we have every reason to believe he is involved in a group that has been carrying out a number of terrorist strikes over the last few years that are made to look like IS.'

Sean frowned, thinking back to his first impression of Rich. A wealthy tosser with wealthy friends, but surely all talk, no action – or so he'd thought. Just one more way he had been taken in by their sick act.

'How do you do that?'

'Oh, it's surprisingly easy. First, you need your genuine event. Say, a car bomb, an honour killing – it doesn't even need to happen, just to be discovered. Next, for every genuine IS supporter there are ten kids whose commitment to jihad extends as far as tweeting *Death to the West* and then getting on with their GCSE revision. They're very easy to frame. Documents are planted, fake computer trails are laid right up to their doorstep, links are forged with genuine IS individuals who are safely out of the country and beyond our reach, and who aren't going to deny it because the publicity is too precious. Presto – a previously undiscovered terrorist cell. Imagine what that does for public confidence.'

'But if you know this—' Sean began.

'Most of the time we can catch it,' the woman agreed. 'But it only takes one or two to slip through – and even if we manage to spot the faked evidence, the fact is, these genuine events are happening and the public is taking notice. The cumulative effect is the same. A climate of fear is created.'

'At first,' the man said, 'Rich faked evidence for events that were nothing to do with him. A house fire that killed the head teacher of a school run jointly by the local church and the local mosque, the brakes failing on a minibus carrying protesters to an anti-war parade – these were genuine accidents that had nothing to do with IS, but he successfully planted the idea in the minds of the media that there was more to them.'

'At first?' Sean repeated nervously. So the guy was a shit, but he hadn't hurt anyone. But if that was 'at first'. . .

'Then he went further and started causing the incidents himself. So far, we believe we can link Rich to a car bomb planted – and discovered – in a vehicle belonging to a prominent human rights lawyer exiled from Syria. A gun attack on a man and a woman who had committed the crime of living together without being married. One lived, the other did not – a note pinned to the body said that they had been breaking holy law.'

Sean felt himself begin to shudder as the list went on. He'd thought the guy was just a harmless tosser – but he was an actual psycho.

'Incendiary devices placed in a couple of restaurants, one of which caused deaths. A suicide bombing aimed at a school – thankfully the bomb went off too soon. Do you see the pattern?'

Sean clenched his fists to stop the shaking.

'He's getting worse,' he said heavily.

'Much worse. Of course, this is all a lot for one man to handle, which is why he delegates jobs to his subordinates. Like the attack on the camp that killed Private Clark.'

Sean sat up sharply. 'That's bollocks! Those were soldiers who died! He's a wanker, but he's pro-Brit! Why'd he want to hit our own soldiers? Why'd he want to hit Clarky?'

'*She*' – the woman held up one finger – 'was *black*' – a second finger. 'That's two reasons someone like Rich would say she had no place in the British Army. But as we say, he delegates. Can you think of anyone else who had a problem with Clark's gender and race?'

Sean could. For a moment, as the one inevitable name came to mind, it seemed like the whole world stopped and ice ran through his veins. Then: 'No. No!' He began to shake his head, pushing himself back in his seat as though they were offering him Clark's dead, charred head to hold. 'No! No fucking way! Heaton? No!'

'I told you we had access to his phone records,' the man said quietly, not blinking, not taking his eyes off Sean's. 'He was on his phone seconds before the attack. He dialled a number for a cheap pay-as-you-go handset. The connection was made and immediately went dead, simultaneously with the explosion. As I'm sure you're aware, bombs can be detonated by phone – you just use a handset as the power source for the detonator. And as I'm sure you're also aware, Corporal Heaton is very proficient with electronics.'

'No!' Sean gasped. If he had been shocked when they told him how he had been set up with Rachel, now he just wanted to hurl.

'So you see, Private,' said the woman, 'terrorists aren't all Middle Easterners cutting off heads and radicalizing our teenagers. They come in all shapes and sizes. Back to Rich. Perhaps he spun you a story about using those rifles for defence. Perhaps, in his own head, it *is* defence – of the way of life he thinks we should all have. However, they will end up being used on innocent civilians whose only crime is to be in the wrong place at the wrong time.'

'Where?' Sean demanded in desperation. 'When? What's he going to do with . . .'

'We don't know that yet. Chop off the head and the body dies. Stop Rich and you stop those weapons being used,' she told him.

'So why's he still walking around?' Sean shouted. 'Nick him already!'

'If our positions were reversed, I'm sure that's what he would do,' she agreed. 'Laws? Who needs them? But the rule of law is there for everyone, and it protects people like him just as much as it protects you and me. That's how we remain better than IS. But there is a downside, which is that we need evidence to make a successful prosecution.'

'And evidence that will stand up in court is very hard to come by,' the man added. 'He's too clever to leave much of it around.'

Sean bit on a harsh laugh. 'Hey, come on. You can get a warrant to read all Heaton's phone calls and credit cards but you can't get one for his?'

The identical looks they gave him were so neutral that they were like an admission.

He stared at them. 'Shit. You mean, you *can't*? *That's* how powerful he is?'

'But if we had a man inside – then we'd be in business.'

Sean frowned as he noted their expressions, then realized what they meant, and recoiled. 'What, like a double agent? Working undercover?'

'This is army business, not James Bond,' said the man. 'It won't be gadgets and sexy women and sports cars. It will be a risk.'

'Are you fucking mental? If I got found out, I'd be dead!'

'So you're in?'

Sean looked away. 'Don't have much choice, do I?' Though, he thought bitterly, he did. He could always just go to jail until he qualified for his old age pension.

And then he remembered – he had never really forgotten – holding Clarky's mutilated, barely alive body in his arms. Anger – sheer violent, homicidal rage – flooded through his veins. No, he had no choice, because passing up on this chance to get back at the *fuckers* who had done that to his mate wasn't an option.

'This isn't what I trained for,' he said. 'You'll have to tell me what to do.'

'Be yourself, Private,' the woman told him. 'You've a criminal history, you've been inside, so you have at least some understanding of the people you will meet. And you're a trained soldier. You're smart. You're streetwise. You know how to read a situation. You can handle yourself with and without a weapon. You're physically fit. In many ways, you're perfect already.' She laughed, then added, 'And that's not flattery. It's just a simple fact.'

'Now,' the man said, 'show me your phone.'

Sean frowned, but shrugged and pulled his phone out. The man studied it, then pulled a briefcase from under his seat and fingered through a selection of different models until he had one that looked similar. He popped the casing and inserted a SIM card, then handed it back.

'It's pay-as-you-go,' he said, 'and it has only one number programmed in, which goes through to Sergeant Adams. From now on, he is your contact. He's been briefed.'

'The sergeant?' Sean exclaimed.

'Do you have a problem with that?'

He had no more problem with that than he did with the entire mess he had managed to make of his entire life. In fact, it was pretty trivial in the big scheme of things.

'Just don't see Sergeant Adams as a spook . . .' He couldn't see Adams as anything less than one hundred per cent straight up. And he couldn't see the man who had believed in him enough to get him into the army wanting to have anything more to do with him.

'So what do I do, then?' he asked.

'Exactly what you have been doing,' said the driver. 'Work with Heaton and whoever he is involved with—'

'Work with Heaton?' Sean repeated in disbelief. '*Work* with *fucking Heaton*? After what you told me? I'll kill him! I'll—'

'Manage your anger or go to jail,' the man snapped. It was like a slap, just enough to bring Sean back to his senses. 'Find out everything you can, without drawing attention to yourself. And report everything back to Sergeant Adams.'

'And you two?'

'There is no "us two",' the man said simply. He checked the clock on the dashboard. 'Now, what did you tell your muckers you were off to do?'

'Said I was going to get a present for my mum.'

'Then that's what we'll do.'

He closed the windows and switched on the engine, reversing out of the space.

In the supermarket, the only thing Sean was really aware of was the new phone in his pocket. *That* was all he was getting as preparation for going undercover? It didn't seem much. What if things went wrong? What if he was discovered? What if Heaton found out and shopped him to Rich? What if he ended up being on the receiving end of one of the SA80s? Or one of Heaton's IEDs?

Too many what-ifs. Sean found a cheap box of chocolates and went back out to the taxi.

'You need to understand,' said the spook as they headed back towards the barracks, 'that this is highly secret. And dangerous. If anyone suspects anything, I – indeed anyone else involved in this investigation – will be unable to help you. And if the ones we are trying to catch get even a whiff of something amiss, then I wouldn't count on them being forgiving.'

'Makes me feel so much better,' Sean muttered. 'So what exactly am I looking for and how will I know when it's all over?'

'The answer to both those question is that we don't know. We desperately need grass roots intelligence, just to understand what we're up against. We want to stop Rich, to prosecute him – but we don't yet know how. We know what kind of person he is, but what makes him tick, what he wants – that's another matter. So, feed us everything you learn, and we'll do the rest. The more we know, the better.'

The barracks were up ahead now. Although the hangover was gone, Sean was feeling sick again. Frying pan and fire sprang to mind. He needed to lie down. To sleep. To forget about all this, wake up and find that it was all a dream. Except that wasn't going to happen, was it?

'You, Private,' the man added, 'are our best lead in months, if not years.'

'How much danger am I in?' Sean asked as the Prius pulled in to the kerb.

The driver turned round, stared hard at Sean, the engine on idle. 'You are a soldier,' he said, voice flat, no emotion. 'You are trained for dangerous situations. It's not all about humanitarian aid and rescuing children from burning houses. So you will be in danger, yes. But that's what you signed up for, isn't it? You made your choices.'

Sean opened the door.

'You can't just leave,' said the man.

'Why?' Sean asked.

The man pointed at the timer on the dashboard.

'I have to pay for this?'

The man stared, said nothing, and Sean realized that of course they were in view of the guards. Everything had to be normal, and that included returning squaddies paying off the taxi driver.

He settled up. 'Keep the change,' he muttered, and slammed the door.

Chapter 25

If Heaton was going to tell him anything at all, Sean knew it would be at the weekend. That was when it had all gone down before – when they were off duty and could get off base with no questions asked. And so half of him wanted, more than anything, for the weekend to come, and the other half dreaded it.

And sure enough, half an hour after knocking-off time on Friday, Sean was round at the flat and wishing like hell, after what Heaton had just told him, that he wasn't.

'What do they need an RPG for?'

He thought his question was natural, even if he was supposed to be working undercover. Sitting in Heaton's kitchen, he didn't feel undercover. He felt about as above cover as it's possible to get. How could Heaton not tell just by looking at him?

I know what you did to Clark, you fucker . . .

But after the time he'd spent with Copper, Sean had

learned to keep his feelings to himself, not letting on. And so he sat there, and kept his expression impassive, and listened to the corporal talk.

'Who cares?' Heaton answered. 'Think of the money!'

The week after the interviews had gone by as if nothing had happened. On the Tuesday, the platoon was on a forced march that had most of them dead on their feet and close to throwing up. The next three days went much the same way, though instead of trying to kill them by running them into the ground, Franklin and Adams had them all going through numerous close quarter combat drills.

At those times, the theft of the SA80s was like a memory of something Sean had seen in a movie. But at night, when he could lie in bed and stare at the ceiling, it all came back. Then he was acutely aware of the two lives he was now leading. One as an ordinary soldier, the other as the bloke who, thanks to some very bad decision-making, had ended up working secretly for MI5 to find stolen weapons and terrorists.

Sean stared at the man he had once almost liked, and for the thousandth time the rage that had consumed him ever since the meeting in the cars flared up like an acetylene flame. He quickly sat on it.

'I can't just think of the money,' he replied. 'No one *needs* an RPG. Not to defend themselves – unless they're in the middle of a firefight, or into some seriously dodgy shit.'

Heaton pulled a couple of cans from the fridge and tossed one over.

'So what's he want it for?' Sean asked him again when it became obvious that he wasn't saying anything else.

'Let's just say that it's for a cause we both care about.'

'Well, that's vague as fuck.'

Heaton sipped his can. 'No it isn't. It's exactly what we talked about before we hit the Reservists. It's about protecting what we value from those who would blow it all to shit.'

Sean didn't reply.

'Think what happened to Clark,' Heaton said, and Sean almost threw the beer in his face. That was exactly what he had been thinking.

'What's this got to do with that?'

'Everything,' Heaton said. 'Because Rich's whole thing is to stop people who do stuff like that.'

The smell of bullshit in the air was growing stronger by the second.

'You're having a laugh, mate.'

'You see me laughing?'

'You know what I mean.'

'Well, don't let it bother your pretty little head,' Heaton said. 'I was only letting you know about the

RPG. I'll be the one sourcing it while you're off in London enjoying yourself.'

Sean blinked. 'While I'm what?'

Heaton grinned and raised his can in salute. 'Rich wants to meet you alone, golden boy. Congratulations. He's forgiven you for the rug, by the way – says it was his wife's and he never liked it anyway. I said you'd be in Trafalgar Square at fifteen hundred tomorrow.'

Chapter 26

'The simple fact is, we are at war.'

Rich finished his double espresso and delicately dabbed his lips with a napkin. 'Our borders are open gates and the enemy are already here. And yet we welcome them with open arms while we grind our own people into the dirt.' His eyes burned into Sean's as he spoke.

Sean wasn't sure if some response was required. 'Uh-huh,' he said hesitantly.

They sat on folding chairs outside a coffee van in the shadow of the National Gallery, and looked out across Trafalgar Square. Sean, Rich – and Malcolm, wearing the same hard-bastard look as he had the week before.

The square was thick with tourists, all vying for photographs, swarming slowly around the fountains and Nelson's Column and the four giant lions. It was a warm day – the only blessing on the Underground had been the blasts of cool air as the trains punched their way out of their tunnels and into the stations – and the tall buildings trapped the heat and made it almost suffocating.

A couple of pairs of armed cops were on a slow patrol, bulky in body armour, with Heckler & Koch MP5s cradled casually in their arms. The amount of flesh on show in the crowd was both good and bad, depending on where Sean looked. There were some fit girls about, and on a normal day he would have enjoyed eyeing them up. And they might have eyed him back, if he hadn't been sitting with one guy who could have been his dad, and another who looked like he hated them all.

Rich had been waiting by the coffee van, which looked more vintage vehicle than state-of-the-art café. They were served by a man wearing an expertly manicured pencil-thin moustache and a striped apron. It was all about as fake as Rich himself.

With MI5's briefing in mind – and as he wasn't pissed this time – Sean was seeing Rich in a different light. It was like all the smiles and posh accent and general hospitality were a thin plastic shell over something deeper and far worse. The smile was now thin and cold, and the eyes above it were hiding something. Sean didn't want to know what, but he had to try and find out.

'You don't sound convinced,' Rich observed. The smile was colder.

'I'm sorry,' said Sean. 'I just didn't realize there was a war on.'

He had reported this meeting via the phone to Adams and the spooks. The answer had been simple: *Report back ASAP afterwards.* So not a lot to work with. He wanted to get Rich talking, which meant questions – but too many questions can start to sound like doubt, and he didn't like to think what Rich might do to doubters. Was he saying the right or the wrong things? Shit, it was like walking through a minefield.

Rich looked around, and his eyes settled on someone. 'If we weren't at war, would there be people like *him* around?'

Sean followed the nod of his head. A homeless guy was shambling through the crowd. He was ragged and grubby, his clothes betraying a life spent on the streets. The bags he pulled behind him on a broken trolley were his only possessions. By his side a little dog trotted along, attached to him by a lead made from a piece of frayed rope.

'Sure there would,' Sean said, 'because there'll always be rich tossers who don't give a shit.'

Rich stood up abruptly. He clicked his fingers at Malcolm, who slipped his hand inside his jacket and handed over a black wallet. Rich pulled out a thick wad of notes, twenties by the look of it, and handed them to the man with the dog. The homeless guy looked down at them, looked up at Rich, looked back at the money. Rich stepped away deliberately, hands held out as if to disown the cash. The man shuffled off at a surprising speed, the wad magically disappearing before Malcolm could beat him up and take it back again.

Rich returned to his seat. 'Well,' he said softly, 'apparently I'm a rich tosser who does.'

Nice performance, Sean thought. He somehow couldn't see Rich handing out money to every poor guy he passed.

He wondered if he had successfully steered between two mines, or was standing poised with one foot just resting on the trigger mechanism.

'Uh,' he said. He tried again. 'Look, I hope you understand that, well, I've been dicked about by people in authority before. I need to really know that you're different. And unless you're all about free handouts to homeless dudes, I've no idea what you even stand for. I know what you like and what you don't like, but I don't know what your cause is.'

A light flickered in Rich's eyes, like a flame in a furnace. 'Our cause is simple, Harker,' he said. 'To make the public want what we want. A Britain where no decent person has any need to be afraid – but where life is intolerable for those who are not decent. In short, the exact opposite of what we have now. Does that sound so bad?'

No, Sean had to admit, it didn't – not put like that. Not if you didn't know exactly how Rich intended to achieve that aim – through terror and murder.

Rich stood and cast his hands wide to gesture at the whole square. 'This place stands for everything that's wrong with this country. Built to commemorate our greatest ever naval victory, a victory that should have made Britain secure for ever – and now look at it. A tourist trap full of people conned into thinking they are protected, when in reality they are little more than slaves for exploitation, a commodity to be bought and sold on the lies of self-serving politicians!'

He sat down again. 'Picture a million citizens marching on Downing Street, fed up with the terror, wanting only peace and security. Our politicians will be forced to deliver, or face revolution. The military on the streets. Suspension of civil liberties. Democracy restricted to those who have earned the right to vote. That is our cause.'

And that is the real Rich speaking, Sean thought. *Thanks for clearing that up*. Rich's eyes bored deep into his, and he returned the stare. Fortunately he knew how. He'd had practice with meth-crazed psychos back on Littern Mills: stare them down but stay neutral, don't give them anything to latch onto. And Rich was just as crazed – it was just that the stuff turning his brain to scrambled egg was ideas, not drugs. Sean now knew exactly what he was dealing with. Rich was mad. As was anyone who was involved with him and believed his shit.

'Now, I have a task for you,' Rich said, his eyes still on Sean.

'Er – OK?' Sean made himself pay attention. 'You going to give us the next job, then?'

Rich shook his head gently, and smiled like a cat at the mouse whose tail it has just caught under its paw. He nodded to Malcolm, who slid an envelope across the table. Sean opened it and immediately recognised the Monty.

'That,' said Rich, 'is your objective.'

Sean felt his throat dry up as though a hot coal had been forced into his mouth. He had to swallow several times just to get something like words out. 'Objective? How do you mean?'

'I mean what any of your officers would mean if they described something as an objective.'

He let it sink in for a second while Sean stared at the photo.

Shit and fuck. 'Objective' meant 'target'. He was going to be expected to attack this place.

'Consider it a little test of our relationship, to ensure that my trust is not misplaced. Let us not delude ourselves – we both know you became involved in our cause through the desire to make a little more money, not through your deep-seated convictions. Whatever it is that drives you, Sean Harker, I need to know that when I require something of you, you will deliver.'

Sean held up the photo. 'But . . .'

Thank God he had the phone on him. He could feel it in his pocket. He had to find thirty seconds to call up Adams, spill the plan. Once he knew what the hell the plan was.

'Let me describe the rest of the day to you,' Rich was saying. 'You will return to Andover with Malcolm and do as he tells you.' His eyes bored into Sean's. 'No offence. You understand why you must be supervised.'

Sean swallowed. 'Goes without saying,' he croaked.

Rich gave a simple nod of satisfaction. 'Malcolm will escort you to a safe place. At ten p.m. he will take you to the target and provide you with the means for accomplishing your task. It will be well within your skillset. Afterwards – and you have my word on this – responsibility will be claimed by some little-known jihadist group.'

'But . . . soldiers . . .' Sean stuttered. Soldiers were ninety-nine per cent of the Monty's clientele. 'Why? You can't just kill—'

'Our cause must be advanced,' Rich said, eyes burning. 'Remember, the purpose of this is to mobilize our government into action against IS and our other enemies. Soldiers are trained to fight and to die. There will not be one man or woman in that pub who would not lay down their life for their country if their duty called for it, and that is what will happen.'

Sean knew he couldn't refuse. But the Sean they thought he was – the recruited patriot, the East London lad, not the guy forced to work for MI5 – still wouldn't just give in. So this Sean didn't, either.

'I can't . . .'

Rich sighed, and Malcolm slid another envelope towards him. Another photograph.

Sean stared at it. 'This is my—'

'Yes, it's your mother,' Rich confirmed.

She was behind the counter at the shop, passing a bag over to some bloke, no idea that she was the star of her own exclusive photoshoot.

'She too could be an unfortunate victim of the kind of people we're fighting, you know. You've seen the videos these murdering filth like to post. The mother of a serving soldier would really get people talking, wouldn't it?'

Rich stood up. 'I will expect to hear from Malcolm at ten-thirty p.m. – and of course I'll be watching the results on the national news shortly after.'

Malcolm rose to his feet and jerked his thumb. Sean, sick to his stomach, got up to follow him.

Chapter 27

Waterloo Station was heaving with crowds starting to head home at the end of a Saturday in London. If Sean had wanted to give Malcolm the slip, now would have been the time. Problem was, he didn't want to – at least, not permanently. But he had to find some time to send Adams a text. Just one simple little text. How hard could it be?

Answer: harder than it looked. Malcolm was cutting him no slack at all. Since they'd left Trafalgar Square, there had never been more than about a metre between them. Several times Sean's hand went to the phone in his left pocket. Spook phone in his left pocket, own phone in his right. His fingers brushed the smooth screen. And every time he was aware of Malcolm's unwavering gaze on him.

It was twenty minutes until the next Andover train. They lounged by a metal pillar and waited. Without moving his head, Sean could see four or five people on their mobiles. Wouldn't it be natural to take the spook phone out, start using it?

But suppose Malcolm wanted to inspect it? And found exactly one number on it?

Thanks, guys, Sean thought bitterly. MI5 had been just too clever. Why couldn't they have just given him the number to put on his own phone? Eh?

There was only one way he was going to get anything like privacy.

'Going for a slash,' he announced. He set off without giving Malcolm a chance to object. He didn't look back, but he could tell that Malcolm was following him. All the way over to the gents and down the stairs. He even produced his own 30p for the turnstile.

The toilets were hot and crowded and smelled of disinfectant. Sean headed for one of the cubicles. He pushed the door open, stepped in, turned to close the door—

And suddenly it was jammed. Malcolm had his hand on the other side. 'You said a slash.'

'I'm a nervous pisser,' Sean said. 'You going to stand and watch? 'Cos people in public toilets notice when guys do things like that.'

Malcolm took his hand away. Sean pushed the door shut and locked it.

Alone at last, thank God! He had about as long as it

takes to have a normal piss. He pulled out the phone, swiped the screen, and—

NO SIGNAL.

The toilets were underground. Deep enough to cut off electronic signals from outside.

There was nothing he could do about it. Sean flushed and turned towards the door. He hesitated, and then unzipped himself. *Then* he opened the door and zipped himself up again, making sure Malcolm saw the action. He gave his jeans a little tug just to make sure he was in character.

And he washed his hands.

It was a long, silent train ride.

Sean waited twenty minutes into the journey, then stood up. 'I need a piss.'

Malcolm opened his mouth, looked around the crowded carriage, closed it again. But he stood up and followed, as Sean had guessed he would.

There was a bit more privacy outside the compartment. Malcolm put his face close to Sean's and spoke in a low growl. 'You've been once.'

'Could be, you know, I'm just a little bit nervous?' Sean returned his gaze without blinking.

Malcolm nodded. 'This time you're keeping the door open.'

'Bollocks I am,' Sean exclaimed. He stood back to let a mother with two small children push past towards the buffet car. Witnesses, witnesses, lots of lovely witnesses. He let them get a short distance away, and lowered his voice. 'There's words for old guys who like to sneak a look at young guys' dicks. Do you want me to shout some of them out, real loud?'

Malcolm's eyes narrowed, but he considered the point. 'If I hear that door lock, I'm knocking it down. If you're still in there when we get to a station—'

'You're knocking it down,' Sean agreed. 'With you. Orders received loud and clear, strength five. That's Harker, going into the bog and leaving the door unlocked. Shit—'

Malcolm put his hand out to block Sean's way. 'And I'm taking your phone.'

They locked eyes, and then Sean shrugged, delved into his right pocket and pulled out his phone. *His* phone – the one that didn't have anything on it except general stuff and a little porn in the search history. He silently handed it over, and then took pleasure in shutting the door in Malcolm's face.

He called up the one number in the MI5 phone's memory, selected SEND TEXT.

Hit on Monty 2200 tonite dont kno how.

SEND.

The message vanished, replaced by a slowly rotating hourglass and the message, SENDING.

Sean grinned and watched it spin. Any moment . . .

SENDING.

C'mon, c'mon, c'mon . . .

SENDING.

Oh for fuck's sake, send already! he shouted inside his head.

SENDING.

And then he looked at the signal strength. There was half a bar, flickering on and off. What totally crap network did MI5 sign their phones up to? Or was it something to do with the train?

He'd taken as long as it took to pee. Malcolm would be waiting. Sean groaned and shoved the phone back into his pocket. Then he took it out again. Supposing Malcolm searched him? Or just noticed its outline in his pocket?

It wasn't a crime to have two phones, but he would have to delete the message from the log. Except that first the message had to *fucking send itself.*

He looked around, desperately seeking inspiration in the narrow confines of an Intercity 125 toilet. Finally he left it behind the door, on top of the towel dispenser, still bravely trying to send its message. He flushed the bog, washed his hands and opened the door.

The train pulled into Andover and disgorged travellers going home for their Saturday evenings, plus Sean and Malcolm. They shuffled their way through the crowd towards the exit and the car park. Malcolm jerked his head, and they made for a white van parked over to one side. He gave the side door a heave.

'In.'

Sean climbed in nervously and peered about. The rear windows were tinted and there were none at the side, so the interior was dark. He could make out some cushions.

The driver was a man with a shaven head and tree-trunk arms covered in tattoos. He gave Sean a curt nod, then another that was only slightly warmer to Malcolm, who climbed into the passenger seat. The driver gunned the engine and Sean quickly sat down on the cushions as the van lurched into motion.

It had been 18:00 when the train arrived in Andover. The next four hours were the longest of Sean's life, and that was saying something when he thought back to sitting in a police cell waiting to be charged, and his time in solitary.

From the floor of the van he couldn't see where they were going, though he tried to follow the route. They stopped at a McDonald's and Malcolm bought burgers and fries for three. Then they drove off somewhere else to wait.

Sean tried to use his senses to work out where the fuck they were. He was pretty certain he could hear the steady rumble of traffic. Were they near the A303? It was a major dual carriageway a couple of miles south of Tidworth, linking London, the M3 and the West Country – there was always traffic on it. But just being near it didn't narrow it down.

After two hours he heard a car pulling up next to the van, and his ears pricked up. The engine sounded very familiar. Of course, the Matiz was an inexplicably popular vehicle so it could belong to anyone . . .

Malcolm wound his window down. 'You're late.'

Heaton's voice spoke a couple of inches away, heavy with sarcasm. 'Yeah. They've actually got security on these things. Crazy or what?'

'In the back.'

The side door opened with a rush of metal, and Heaton and Sean stared at each other. The corporal was carrying a large, ribbed plastic box, as thick and high as a suitcase but twice as long.

'Guess I don't need to leave instructions, then,' he

murmured. He dumped the box next to Sean and pulled the door shut again. A moment later, the Matiz drove away.

Malcolm turned his head. 'The box. Open it.'

Sean knelt and pulled the box towards him. It was heavy, but nothing he couldn't handle. He reached down and undid two simple clips to open the lid.

Holy shit . . .

Lying in the box was a Carl Gustav AE84-RCL recoilless rifle – what a layman would call an RPG. It was like a short drainpipe, painted light green, with a couple of pistol grips and a trigger, the tip of a rocket just poking its snout out at one end.

Sean hadn't been trained in its use, but he didn't need to be. He knew his way around a weapon well enough. And bearing in mind that these things were meant to be used against tanks wrapped in steel armour inches thick, he could only imagine what it would do to a brick building.

And he had to use it on the Monty or his mum was . . . Well, he didn't want to think about that. At all.

He closed the box again. The driver switched on the radio. After that the two men just sat in the front, waiting. Apparently they were quite prepared to do that for another two hours.

Sean lay back and stared at the roof of the van. In his

mind, that spinning hourglass from the phone was being projected up there. SENDING . . . Had it ever sent? Had MI5 been alerted? Had they had time to do anything about it? Should he have kept the phone on him and tried to send the text later?

The sound of a phone going off in the van's grave-like interior was like the opening chord of a heavy rock gig. Sean spasmed into a sitting position. It wasn't just that a phone had gone off – it was *his* phone.

Malcolm calmly pulled it out of his pocket and looked at the screen. 'Do you usually answer the phone at this time on a Saturday night?'

'Huh? What?' Sean demanded. The question was so ordinary that he had difficulty pulling the brain cells together to answer it.

Malcolm turned and gazed at him. 'It's important that you stick to your usual routine. It's a simple question. Yes or no?'

'Uh – then, yeah. Yeah, I do.'

Malcolm handed the phone over. 'Then answer it.'

Sean reached out for it, already pre-emptively running through excuses in his head for why, no, he couldn't come out on the piss right now. It had to be one of the lads. They would have clocked that he wasn't in barracks.

His eyes bugged out when he saw the name on the screen. 'Mum?' It came out almost like a scream.

'Hi, sweetheart!' Amazingly, she didn't sound like she was about to burst into tears, which was what usually happened when some crisis made her call him. She sounded almost . . . happy. 'I just wanted to thank you for the flowers. They're beautiful.'

'*F-flowers?*'

'*From Sean and all his mates*, it says here.'

There was a few seconds' silence as his mind raced.

'So – what are you up to tonight?' she asked, when he still hadn't said anything.

'Mum . . .' He struggled to think.

The Guyz were sending flowers? Matt and Copper? Come on!

The lads in the platoon? They hardly knew she existed.

The only alternative was . . .

His eyes locked with Malcolm's. The phone wasn't on speaker, but it was quiet enough for the tinny voice to fill the van. The men in front had heard every word.

'Perhaps you should ask if it says anything else,' Malcolm suggested.

And because Sean guessed Malcolm wasn't one to make casual chat, he passed it on, dreading what the answer might be.

'Ooh, hang on . . . Yes, it says, *World's best Mum. We always know where to find you*. It's so sweet, love.'

'Yeah,' he said harshly. 'Gotta go.'

288

'Oh – right – of course. Didn't want to bother you, just—'

He jabbed the screen to end the call.

We always know where to find you. Rich just making his point. He didn't even have to send Malcolm round to do his dirty work. He could send a bomb through the post. Even the Guyz couldn't protect her against that.

Flowers? You shouldn't have. No, really.

He mutely handed the phone back to Malcolm for safekeeping, and went back to waiting.

The icing on the cake was that by the time 22:00 came round, he was bursting for a piss. He hadn't actually been all afternoon.

'It's time,' said Malcolm. Sean looked at his watch as the van started moving again: 21:53. 'Five minutes. Get ready.'

'Right,' Sean replied. He reluctantly lifted the weapon out of the box.

He couldn't even fake missing the pub. Once the van stopped, he would have to open the door, fire, and know that the rocket he had just launched was dead on. Anything else wasn't so much inexcusable as just unbelievable. And Rich, Sean now knew, would not take kindly to the unbelievable.

The van started to slow.

'Two minutes. Put this on.'

Malcolm handed Sean a black balaclava. Even with everything swirling around his head, he could see it made sense. Someone might catch a glimpse of the guy inside the van, might even recognize him.

Sean reluctantly pulled it over his head. The wool was scratchy against his face and it smelled of sweat. Not his.

'Stand by.'

He checked the weapon – not that there was much to check: a basic trigger mechanism and a flip-up iron sight that did little more than get in the way.

He had to do this. He had to trust that the signal had got through – that the phone had finally sent its message, that the spooks had been able to arrange something. He was more in the dark than he had ever been before. He would never have gone into a job with the Guyz with as little information as this. That was how you screwed up; that was what got you arrested. He would have simply refused until Matt or whoever came up with a plan that actually made sense. But now he was in one place at one moment with one job, and he had to do it. *Shit.*

The van slowed and stopped. Malcolm and the driver both pulled on balaclavas of their own and suddenly leaped out. A moment later, both the side door and the rear doors were pulled open. *Of course*, Sean thought. *Got to ventilate the exhaust . . .*

And there was the Monty, right in front of him. They'd pulled up just at the entrance to the car park.

Malcolm was at the side door. 'Now!'

Sean gave himself no time to think, no time to pause. In a smooth move, he had the Carl Gustav on his right shoulder and was staring down it towards the Monty. In the brief seconds between aiming and firing, he noticed the cars outside the pub, the shadows of figures in the windows. Music pulsed faintly from inside. The wind was warm, scented with the remaining heat of the day and something delicious from the pub restaurant.

Sean pulled the trigger.

Chapter 28

The rocket shot out of the end of the launcher like a greyhound from its cage. The backblast filled the interior of the van with fumes, even though all the doors were open. Sparks flew from the rocket as it ignited and gained speed, racing towards the pub.

The doors slammed shut a split second later, so Sean didn't get to see the explosion. It wasn't as dramatic as he had expected – a dull thud, followed by a sort of thumping pop that made the van rock, then the immediate chorus of car alarms set off by the explosion.

A moment later the driver and Malcolm were back in. Sean toppled over as the driver pulled away, and over the noise of the engine he heard the first screams and shouts.

No one said anything else. Sean didn't even stop to ask where they were when they pulled over and Malcolm indicated with a jerk of his thumb that this was where he left them. Once he was out in the fresh air, he recognized that he was a five-minute walk from the main gate. Malcolm silently handed him his phone through the window.

As the van drove off, he dropped to his knees and threw up at the side of the road.

When he got back to barracks, Sean had hoped for solitude – somewhere he could just collapse and make sense of everything. No such luck. He was in a block of single rooms that all opened into a common area. Ravi Mitra and Curtis West were there, watching a movie.

Mitra looked up in alarm at Sean's appearance. 'Shit, you look bad!'

Sean grunted and went into his room, wiped – not from exertion; from the battering his emotions and nerves had taken.

Rich was right – he was trained to kill. He was a soldier. It was what he would be asked to do if necessary, and he would do it well. But what he'd just done had no connection to that. Launching a rocket at a pub on British soil? It was insane. It was unbelievable. There was no way such a thing could ever happen. Except that it had – and he had done it.

Sean wanted to cry, wanted to scream, wanted to kick the living shit out of anything he could, just to let out his rage and confusion.

He became aware of raised voices outside. Fists knocking on doors. Then, after a single cursory knock, his door flew open and Sergeant Adams filled the frame.

'Harker,' he said. He jerked his head towards the common area. 'Outside.' He disappeared immediately, going from door to door to deliver the same message.

Sean slowly got up and went out.

The others from the platoon were filing out to join the ones already there, all obviously wondering what had happened.

'This everyone?' Adams asked. 'Right. There's been an attack on the Monty. Some kind of explosive. I'm just doing my rounds to check names.'

'Oh my God!' Mitra exclaimed.

Sean forced his dry mouth into action. 'Was anyone hurt?'

'Yes. A few.'

Sean closed his eyes and felt his guts clench. He wanted to hurl again.

'All minor,' the sergeant said distinctly. Sean opened his eyes again, not quite believing it. 'The front bar that got taken out was closed for redecorating. Everyone was in the lounge bar at the back. Lucky, eh?' He was looking in Sean's direction, holding his gaze a fraction longer than necessary – long enough for Sean to get it and the others not to notice anything. 'Minor injuries only. You know. The kind of thing we're so good at faking for our exercises. Sounds like a real catastrophe was averted.'

Suddenly Sean had to fight to hold it together. He was nowhere near as good at it as the sergeant. The gush of relief that ran through him was like cool water after a twenty-mile march.

Mitra had switched the TV to a news channel. It was still too soon for pictures, but the basic facts scrolled across the bottom of the screen as breaking news. They painted a grimmer picture than Adams was describing. *Substantial damage . . . Number of casualties unknown . . . Statement expected . . .*

Well, Sean thought, if MI5 were in control of the scene, it stood to reason that they would want to big up the damage as well. Let Rich think it had been a lot more successful than it was.

'Oh, fucking hell!' Mitra exclaimed. 'Clark and then this? What's next?'

Adams patted him on the shoulder. 'Don't fuss yourself, Kama Sutra. The world's a shit place, end of. They hit at us – it just makes us stronger. Right, lads?' But he looked at Sean again as he said it.

'Right!' Sean happily added his voice to the chorus of agreement.

One by one, or talking together in outrage, the platoon dispersed back to their rooms. Adams half turned to go, then came back. He delved into his pocket. 'Oh, Harker, I think you dropped this. Take more care – I'm not your nanny.'

And he handed over the phone. The spooks' phone, retrieved from the train. They must have tracked its signal.

'Wow. Thanks.' Sean took it, slipped it into his pocket. 'I've been looking for it everywhere.'

'Now get some kip,' said the sergeant. 'You look exhausted.'

And with that, he was gone.

Sean went back to his room. Adams was right. He was exhausted, and his relief at the news had simply added to his tiredness. It meant that all the adrenaline that had been keeping him going was no longer needed, so it could just drain away and leave him running on empty.

He fell onto his bed, and his phone – his own phone – buzzed in his right pocket. It was a text from Heaton:

I owe you a drink. Pick you up Tuesday evening 1900.

Sean immediately wanted to be sick again. Trouble was, he had nothing to bring up.

And he still had a job to do. He pulled out the spooks' phone, and called up the text menu.

Chapter 29

Testing, testing . . .

Sean wanted to say the words out loud and hear the reassuring confirmation that he was getting through. The glitch with the phone on the train had dented his confidence in MI5's electronics.

But he was sitting next to Heaton in the Impreza, crawling slowly at the tail end of the evening rush hour, on the way to a rendezvous with madmen. He was being forced to trust again – trust them to have set up the wire correctly, trust himself to have turned it on right.

It was a neat device – a gadget the size of a credit card sewn to the inside of his shirt. The microphone was one of his buttons. It meant that if he got searched – if he had to take his shirt off – then it wouldn't be like the movies where the guy always has trailing leads and an incriminating box taped to his stomach.

But it was still there – it was still discoverable if he got careless. It seemed appropriate that the gadget lay more or less over his heart. Whenever it brushed against his skin and reminded him of its presence, it felt like a great big target saying *Shoot me now.*

Heaton had picked him up as promised, but it hadn't been for a drink. They had headed straight for the A303 and London. Rich had summoned them again.

Heaton had headed for the M25 and they had circled London anti-clockwise before coming off. They were now somewhere near Peckham. After numerous stop-start traffic lights and junctions, Heaton turned into an ordinary-looking light industrial estate. It looked pretty new, with nice shiny metal surfaces to all the units. He drove slowly, looking at the numbers painted on the front faces of the units. There was only one with cars parked up outside, and sure enough that was where he stopped. Sean instinctively scanned the vehicles – a top-of-the-range Jaguar XE, a much more modest Mondeo, and a Yamaha motorbike.

'This is it.' Heaton switched off the engine. 'Front line of the war!'

'You mean,' Sean couldn't help saying, 'front line to a tidy profit.'

Heaton grinned and shrugged. 'Demand's going to shoot up, mate. Someone's got to supply it.'

'What's next, then?' Sean asked as they got out, for the benefit of the microphone. Making casual conversation with Heaton was almost impossible without wanting to simultaneously throw up and kick the shit out of him. But at least trying to gather intelligence made talking easier, and he could only hope it brought forward the time when MI5 had everything they needed to come in with all guns blazing.

He pushed his door shut; the Impreza beeped as it locked itself.

Heaton grinned. 'The big one, Harker. Exciting times.'

The unit had a large sliding shutter for vehicles, now closed up, and a smaller door to one side for people. Sean took a deep breath and followed Heaton through this one.

Inside, the space was occupied by four large, long-wheel-base Transit vans, parked facing the shutter. White, no signage. Beyond them was an office. It shouldn't have surprised Sean, but still his heart sank at the sight of Malcolm waiting outside. The Doberman indicated with a jerk of his head that they should go through.

'Come in, dear lads, come in!' As they entered, with Malcolm hot on Sean's heels, Rich turned away from two other men.

Sean stopped dead when he saw who the company was. They stood there with big grins on their faces and

Sean wanted to kill them both, even while he went into acting mode and shook Rich's outstretched hand.

'I believe you know these two gentlemen?'

'Copper. Matt,' Sean said with a nod. He wanted to say more. He wanted to say, *What the fuck do you think you're doing getting involved in this bullshit?* and *Are you fucking mental?* and lots of other stuff too. He wanted to lay into them, beat the crap out of them, kick them out of the unit and all the way back to the petty crime that kept them occupied back on their own turf.

'Surprise, hey, Seany?' said Copper, and gave him a big-man hug that almost cracked a rib.

Matt gave him a fist bump. Sean nodded, still fighting the urge to punch their faces for being such tossers.

'If Gaz could see us now, eh?' Matt murmured with a wink, and Sean had to stuff his fists into his pockets so that the urge to use them didn't overwhelm him.

'Yeah,' he managed to say.

'Good, good,' said Rich. 'Shall we get on?'

'Sure,' Sean said. 'Tell us about the big one.'

Rich cocked an eyebrow at him and he froze inside, keeping the smile plastered on his face. Oh, shit, had that been too eager? Had he aroused suspicions?

'All in good time.' Rich waved a hand over to one corner of the unit. There was a screen there, and a pile of DVDs, and some bean bags. 'For the moment – food will be arriving shortly and there is enough there to keep you gentlemen entertained for the night. You will be sleeping here. Tomorrow is, as Mr Harker puts it, the big one.'

'Yeah, but what is it?' Matt asked. Now he was the recipient of the cocked eyebrow.

'It is something that will cause terror and chaos stretching far beyond London itself. This will be world news. The media frenzy will be enormous. People will at last realize that they are not safe at home. They will demand changes. I'm not talking about a revolution – nothing so grand. Just sensible laws to protect law-abiding folk and suppress undesirables. A little less democracy and considerably more investment in our armed forces. Soldiers on the streets to protect us.'

'Hey, Sean,' Matt said, 'you might get to be a useful member of society after all!' He and Copper high-fived each other.

Why? Sean wanted to shake them and scream the question in their faces, though he could already have a go at guessing the answers. Heaton – for the profit and for himself, like he had just said. Copper – because he was messed up and this was messed up, and people who weren't him would suffer and die. But Matt? Matt had always had a calmer head than Copper. Copper must have recruited him and made him think that there was

301

something in it for the Guyz. In the world that Rich wanted to create, the Guyz could fly high.

'Before we go any further,' Rich said, 'I believe Mr Harker has a phone call to make?'

Suddenly it was like the air conditioning had come on, full blast. Sean felt the blood drain from his face and the moisture from his mouth.

Fuckity-fuckity-fuck-fuck-fuck . . .

'I do?' he whispered. He barely made any sound, and he had to cough and force volume out of his throat for another try. 'I do?'

He was conscious of five pairs of eyes all trained on him like lasers. How did they know about the phone? And if they knew, how was he still alive?

'You will all be spending the night here,' Rich said, as though explaining something to a child. 'You can't just go AWOL from the army – they will ask questions. Corporal Heaton has already booked a day's leave for tomorrow, on my instructions. But you need to call the adjutant and tell him that your mother has been taken ill, so you need to request emergency leave.'

The sheer gush of relief made Sean's heart thump so loudly that he wondered no one could hear it. It was backed up by an equally strong surge of revulsion at the thought of spending the night with these crazies. But there was nothing he could do about it. MI5 wouldn't pick this lot up until they absolutely knew what was going down. Until that happened, he was still in it.

'Uh. Yeah.' He smiled faintly. 'I'll make the call now.' He pulled away, stepped out of the office and into the dim interior of the unit. Took two or three deep breaths. The air tasted of plastic and petrol, but it still seemed cleaner than what he'd been breathing.

He sensed rather than heard a noise behind him. Malcolm stood in the doorway, watching. He silently extended a single finger and pointed to where Sean was standing. It was an obvious message that he was to go no further.

So Sean pulled out the spooks' phone and dialled, with a friendly smile at his watcher. It rang twice, and then he heard the unmistakable voice of Sergeant Adams on the other end.

'Yes?'

'Uh. Hi. This is Private Harker.' Sean rattled off his army number, and gave Malcolm another smile. 'I need to speak to the adjutant's office. It's an emergency . . .'

Chapter 30

It was a long, long night spent on a mat on the warehouse floor. Sleep wouldn't have been easy even if Sean hadn't been surrounded by murderers who wouldn't think twice about offing him if they knew the truth. There was still speculation about what they were doing here – though Sean had twigged one thing. Four vans, four of them. That had to mean something.

Rich had disappeared before they turned in, and Sean actually found himself wishing he hadn't. His absence meant that Malcolm was in charge.

But sleep did come, and it came so deeply that when they were kicked out of bed at 05:30, all Sean really wanted to do was stay in his sleeping bag – sleep in and pretend that none of this was happening.

Except that he couldn't. They all stirred blearily and stumbled into life, knocking back coffee and pizza which Malcolm provided. And far too soon they were lining up beside the vans, awaiting instructions. Sean had guessed right – they were drivers.

Malcolm handed out four plastic envelopes: Sean, then Copper, Matt and Heaton. Each one had a CD in it.

'These are your orders,' he said. 'You will each take one of these vans. Your destinations are in the satnavs – just follow directions. Play your CD when you are in your van. Stick to the schedule. Arrive when you've been told to arrive, leave by the route you're given.'

With nothing left to say, Sean gave a nod to the others, then climbed into one of the waiting vans. He couldn't see whatever was in the back as it was blocked off from the driving compartment.

Time to go. Malcolm thumbed a button on the warehouse wall that made the shutter rise up to reveal the early sun of a September morning. Sean fired up his engine and, one by one, the vans began to roll out. Sean was third. He gave the last driver, Heaton, a nod, and put the vehicle into gear.

The little convoy trundled slowly off the industrial estate, picking up speed until they could pull onto the main road. The van handled slowly and heavily. Whatever was in the back weighed a lot.

'OK,' Sean said loudly, for the benefit of the wire he was wearing. 'Playing the CD now.' He pushed it into the slot on the dashboard and waited. A moment later, an artificial-sounding voice filled the cab. Sean guessed the instructions had been typed into a computer's voice synthesizer. There was nothing here that would link it to Rich.

'*Your satnav is taking you to the southern entrance of the Blackwall Tunnel. Arrive at 06:55. Enter the tunnel. Halfway along, at the deepest point, pull the van over across both lanes to block the traffic flow. Abandon the van and proceed northward on foot. The van will explode at 07:00 hours.*'

Sean's eyes went wide. There was a *bomb* in the back? He had been assuming it would be another Monty job. Suddenly he fancied he could feel its malevolent presence lurking behind the bulkhead. The van hit a slight bump in the road and he stifled a scream.

And, of course, Sean thought, remembering what MI5 had told him, it would all be pinned on non-existent IS supporters.

The voice was continuing:

'*In the meantime, please note that the device is attached to a GPS tracking mechanism. If this vehicle diverts from the intended route, it will explode. I apologize for this necessary precaution. I look forward to seeing you again, and to thanking you in person.*'

Well, fuck all this – this was right off his pay grade.

Adams and MI5 would have heard all that on the wire, but they couldn't talk back to him. Sean grabbed the spooks' phone and dialled, then drove single-handed with it pressed to his ear.

Adams answered almost at once.

'You'd best have a plan, Sergeant,' Sean said, 'because I'm all out of ideas.'

The screen of the satnav showed him the route he was taking. At the moment he was crawling along steadily towards the A2 south circular. ETA at the tunnel now just under forty minutes.

'We're working on it.' A pause, with murmured voices in the background. Adams was not alone. Sean tried to imagine him sitting with the spooks, who were channelling all that precious information where it needed to go. 'Keep going. Please confirm that there was no hint of where the targets for the other vans are.'

'Nope. No idea.'

'OK. Each of you has a drone tracking him from above – pisses off Heathrow no end, but that's their problem. We're projecting along the routes the other three are taking for likely targets so we can intercept them. The Bomb Squad are scrambling as we speak.'

'OK, cool. What about me? Just give me directions where I can hand this over to the Bomb Squad and I'll be fine.'

More muted conversation.

'You're not to divert from the given route, Sean. You heard the instructions about the GPS.'

Oh, shit. Adams had called him Sean, not Harker. Oh *shit* – that had to be bad. You only started to be nice to someone if you weren't optimistic about their prospects.

'Well, fine, I'll RV with the Bomb Squad wherever. And do me a favour and keep calling me Harker, Sergeant. Please?'

A pause.

'Harker it is. Of course. Right, listen up. You proceed as per satnav instructions. Our friends are staging a traffic jam. They've hacked into some traffic lights, set them permanently on red. Any moment now the traffic you're in will snarl right up. You'll grind to a dead halt.'

Oh, great . . . Sean thought. Stuck in traffic with the bomb going *tick-tick-tick*?

'And that's where the Bomb Squad meet me, right?'

A pause.

'Negative. That's where you defuse the bomb.'

The sergeant's last sentence floated alone for just a little too long.

'Excuse me, please – what? Could you repeat that, please?'

'You will have to defuse the bomb. We don't have enough EOD personnel to handle four simultaneous targets. You're our man on the ground. We have Captain Fitzallen here, who'll guide you through it. She reckons it'll be pretty easy – probably just a timer attached to a shitload of fertilizer.'

'You're kidding me, right?'

'No,' said Adams. 'I am definitely not kidding you. This is our only option.'

The traffic on the A2 ahead was starting to slow.

'I've never defused a bomb.'

'Then now's your chance to learn,' said the sergeant. 'As soon as the traffic stops, get in the back of the van, tell us what you see. Understood?'

Sean didn't reply as, almost on cue, the road snarled up. Drivers up and down the highway started to vent their frustration in the only way they could: with the car-horn symphony.

Sean jumped out of the driver's seat and ran down the side of the van. A man in a BMW yelled at him to 'Get back in your van, you dick, or you'll just make this worse,' but Sean ignored him. Insults he could take. Explosions, not so much.

He fumbled on the keyring for the key to the rear doors, and pulled them open. And there, innocent as anything, was the bomb.

'F-u-u-ck . . .'

Two rows of waist-high blue plastic tubs, filling the

rear of the van. He remembered Captain Fitzallen's briefing. *Two hundred kilograms of explosive . . . killed thirty people . . . two hundred bags of sugar.*

This was a lot more than two hundred bags of sugar.

Even as his eyes continued to scan it, Sean was back on the phone. Taped to the nearest one with high-quality gaffer tape was a black box with an LCD counter, and a grey slab the size of a phone that Sean immediately recognized as PE – plastic explosive. The counter showed the current time – half past. A black tube was embedded in the explosive, joined to the box by a couple of wires.

'I've found it. Not that it was difficult to miss.'

'OK,' the sergeant replied. 'I'm passing you on to the captain now. Do exactly as you're told.'

There was scuffling down the line.

'Private Harker?' The voice was clipped and professional.

'Yep – uh, yes, uh, ma'am,' Sean replied.

'Under the circumstances, call me Fitz. OK, this is going to be fun. We usually do this in threes and we're all experts. Tell me what you can see.'

Sean described exactly what was in front of him, down to the box and the PE.

'Good,' said Fitz. 'That will be what we have to deal

with. I need you to take a photograph of it now and send it to me.'

Sean flicked up the camera and took a snap.

A yell came from behind him. 'What do you think you're doing taking photos?'

Sean turned round to see a pretty fit woman in a pretty fit soft-top sports car. 'Sorry,' he said, and sent the photograph.

'Sorry?' she exclaimed. 'You're blocking the road! If the traffic starts to move, *you* won't be able to! Get back in your van!'

Sean turned his back on her, the phone to his ear. 'Well?'

'Piece of piss,' Fitz said. 'The black box will be both the timer and the power supply. That thing in the plastic explosive is the detonator. At the chosen time the timer will send a spark down those wires – and *boom!* That looks like some hard-core tape holding everything in place but the wires are unshielded, so they are what we deal with. You'll need to cut one of them. Either will do. Do you have any kind of knife?'

'Sure.' Sean's penknife was in his hand in a moment. He put the phone onto speaker, set it down, and put the blade to the nearest wire. 'Hang on, I'll do it now—'

'*Wait, wait, wait!*' Sean froze. 'I didn't say you

shouldn't take precautions. Cut one without them and there's a chance of a spike in the other.'

And *bang*, Sean guessed. He slowly withdrew the blade.

'I want you to strip down the two wires to bare metal and then twist the two together. That will act as a shunt, so any current from the power source just goes round the circuit and misses the detonator. *Then* you can cut the wire.'

Sean forced a laugh. 'Sure. Shit, I never knew defusing a bomb was like twoccing a car.'

'I have no idea what you're talking about but I'll assume it's all good.'

'Yeah, keep thinking that.'

It took thirty seconds to peel off two inch-long lengths of plastic from the wires. Sean looked at what was in front of him. This was nothing like James Bond. He had no clever gadgets – not even a pair of pliers – just some advice down a phone line while angry commuters yelled at him, unaware of the fact that he was actually trying to prevent them from being blown into a billion tiny pieces. Nearby he heard the sound of a motorbike choking into silence.

Sean took a deep breath. 'Right, I'm going to do it.'

He was aware of someone coming up behind him. He hoped it was the fit woman seeing what he was doing.

Maybe she'd be impressed once she learned what he was up to.

'Be with you in a moment . . .' he said, and twisted the two wires together—

Something clobbered him over the head and dropped him to the ground like a sack of coal.

Chapter 31

Sean opened his eyes just in time to see a booted heel coming down on his face. He rolled out of the way and onto his feet. Dizziness threatened to take him back down and he clung onto the van for support.

His attacker he recognized immediately. He wore a leather biker's jacket and a helmet, but there was no mistaking the eyes that glared through the visor.

'Malcolm? What are you doing here?'

'I never trusted you,' Malcolm stated flatly. 'The day of your test, you shut a door in my face twice. So I followed you.'

'And now?'

For an answer, Malcolm pulled a Glock from inside his bike jacket. He cocked it as he walked right up to Sean and placed the muzzle against his head.

'Whoa!' Sean shouted. He staggered back, hands held high. 'You can't just slot me in broad daylight! Witnesses!'

He looked desperately at the fit woman. She was on her phone now, unaware that anything was going on.

Malcolm glanced around. 'And what will the witnesses see? A vigilante hero whom they can't identify stopping a bomber—'

Sean went for the gun. He knew the move. It had worked on that loan shark Ricky like a textbook exercise.

Malcolm hadn't read the textbook. He simply tightened his grip on the pistol, and it remained glued to his hand, even though Sean strained at it. Then, slowly, he began to bend Sean's arm back. Sean redoubled his efforts, both hands trying to keep the gun hand away.

The Doberman started to move forward, and Sean was being pushed back into the van. The nearest tub dug in below his shoulder blades, and he felt himself bending backwards, further and further. They stared into each other's eyes over a distance of inches. Malcolm's were emotionless, showing as much interest as Sean might when he swatted a mosquito. Then Malcolm brought his free arm up and pressed it into Sean's throat. Sean's head was pinned against the lid of the tub. He heard his breath start to gurgle under the intolerable pressure. Cut off the air to his lungs, cut off the blood to his brain – either would work. Dark spots started to dance in front of his eyes.

Through the roaring in his ears he could hear voices.

'Should we call the police?'

'Oh my God, I think he's killing him . . .'

The witnesses who hadn't bothered Malcolm were hanging back, not quite daring to intervene.

Sean was too weak to keep both hands on the gun now. His right hand slipped off, so he used it to try and lever Malcolm's visor open, claw at those cold, dead eyes. Malcolm simply shifted his head slightly and kept pressing. Sean's arm flopped down. He just had the strength to keep pushing at something, anything – whatever he could reach, which was now Malcolm's groin.

OK, let's really put a stop to you . . .

He clenched his fist and punched.

Malcolm trembled, and grunted, and the pressure on Sean's throat eased slightly – just enough to let him take in a huge, wheezing breath. But he kept squeezing. Malcolm's jaw clenched, and shudders ran through his body.

Sean punched again, and again. Malcolm's shudders grew worse, and suddenly he let go of Sean's neck altogether. Which meant that Sean could get a proper grip. He yanked down as hard as he possibly could.

Malcolm screamed and doubled over. Sean grabbed at the Glock and successfully twisted it out of Malcolm's hands. Before Malcolm could straighten up, he kicked as hard as he could against the side of his helmet. Malcolm staggered backwards and Sean straightened up, holding the gun in the approved manner, both hands on the grip, arms straight, feet apart, looking straight over the sights at his attacker.

'Stay down, Malcolm, or—'

And then there was a knife in Malcolm's hand, and he was running at Sean with an animal howl.

Sean fired, twice, the gun jumping in his hand. Red flowers blossomed in Malcolm's chest, and he crumpled like a puppet whose strings had been cut, dead before he even hit the ground.

People screamed, and Sean was dimly aware of a rapidly clearing area around him as the witnesses fled the killer with the gun. Well, that was one way to do it. For a moment he looked at the body of the first man he had ever killed in cold blood. Then he coughed and rubbed his throat, trying to get his breathing back to normal.

He picked up the phone. 'Still there?' He tried to make his voice sound normal, but he knew it was shaking. What he had just done – there was no way of making it cool or clever, like on TV. It had been a matter of survival. It could just as well have been him lying there dead.

'Still here.' Fitz's voice was a little less dispassionate than before. Presumably everyone had been watching the show via the drone. 'Did you twist the wires together?'

'Yup.'

'Then cut one of the wires between detonator and shunt.'

Sean put down the gun, picked up the penknife. 'Doing it now.'

He put the blade to the wire – and paused.

Was this it? What nearly eighteen years of mostly wasted life came down to? And just when he had started to make good. Again.

He cut the wire as directed.

Adrenaline surged through his body as it realized that it was still alive. He threw back his head and yelled: '*OH – FUCK – YEAH!*'

Then he sagged against the tubs.

Adams was back on the line. 'Excellent. Well done.'

'Sheer fucking A!' Sean shouted in agreement.

'No, fucking Z. Our friends raided the warehouse and found evidence of five – repeat *five* – bombs having been made.'

Sean felt all the energy drain out of him, leaving him with his battered mind and body. 'So where's the fifth?'

'Exactly.'

'Oh. Shit.' Sean sagged against the van. 'But . . . there were only four drivers, and Malcolm's here . . . So that just leaves . . .'

'Maybe he actually wants to get his hands dirty for

once. Press the button on his own pet project.' A pause
while Adams spoke to someone away from the phone.
'The other vans all seem to be heading for destinations
around the City, so that's where they'll concentrate their
search. But it's not your problem, Harker.' Adams was
back to his normal self, a sergeant addressing a private.
'If it blows, it blows. You've done your bit. You need to
stay there until the cops and the Bomb Squad arrive. We
can't leave that thing unattended. And right now the
police are responding to calls from the public about a
lunatic with a van and a gun, so put it away and wait
with your hands on your head. You're standing over a
dead body, so don't give the Met's finest the slightest
excuse to plug you, because it's all they'll need. Just let
them nick you, don't say a word, and we'll come and
get you.'

Sean breathed out heavily. 'Sure. No probs.' He wasn't
going to argue about the injustice of getting nicked for
being a hero. He stuffed the gun into his trousers, aware
that he was aiming a weapon directly at his balls – really,
really hoping that his instructors were right when they
said that a Glock was knock-proof and would only ever
fire if you actually pulled the trigger – hence, no safety
catch. Then he plonked his arse down on the rear step of
the van, linked his fingers on top of his head, and waited.
The sound of sirens tickled his ears. They would take a

while to get through. Well, he had all the time in the world.

He stared at the rows of empty cars in front of him, glanced down at Malcolm's body, and quickly looked away again. 'Yeah, you're welcome,' he said to the sports car belonging to the fit woman.

Fuck that fifth bomb . . .

Something clattered next to him and he jumped. His senses still hadn't quite come down from their high alert. He quickly checked the bomb. Nothing had changed . . .

No – something *had*. A small plastic rectangle lay on the floor of the van beside him. He picked it up and found that he was holding the display from the black box.

Eh?

He peered closely at the box. There was a glistening rectangle where the display had been stuck. He looked at it again, and his heart thudded.

It was just the display off some pocket calculator, stuck onto the box. It had nothing to do with what was in the box at all.

'*Fuck!*' he bellowed, and grabbed the phone.

Fitz answered even before it started ringing. 'What? What's the matter?'

'It's a fucking fake, that's what . . .' Sean trailed off, then leaned forward and peered between the barrels.

Right at the front of the van, where he would never be able to get at it without moving everything else, just behind the bulkhead, inches from where he had been sitting as he drove . . .

'There's another timer. And—'

It hit him in the guts like a blow. 'It's set to ten minutes early! Oh-six-fifty! What's the time now?'

Suddenly he didn't want to look at his watch.

And now he knew that Rich had never planned for any of the drivers to survive. They were all meant to die. Didn't matter if they hadn't quite made their destinations. They would still be surrounded by traffic; it would still be carnage. The press would call them suicide bombers, which would just strengthen the alleged link with IS. It was brilliant. It was brutal. And it was only minutes away.

'Get out!' Fitz snapped. 'Get out of there now!'

Sean was already running, weaving between the abandoned cars.

What else had Fitz said back in that lecture? It was nagging at him. Something else about the Omagh bomb . . .

Deaths were mostly caused by the supersonic shockwave of the blast, and the distribution of shrapnel . . .

Shit. He couldn't outrun either of those. But he could shelter. There had to be a good ten cars between him and the van now.

He flung himself to the ground behind a Volvo estate, skidding on his front on the rough tarmac just as the sky seemed to split open and a deep, roaring boom shook every cell in his body. He lay there, dazed, confused, as dust and debris came raining down. Somehow he knew that his body was in tremendous pain. It told him this, but it wasn't letting him feel it. All the noise – car alarms, screams, a torrent of horror and confusion – was parked a safe distance away too, where his brain could register it but didn't have to listen.

He coughed, as pain and noise slowly came back to their normal levels. His fingers brushed against bits of glass, shattered into tiny diamonds. Slowly he pushed himself onto his hands and knees and looked back. The van was a dark skeleton, consumed by flame, belching thick black smoke. The vehicles on either side and in front and behind weren't much better. Others further down the road were slight improvements. They were only write-offs.

Sean dragged himself to his feet, leaning against the Volvo. His body felt like one big bruise. The sirens were nearer. The emergency services would be here soon. Cool, they could deal with it.

But first he could report in. He felt for the spooks' phone. It rattled. He held it up to his head and shook it. Definitely rattling. Plus the screen was starred and cracked. It was in worse shape than he was – he wouldn't be making any more calls on that.

'OK,' he said out loud. There was still the wire. 'This is Harker, checking in. Hope you're getting this.' He felt for the button that was the wire's microphone, and something gave beneath his fingers. He stared down at it in horror. The plastic was smashed. As he watched, the button fell off, and he felt the loose wire tickle against his skin inside his shirt.

'Oh, crap . . .'

Wondering what to do, he got out his own phone, which seemed to be undamaged – but with the other phone out of action he realized he no longer had the number he needed. He put his hands up on his head again as he thought. The Met would be in an even worse mood now that one of the bombs had gone off. He leaned against the Volvo and sighed. Was it just the one bomb? he wondered. He didn't know. Maybe they had got to bombs two, three and four in time . . .

But there was still that *fucking fifth bomb. Fuck* Rich. He might have known. Nothing was simple. Not in the head of someone like that. He remembered that meeting in London. The signs had been there – the way it took just a few words for Rich to morph from calm and collected to twisted crackpot. *This place stands for everything that's wrong with this country . . .*

Sean stared into the distance. That had to be it. It just had to be. Trafalgar sodding Square . . .

Unless Trafalgar Square was already one of the locations . . .

But Adams had said that it looked like everyone was heading for the City. The financial district – the Bank of England, Lloyds, rich multinationals. It meant that at some point they had all turned northwards to cross the river, probably at Tower Bridge or London Bridge.

Trafalgar Square was west of all that, and if Sean was heading to Trafalgar Square from Peckham then that was the direction he would head. He would cross the Thames at Westminster Bridge, or Waterloo.

So Trafalgar Square had not been the destination of any of the others. It *had* to be Rich's target.

Sean looked at his phone again. How was he going to report this? He thought of just dialling 999 – but would anyone take him seriously? They certainly wouldn't put him through to the spooks . . .

No – he had to get to Trafalgar Square himself. He stuffed the phone in his pocket and began to run from car to car, checking doors, looking for one that still had keys in.

But . . .

He squinted back up the road. None of these cars would be going anywhere. Shit! He needed something that could get through this jam. A bike . . .

Malcolm had been wearing bike leathers.

Sean ran back to the wreckage of the van, which was still blazing away. He hadn't noticed the bike, but he remembered hearing it . . .

And there it was, lying on its side two cars away from the van. The cars had taken the force of the blast and the bike was still intact – a Yamaha Fazer FZ1, smooth black metal lines wrapped around a 998cc engine. It was the one he had seen outside the warehouse. He laughed, remembering the Kawasaki Ninja that had got him into all this trouble in the first place, the night he was caught by the police. Perhaps this one would actually get him *out* of trouble.

He picked up the bike and found the key still in the ignition. He turned it as he swung himself into the saddle and the engine shuddered into life.

It throbbed impatiently as Sean weaved his way between abandoned vehicles, until at last he was clear and the road ahead was empty. He leaned forward, throttled up, and the bike surged forward. Now all he had to do was remember the way.

He pulled left onto the A2, leaning over so that his knee almost brushed the ground. The bike raged and roared beneath him as he hurled it westwards, the opposite way to the route he had been taking to the Blackwall Tunnel.

Traffic crawled along. He hurled himself between gaps and through spaces that looked like they wouldn't have taken a moped. Somehow the cars managed to get out of the way.

Did they still have the drone on him? He hoped so. They might guess where he was going and get there first. Or maybe give orders to any cops to keep out of his way.

Trafalgar Square. Trafalgar Square. If he thought it hard enough, would they work it out?

Through Elephant and Castle, running the red lights, hurtling round the roundabout, cutting off any cars that even thought about having right of way. By now the cops must have been alerted – maniac on a Yamaha, heading west. But what were they going to do? They would never catch him in a car. And if any bike cops gave chase – well, the more the merrier. He would lead them to Rich.

He pointed the bike up towards Lambeth, and almost hit the brakes as he rode slap bang into roadworks blocking the way. With a spin of the rear wheel out to his right, Sean heaved the bike out of the road and onto the pavement. He forced himself to slow down just enough to allow pedestrians to throw themselves out of the way. Most of them had the sense to do just that. Some tried to knock him off, but by the time they reached for him he was already gone.

Past the back end of Waterloo and onto Westminster

Bridge, the Houses of Parliament gleaming in the early daylight on the far bank. The Big Ben clock said it was just coming up to 7:30. He took the interchange into Whitehall completely the wrong way, cutting straight across the right turn rather than politely going all the way round Parliament Square.

And there was Trafalgar Square – Nelson's Column marking the spot at the far end of Whitehall. Sean blazed up the final stretch, past grand, austere government buildings, and the rest of the square slowly came into view. There was no sign of emergency vehicles, which was good and bad. Good, because if the fifth bomb was here, it hadn't gone off yet. Bad because his unseen watchers hadn't guessed where he was heading. He was on his own.

He went across the junction at the end, taking the direct route almost to the base of Nelson's Column. With a dramatic skid that wasn't exactly planned, he pulled the bike up and was off it in a single movement, scanning the area.

It was 7:30 in the morning – the only people around were the ones walking to work. Nothing like as packed as it had been when he was here with Rich. Of course, no one was getting involved. Sean got some sideways looks, but that was all.

But they were still *there*. If a bomb like the one in the

van went off right now, it would take forty, fifty people with it – the blast and the shrapnel cutting right across the open space like a giant blade.

If it was here. Sean couldn't see any stationary vans. He leaped onto the base of Nelson's Column, clambering up to the topmost ledge, eyes scanning all around for any sign. Where . . . ?

A ringing sound caught Sean's attention, though at first he didn't register what it was. Then he recognized the tune. It was his phone. He put it to his ear. Had Adams tracked him down? he wondered. He pulled it out.

'Yup?'

'*Hello, Sean.*'

It was the same synthesized voice that had given the instructions on the CDs.

'Don't do it!' Sean yelled. 'These are innocent people!'

There was a pause. Wherever he was, Rich must be inputting the words in real time.

'*There is no such thing as innocent people,*' the voice said flatly. Another pause. '*You know about the fifth bomb and you are alive. Therefore you have betrayed me.*'

'It's over,' Sean said. It was all he could think of. 'Give up.'

'*The bomb was set for later in the day when the square*

is busier.' Pause. *'Perhaps I should set it off now. What do you think?'*

Sean looked around frantically. 'Where are you?'

'They do not teach observation in the army, then.'

'Eh?'

'How many homeless people have you ever seen with an iPad?'

What?

Sean scanned the square again – and then he had it. Sitting at the bottom of the grand flight of stone steps leading up to the National Gallery. An old tramp, baggy hat pulled down over his face; long, shapeless coat; nothing that could be picked up off CCTV tapes. He could probably ditch the outfit in seconds and become the well-dressed white guy no one paid any attention to.

And he had one hand tucked inside his coat. The other held the coat slightly open, just enough for him to peer in and see what he was doing. The man glanced up at Sean from under the brim of his hat, and pulled the coat open a fraction of an inch. Sean just had a moment to catch the light of a screen before it disappeared again.

The robot voice continued. *'I'm going to turn and walk away. Once I'm safely sheltered I will detonate the bomb. You can come and get me. You can run for shelter. Or you can stay and find the bomb. Your choice.'*

Without looking back, the tramp stood up and shuffled off.

He was two hundred metres away. Sean would never catch him in time. And at this range he would never get him with the Glock. He swore loudly, and scanned the area again in desperation, looking for a clue, any clue.

And then he realized that it was literally right in front of him: the fake vintage van coffee stand, surrounded by metal chairs. It had been moved to the right, in front of the Column. The perfect place to cause as much damage as possible.

Sean ran over and tugged at the door. It was locked. He went round to the front. The shutter was down, the whole thing sealed off – and it was easily big enough to carry the same kind of load as he'd had in the Transit.

This had to be it.

'There's a bomb!' Sean shouted. He waved his hands frantically. 'A bomb! Get away!'

All he got was some odd looks. Fuck, what did it take? Last time he'd had to shoot a guy . . .

Inspiration struck. Sean pulled out the Glock, cocked it, waved it above his head. 'Run! Now! There's a bomb!'

A few bystanders shuffled into something a little more urgent. But still no one was really shifting. He was going to have to fire the thing. That was what had got them going before.

Fire it where? He couldn't loose off rounds in a crowded city and not hit someone – not even into the air. They would come down somewhere. The only thing he could think of that would absorb the shots was the coffee stand, and he wasn't going to fire at something that might explode.

And then he had it. He ran over to one of the fountains, leaped up onto the balustrade, and fired two shots into the water. '*Bomb! Bomb!*'

He fired again.

And now people were moving. They began to scatter, slowly at first, then faster and faster, screaming as the panic spread. Sean fired again. Then he ran over to the other fountain, and repeated the performance. Everyone fled, shrieking, as he approached. The square was finally clearing.

Would that stop Rich blowing it?

He couldn't risk it. Rich was only giving him this chance to toy with him – give him the impossible choice of trying to save people, or saving his own skin. He would want to make whatever grand, final gesture he could – his way of saying, *Fuck you all*. Meanwhile Sean was now a target for any Met officer with a gun of his own. This close to Whitehall and Downing Street, there would be plenty of them around.

Well, I'm a soldier. We lay down our lives if we have to.

He fancied he could already feel the laser sights dancing on his chest. On his back. Anywhere. But he fired until the gun was empty. The area was clear; there was nothing more that he could do.

How long had that all taken? Thirty seconds? A minute? He had to be out of time. His shoulders sagged as he looked around. The edges of the square seemed to recede as the empty space grew bigger. He had to get across it, out of the bomb's range. Oh, fucking hell, couldn't he just lie down and rest . . . ?

He sighed, and started to run. Met marksman or bomb blast, one of them would probably get him, but he was fucked if he was just going to lie down and take it.

The world lit up . . .

Chapter 32

The third time Sean woke up, he could speak and think.

The first time: bright lights, whiteness blinding him. A human shape. A nurse, telling him to rest, gently pushing him back as he struggled to get up; he was trying to explain that he didn't need a fucking rest, he needed to fucking get out there and fucking stop the fucking-fuck-Rich-Malcolm-bike-bomb-coffee-ow-don't-stick-a-needle-in-my-arm-you-cow . . .

The second time, the white lights began to fade, going down to grey, other colours edging in, forming shapes. A room with white walls, furniture that had seen better days, a television high up. A nurse at the end of his bed, reading his notes. It had to be the infirmary at Burnleigh. Funny, he didn't remember having an accident. Then he frowned. Burnleigh – hadn't there been other stuff in his life since then? Something had happened, but he couldn't remember so it probably wasn't important. The nurse looked fit. He would ask her the next time he woke up . . .

The third time, he recognized the person dozing in the chair next to his bed.

'Mum . . .' he croaked. His throat was dry as dust.

She was awake in a moment. 'Sweetheart! Darling! Here . . .' She held his head up so he could take a long sip of water out of a straw in a bottle. Then she pinched his cheek. 'And, happy birthday! Eighteen today! My little boy.' Her face fell. 'Oh, love, I was so worried—'

Eighteen? Where was he? How long had he been out for?

'What happened?'

'There was an explosion in Trafalgar Square,' she said. 'What were you doing in Trafalgar Square? If you were in town, you could have come and seen me.'

'Explosion?'

'Oh . . . yes . . . Doctor says you got hit by a . . . flying metal chair? Concussion and bruises, nothing too serious, they say. Nothing too serious, my arse! If it knocks my little boy out, then that's what I call serious. I'll go and let the nurse know you're awake. Oh, and here's your friend. I'll let you two have a chat.' She leaned forward and whispered into his ear. 'Bit of all right, isn't he?'

Sean frowned, still trying to remember. Trafalgar Square . . . something really important . . .

And then, like it had just been uploaded into his memory, it all came back. Not just Trafalgar Square, but what he had been doing there.

'Mum!' Sean said suddenly. He clutched feebly at her arm and fought back the panic. 'Don't go . . .' He couldn't see round her to make out who this friend was. It was Rich, had to be, come to pay him back. He would only need a few seconds, and Sean would be completely helpless . . .

But his mum had moved away, out of the room, and he recognized the visitor.

'Sergeant?' he said in surprise.

They gazed at each other. Adams had a large envelope and a newspaper under his arm.

'Well, you remember me, at least,' he said finally. 'Do you remember this?'

He unfolded the newspaper. It was the *Evening Standard*, and the front page read: MASSIVE EXPLOSION IN TRAFALGAR SQUARE.

'I kind of missed the moment it went bang,' Sean said weakly. And he was eighteen today – which meant he had been out for three days. 'Why aren't I dead?'

Adams flicked the paper open and scanned through it. '*Blah, blah, blah . . . unnamed member of the Special Forces* – and do not let that go to your head, laddie, because I promise you it no longer applies – *who was believed to have been in the blast shadow of Nelson's Column, was taken to . . .'* He folded the paper with a flat smile. 'So, shockwave couldn't get you, but never underestimate the range of a flying metal chair.'

'Ha. Funny.' Sean frowned. Even that made his head hurt, but he knew there were gaps in his understanding and he wanted them plugged. 'What happened to the other bombs?'

'We got all three vans, all defused. Two of the drivers surrendered without a fight, including Corporal Heaton. One, a red-headed man' – Adams paused – 'resisted, with an army-issue Glock. The snipers had to take him out.'

Sean closed his eyes. *RIP Copper.* 'And what about Rich?'

Adams paused, looking hesitant for the first time since Sean had known him.

He closed his eyes and groaned. 'Oh. Fuck. He got away?'

'Remember, my involvement with MI5 stopped the moment you were no longer useful to them, which means that so did my access to information. But as I understand it—'

'He got away,' Sean said again.

'Yes. On the other hand, the spooks got a lot of useful information on him. He won't be picking up the old cosy life in Guildford again.'

'Any more good news?'

'Actually, yes.' Adams brandished the envelope. 'I came to wish you a happy birthday.'

'Aw, you shouldn't have.'

'That's all right. I almost didn't.' Adams passed the envelope over. Inside was a card, and a colourful badge: 18 LEGAL FOR ANYTHING. There was a hole on the front with the caption: *Guess who this card's for? Put your finger here to find out.*

He followed the instructions and opened the card. It was signed by all the lads, and his finger stuck out from the groin of a cartoon man. The caption read: *It's to a REAL dick.* He waggled his finger up and down, and tried to smile.

'Jeez. Guess I'm all grown up now.' He leaned over to put the card on his locker.

'Officially adult,' Adams agreed. 'Which means we can officially court-martial you.'

Sean looked at him. Then he looked around and took in the complete absence of handcuffs, Redcaps or any other kind of security. 'But you won't,' he whispered. Suddenly he had to turn his head away as tears filled his eyes. *Shit.* He had always known this would come, but – *shit.* 'You're just going to throw me out quietly, aren't you?'

And why shouldn't they? he thought bitterly. If he

remembered Trafalgar Square, he also remembered how he had got involved in all this in the first place. Basically blackmailed into it by MI5, with the threat of a long jail sentence which he totally deserved if he didn't comply. And he had failed to stop two bombs.

But even before that – everything the army had done for him he had just thrown back in its face. Even after he monumentally screwed up, even after he was busted by MI5, he remembered Franklin and Adams standing by him in that interview room. Not leaving him. Backing him up.

He had briefly been part of a family that would support him unconditionally for the rest of his life – and he'd chucked it away because for some insane reason he had preferred the old lifestyle. Contrast that with the Guyz, whose continued friendship could only be bought with stolen money.

'Now, why would we do that? What's the poor civvy world ever done to deserve having you unleashed on it?'

Sean stared at him, eyes wide.

'Your actions,' said the sergeant, 'saved lives. Even though two bombs exploded, no deaths have been reported. The way you discharged your weapon safely showed an exemplary regard for public safety and no thought for your own. You know there are armed cops everywhere in the West End? You could have been shot yourself at any moment. In short, there's too much good soldier in you to waste. And it helps that Mr Franklin has been putting his own career on the line, saying that if you go, he goes. And he is far too good an officer to chuck away. Here . . .' He leaned down and pinned the 18 badge onto Sean's hospital gown. 'And that's the only medal you're getting, because there isn't one for being a lucky bastard, who doesn't have the sense to call up the authorities before going all vigilante on his own.'

'Didn't think they'd listen,' Sean said weakly.

' "Hi, I'm the gun-toting nutter who just blew up a van on the south circular." I think you'd have got their attention. I know you don't have the best impression of authority, but try to remember they're not all stupid.'

Sean looked down at the badge. Turning eighteen was no big deal – it wasn't exactly going to change his life. But having Adams pin something on him with his own hands – that counted for a lot.

The sergeant smiled. It was an unusual sight. 'You've been lucky, Harker. You were offered an olive branch, you took it. If you hadn't, then right now you would be with your friends and looking at the best part of your life behind bars.'

'I killed a guy,' Sean said quietly.

Adams's face turned to stone. 'I witnessed it via the drone. So did a lot of other people higher up than me.

We all saw a soldier on active deployment using reasonable force to defend himself. I would say the circumstances ticked every box in the Rules of Engagement.'

Sean nodded. Words weren't needed. Not now. He was too tired anyway – he just wanted to go back to sleep, if he was honest. And his head was hurting. But he had one more question.

'Why did the spooks lump you with me, Sergeant? Thought it would've been the lieutenant's job.'

'It was. I volunteered.'

'You . . . Why?'

'I inflicted you on the army. I believe in clearing up my own messes.' Adams grinned. 'And of course I also like to take credit for my success stories.'

Suddenly Sean couldn't meet his eyes. He turned his head away and blinked rapidly again. 'Really let you down, didn't I?' he murmured.

'By being a thieving dipstick? I already knew that. One thing I didn't have you pegged as was a murderer and a traitor – and, guess what, you're not. Well, enough of these pleasantries. I'd best be going. Let you get some rest.'

Adams drew himself up into NCO mode. 'Private Harker!' he barked.

Sean lay at attention in bed. 'Sergeant!' he shouted at the ceiling.

'Get better!'

'Yes, Sergeant!'

'At ease.' With a half-smile on his face, the same one he'd had when they first met, Adams turned away. Sean lay back on his pillow with a much larger smile of his own.

So he was still a Fusilier. For the first time since he'd joined up, that was more important than being one of the Littern Guyz.

Sean had been one of the Guyz since the day he was born. The streets had shaped the way he grew. Look how easily he had slipped back into acting like one of them as soon as Heaton came along with his money and flash car.

That little lapse had almost got him killed.

It was one more item to add to the charge sheet against the gang that was growing inside his head. Basically he'd let them quietly screw him for his entire life.

But the army had shown him another way of getting through life, and it was infinitely better. So even if the Guyz were still an ongoing concern – if they didn't just collapse when the news about Matt and Copper came out, or get muscled out by some other outfit . . .

'I'm not one of the Guyz any more,' Sean murmured, and it was as if a weight he hadn't even noticed had fallen away from him.

It lasted about a second – until he thought about his mum. There was no way they were going to look after her now. And he didn't want them to. That would mean owing them something.

So it was down to him. He would just have to get her out of there. Set her up in a flat of her own.

But do it honestly, and on his pay. It would be tight. He needed to think it through . . .

His eyes were growing heavy, his thoughts muzzy. His battered body was demanding sleep, and there wasn't much point fighting it. Not if he was going to obey the sergeant's order.

Whatever. Bring it all on. He could take it.

AFTERWORD

By the age of 16, I was in juvenile detention and going through a pretty similar experience to Sean's at Burnleigh YOI. I had been abandoned as a baby, and then grew up with foster parents in South East London. I went through nine schools in seven years, didn't fit in and didn't see the point of any of it. All I angrily knew was that I didn't have much in my life, and there were people that had a hell of a lot more.

We were no great criminal masterminds. Burgling the same block of flats several times was always going to end up with us getting caught. The government's way of dealing with 'teenage delinquents' at that time was to lock us up in a Young Offender Institution and deliver what was labelled as the 'short, sharp shock' – a boot-camp-style, brutal regime designed to scare us into not reoffending. It was later abandoned when they worked out it wasn't working as a strategy, but it wasn't much fun at the time.

It was whilst I was in juvenile detention that the army

recruitment guys turned up and offered us an early release if we joined up. It sounded better than prison to me, so off I went.

Little did I know that joining the army would change my life. It showed me that there were opportunities to make something of myself, if I was willing to put in the effort. I discovered that I had the reading age of an eleven-year-old, six years below where I should have been, and learning to read was the first step in changing my life. I think Sean is probably a bit ahead of me on that. And he's smart. But he still shows that it's not always easy to leave your past behind and it's not easy to make the right choices. It takes a lot of guts.

These days, I spend quite a bit of time visiting schools, prisons and workplaces, as well as army bases and businesses, talking to them about my experiences and encouraging them to start reading and writing. I see people just like me – and people like I used to be – and I tell them, 'If I can turn my life around, then so can you.' Every time you get a bit of knowledge, you get a bit of power to make your own decisions and take control of your life. Just try it.

Andy McNab
26 January 2016